**W9-AHZ-303**

Please
return
my
book

Via Cintron Ashmeade

Silent
Fury

Silent
Fury

Linda
McHugh

TOR

A Tom Doherty Associates Book
New York

SILENT FURY

This book was printed on acid-free paper.

A Tor Book
Published by Tom Doherty Associates, Inc.
175 Fifth Avenue
New York, N.Y. 10010

TOR® is a registered trademark of Tom Doherty Associates, Inc.

ISBN 0-312-85319-X

Printed in the United States of America

To my Hero—
and my Mother—
Rosemary Ellen Hartigan

Acknowledgments

A special thanks to Father Andrew M. Greeley, who made everything possible, and to my family and friends for their unflagging encouragement and support.

Prologue

"Oh, how decadent!" Meg cried. "Farrell! Did you know Jan had left these?"

Farrell shook her head. "She must have set them down when we were looking for the umbrella. I wonder why she didn't just bring them along."

"I don't know." Meg smiled sheepishly. "But as long as they're here . . ."

"Oh, go ahead," Farrell urged. "You can certainly afford the calories."

"But right before bed?"

Farrell shrugged.

"Okay, you twisted my arm," Meg teased, plucking a brownie from the plate. "They really are decadent!" she cried again, heading back to her room. "They have chocolate chips in them, for God's sake. Good night, Farrell," she called. "Sweet dreams!"

"Sweet dreams, Meg," Farrell answered softly.

In her room, Farrell undressed and pulled her emerald-satin nightgown over her head, then reached back and freed the mane of copper hair that had become trapped in the neckline.

Out of the corner of her eye, she caught a sudden movement. Startled, she whirled around . . . and confronted her own reflection. Well, I've lived here for only twenty years or so, she chided herself. Naturally that mirror would frighten me. She crossed the room to study herself more closely. Her eyes, the same brilliant green as the gown, looked huge in her drawn face, and were smudged with telltale circles.

I look—she paused, searching for the appropriate word—haunted, she decided as she pulled back her covers and climbed into bed. And I'm so tired. But each time she closed her eyes, she was assailed by horrible images of the past weeks. Finally she sat up and turned to stare out at the night through her open window.

"Where are you, Max?" she whispered, again feeling the pain of his sudden departure. A faint breeze wafted through the pines. Normally, the stirring of air would be enough to fill her room with the damp green musk of the evergreens . . . but this summer's drought had burned the life out of everything.

Turning, she laid her head back down on her pillow and tried to concentrate on the soft hush of wind through the trees.

Outside, a dark shape separated from the shadows. It was time! The wait had been unbearable! Minutes had crept by like hours . . . like years.

The house was dark, as it should be. She glanced at the glowing numerals on her watch. It was midnight, the witching hour. How appropriate; even time was on her side.

Fortunately, the window she had used that afternoon was still open, and the screen was as she'd left it. It was almost too easy, she thought as she removed the tape and entered silently. She went first to the dining room to check the brownies.

They'd eaten some, she was sure of it! A quarter of one should have been enough if—she faltered for a moment and felt a wave of panic—if I mixed them properly. Oh, but of course I did! She dismissed her irrational fear. "Of course I did," she whispered.

She went to the living room and set down her supplies as she took it all in for one last time: the gleaming oak floors, the massive stone fireplace, the magnificent view of the silvery blue lake. God, how she hated these people! It was time to put things right. She began to feel the power growing deep inside.

The strength was coming on in steady waves . . . pulsing through her. It almost seemed to vibrate in the air around her. Her vision seemed different somehow, in sharper focus; and it felt as though she were standing higher up off the ground than usual, as though she'd suddenly grown taller.

Reluctant to let the moment pass too quickly, she stepped out onto the balcony to revel in the night and the soft, warm breeze. As she crept out, the screen door slipped from her grasp and closed with a loud bang.

She held her breath and waited in the darkness.

Something dragged Meg up from sleep. At first she thought a sound had awakened her, but as she struggled to the surface, she realized that instead, a feeling had roused her. Once again the awareness of evil had her trembling in her bed. Something's wrong, she thought; Farrell's in danger . . . we're *both* in danger!

She was so groggy that the simple act of opening her eyes seemed a Herculean feat. What's wrong with me? she wondered, vaguely aware that this was no ordinary lethargy.

Someone was moving about in the living room. She tried to lift her head, but it was too much effort. She called Farrell's name, but her voice was only a whisper. She realized that the darkness was closing in again and that she was helpless against it. She was slipping back, slowly, slowly. So tired. Maybe if I rest my eyes, just for a minute . . .

Minutes passed, but no one came. She breathed a sigh of relief and walked over to the edge of the balcony.

She stood there, staring out at the lake, when suddenly something moved on the surface of the water—a silver flash. A bird, she decided. Something small.

Her heightened senses were reassuring. Her vision was

such that she imagined she was seeing not only the gently rippling surface of the water, but clear through its depths to the wavy ridges of sand that lay beneath.

She gripped the heavy wooden railing with small white hands. If I squeeze, she thought, I'll snap it.

Turning from the balcony, she reentered the living room. A wooden crate lay in the corner. She heard a faint rustling sound within it.

A smile crossed her face.

She retrieved her supplies, unaware that she was humming a meandering, discordant tune. She reached into her pocket for the matches. Approaching the corner, she lifted the can of gasoline, and trembling with excitement, her entire body pulsing with the power, she began to pour . . .

Part
I

One

The dark child stood watching in the sun-dappled shade of the neighbors' backyard apple tree. The older girls were busy building kingdoms in the sandbox, while the boys were engaged in warfare, using armloads of rotten apples for ammunition and drawing occasional sharp scoldings from their young mothers.

The women, in their crisp, spring cottons, were arranged haphazardly, like scattered buttercups, on the rough cement of the back steps. They were discussing Korea: how serious a threat was it? Could their husbands be recalled? They wanted no more interruptions in their young lives. Still, the possibility seemed remote on that bright spring morning in 1950. They turned their faces to the sun, reveling in its warmth and the boon of each other's company.

She watched, and listened—to the boys shrieking and making noises like bombs exploding, to the comforting hum of the women's voices, to the high-pitched bickering as the girls argued over who would be a prince today, or a lady, or a countess. There would be no discussion over the role of princess. It went without saying that "The Beauty," her sister Eileen, would have that coveted role. Eileen, six years her senior, was, at eight, already considered breathtaking.

She glanced briefly at her brother, Junior, the only child besides herself not playing. But, unlike her, Junior was resting. Soon his muffled snoring would grow loud enough to draw scornful attention from the other boys—not that it would bother him. At nine, Junior was so cocooned by his unwavering assumption of superiority that no amount of teasing could faze him.

In spite of his indifference, she threw a stick at his round tummy. He turned, grumbling in his sleep, and stopped snoring.

Dismissing him, she once again focused her full attention on the sandbox, or rather, on the air around it. She stood as before, motionless, watching and waiting for the something that she was sure would happen. She was readying herself for the instant of recognition that she understood would come upon her before "the happening" occurred. That second, she knew, could quite possibly make the difference between tragedy or a mere mishap.

She was so intent upon her vigil that she did not feel her grandma's eyes on her, or sense her worry. For Grandma Kate knew her son's youngest child better than anyone else. On the day that Meg was born, she had taken one look, turned to her beloved daughter-in-law and said, "This one's an old soul, Lucy. She's been here before."

Lucy hadn't understood, and Kate had seen no reason to alarm her by explaining. She would know soon enough anyway. But Kate knew, and Junior, too. Kate laughed to herself at the thought of Junior having such sensitivity. The fact remained, though, that the boy had been uncomfortable in Meg's presence since the day she was born.

Kate glanced over at Lucy, more like a daughter to her than an in-law, and smiled to see her getting on so well with the neighborhood ladies. After seven years in this southside Chicago parish, they were finally getting over the stigma of being "newcomers," and from the old neighborhood yet! Not that they were competing with old money or lineage. Far from it! But some of the stuffiest and most elitist of their neighbors had beaten them here from the back-of-the-yards ghetto by a scant year or two.

With grim satisfaction, Kate watched the women opening their ranks to Lucy. She understood instinctively that despite her daughter-in-law's genuine charm and ready laugh, their friendship was being proffered as a direct result of her son's considerable monetary success.

She thought of her only child with the all-consuming pride of a single parent. So different from his perpetually intoxicated father, who mercifully had died before their child was six.

Patrick Sweeney, God bless him, was a redheaded, green-eyed giant of a man who rarely touched a drop, and whose awesome work ethic, his eye for real estate, and his timely purchase of a string of filling stations had rescued them from the tenements and squalor of the stockyards.

She could see their house from here, the finest on the block. A two-story red brick on a corner lot (and with a finished basement!). Her son had done her proud. Not just with the house or his kind heart; he'd given her the further gift of marrying a girl whom she was thrilled to call her daughter, and then the added blessings of the children . . . Ah, the children. Kate had no doubt that if it hadn't been for the war taking Patrick away for those three years, she would have six grandchildren now instead of three. Patrick and Lucy were besotted with their offspring, each of them blinded by a fierce, protective love. Kate was the only realist in the house; although she adored the children, she saw them for what they were.

Patrick, Jr., whom they'd intended to call Pat, had somehow ended up being called "Junior." It just seemed to suit him.

Junior was lazy, so lazy that he had refused to walk until the age of three. His despairing mother had carted him around the city from one specialist to another until Kate caught him (by spying on him through a keyhole) walking around in his room. Junior was clever, but not smart. He would often expend more energy in trying to get out of a job than he would have used had he just gone and done the work in the first place.

Eileen was the beauty of the family, and a rare beauty she was. Even at eight, she was breathtaking. She had glowing russet hair and clear, amber eyes, almond-shaped like Lucy's but turned up at the corners like her grandma's. Her face was finely sculpted, with prominent cheekbones, a pert little nose, and full, sensuous lips.

Meg was another being altogether. A tiny wisp of a child, with her mother's dark hair and huge, soulful black eyes. She looked out at the world with such a level gaze and earnest expression that it tugged at your heart just to look at her.

Kate stared at her now, precocious little Meg, and knew beyond a shadow of a doubt that the child's sixth sense had been somehow activated, and that she was on alert.

Meg felt the currents more strongly now, like the rush of wind in a falling dream; she could feel them building . . . building. Then all at once, in a flash of light, she saw what was about to happen. She heard the sudden, deafening crack of the branch that shaded the sandbox, she saw it plummeting toward earth, toward the unsuspecting girls . . .

She screamed.

The girls, alarmed by her piercing cry, jumped back, and the enormous branch fell and crushed a kingdom, but not a single child was harmed.

The women never knew. They heard the scream, they saw the branch crash to the earth, and they never realized that the scream had come first.

But the children knew.

It wasn't until a year later, when Meg was three and already quite fluent, that Lucy began to understand.

Meg burst into the kitchen one morning. "Mommy!" she cried urgently, tugging at Lucy's skirt. "Daddy needs you!"

Lucy looked down at her and smiled. "Daddy's at work, honey. He left hours ago."

"But, Mommy," she persisted, her tears making dark pools of her eyes, "he's calling you! He needs you!"

Lucy reached down and lifted the sobbing child. "Honey, it can't be Daddy. Maybe you heard one of the neighbors calling somebody." Meg wiggled out of Lucy's arms and ran from the room. Lucy looked over at Kate and shrugged. "What do you suppose that was about?"

"I can't imagine," Kate answered.

An hour later someone was pounding at the door, and Kate and Lucy, with sudden unspoken understanding, ran as fast as their legs could carry them. Meg was already there, jumping up and down in frustration at not being able to reach the knob.

Lucy fumbled with the lock, then pulled the door open, and there on the steps stood Patrick, leaning heavily on his closest friend, Captain Shay.

"He's right as rain, right as rain!" boomed the Captain, his brogue as thick as cream, as it was wont to become when he was overexcited. "Just a bit shaken up and a wee bump on the noggin, nothin' a-tall, nothin' a-tall! Lucy, my love, perhaps you'll be wantin' to put your man to bed."

Lucy slipped an arm around Patrick's waist and led him off. Then the Captain turned to Kate.

"Ah, Katie! I almost didn't see ya! And you're lookin' as lovely as the flowers in spring!"

Kate knew how much the Captain loved her son and that it was nerves and fear that kept him babbling. "What happened?" she asked. "Wait, never mind. We'll wait till Lucy comes back from bedding him. Come, I'll make you some tea."

"Perhaps something a bit stronger," the Captain suggested hopefully, following her into the kitchen.

A few minutes later, Lucy joined them.

"He's lying down now. He'll be all right, Mom," she said to Kate, and then she turned to the Captain. "Captain, thank you," she began, and dissolved into tears.

"Don't be silly, girl," he told her. "I love the man."

"I know. It's just—" and she broke down again.

At last the Captain was allowed to explain what had happened. It seemed that Patrick had pulled out of the gas station that the Captain managed when off duty, only to be

struck by an oncoming car. The other driver was so intoxicated that he had passed out behind the wheel.

"It was a hell of a crash!" said the Captain, completely
forgetting himself. "Nothing left of either car, just two
great heaps of junk. I say it's a miracle either of them
lived!"

"What about the other driver? Was he hurt?" asked
Kate.

"The bum walked away without a scratch!" Clearly the
man's good fortune didn't jibe with the Captain's sense of
justice.

"You know," he said, turning to Lucy, "I'd have
missed the whole thing if Patrick hadn't called for you."

"What are you talking about?" she asked, aware of a
prickling sensation traveling down her spine.

"Well, I had me back turned, but I heard him yell
'Lucy,' so I spun around to see if you were there."

"He called my name," Lucy said to Kate.

"Over and over," nodded the Captain.

"What time did this happen?" Lucy asked reluctantly.

"Eleven-thirty sharp," the Captain answered, scratch-
ing his bald head and looking from Lucy to Kate.

"Mom?" Lucy's voice trembled.

"She's fey, Lucy," Kate answered.

"What do you mean?" Lucy asked, her heart pounding
with fear. "What does it mean?"

"It just means that she's more sensitive than most
people. She'll know things before others do," Kate explained.

"How can you be so calm about it?" Lucy exclaimed.
"You act as though you knew!"

"I didn't know for sure, but I suspected," Kate said.
"It's not so strange to me. My great-aunt Celia had the gift.
It's not a bad thing."

At this, the Captain interrupted. "May I ask if you're
referring to one of my little darlings?"

The Captain was a confirmed bachelor. At thirty-
eight, he lived with his mother and his forty-two-year-old
invalid, spinster sister. He'd brought them over from Ireland the moment he could afford to, and now he sup-

ported them with no trace of resentment. He treated each of them with unfailing kindness and devotion. He was a policeman, though not yet a captain; everyone called him by the nickname out of respect and through recognition of the fine gentleman he was.

He considered the children as much his as anyone else's and, in fact, was godfather to each of them. He loved them with all of the tenderness his warm heart had to offer.

Lucy answered him immediately, for they kept no secrets from this man.

"It's Meg," she acknowledged. "She told me that Patrick needed me this morning. She was almost hysterical."

"About what time was it?" he asked.

"Eleven-thirty exactly," she told him.

"Well, then, Katie, I expect you're right. Now, my mother claims that her cousin, Mary O'Donahue, had the second sight. But then"—his blue eyes twinkled—"my mother likes a bit of attention now and again."

It was true, Meg was a bit fey. In time, the fact was accepted as a part of their lives, like Eileen's dazzling beauty and Junior's temper tantrums.

Meg had funny little ways about her, but her small quirks were harmless and, in fact, sometimes came in quite handy. She would announce visitors ten minutes before their arrival. She always knew whether it would rain or snow, and when the telephone rang, she could often tell who was calling.

Patrick's accident was the most remarkable event involving Meg's "gift" until September of 1954, when the time came for her to begin school. Like most little girls, and especially those with older siblings, Meg was positively gleeful at the prospect of first grade.

Finally, after two years of the acute agony inflicted by watching her glamorous older sister strut off each morning in the coveted maroon-plaid uniform jumper, now she, Meg Sweeney, in a jumper all her own (albeit Eileen's hand-me-down), was going to school!

The children were seated at the kitchen table, fidgeting and wiggling in that state of high nervous excitement that infects young people each year on the first day of school.

Lucy was bustling around the kitchen, frying eggs and stirring oatmeal, while Kate was pouring juice and admonishing Junior, insisting that three bowls of oatmeal were quite enough and, yes, she was well aware of the fact that he was a growing boy.

Finally it was time to go. Lucy hugged Meg on her way out the door, and asked quite routinely, "Nervous about school, honey?"

"Not about school, Mommy!" Meg squealed.

"Well, what about then?" Lucy asked, smiling.

"Today I'm going to meet my husband!" Meg announced, her eyes dancing with joy. She skipped down the steps, blissfully unaware of her mother and grandmother's dumbfounded expressions.

Meg came home that day utterly crestfallen.

"He wasn't there!" she cried. She ran up the stairs, straight to her room, collapsing in tears on her bed.

Every year was the same. She would go off on the first morning of school full of confidence and hope, and come home bitterly disappointed.

Every year, that is, until she began fifth grade. By now, Lucy and Kate had learned to dread the first day of school because of the effect it always had on Meg. So when at the end of the school day, Meg burst in, they were braced for the usual misery, totally unprepared for what happened.

"He's here!" Meg sang joyously. "He's finally, finally here!"

She went on to describe him. "He's tall, very tall, almost as tall as you, Mom. He's got my color hair, but lighter eyes. He's so handsome, you wouldn't believe it! He's got the nicest smile, and his name is Daniel William Conner. He was supposed to come to my school in first grade, but his dad got sick, so he had to go to public school, but his dad's all better now."

That was it. As far as Meg was concerned, from that moment forward, her fate was sealed. There would never be anyone for her but Daniel William Conner. She'd waited this long, and she was fully prepared to wait forever, if necessary, until he got around to noticing her.

It took years. For Daniel was the sort of boy who was far more interested in football, baseball, and basketball than he was in girls.

Meg didn't push herself on him, but she never missed a game if Daniel was playing. And in the meantime, she went quietly about her own business, developing into quite a talented artist while she waited, secure in the belief that Daniel would someday be hers.

Two

While Meg was in the sixth grade, waiting for Daniel to come around, and Eileen was, at seventeen, fast becoming a spectacular beauty, Junior became the first Sweeney in history to go to college. Though his grades throughout high school had been abysmal, in 1959 attending college was considered a mark of privilege and wealth, and Junior was hell-bent that he should bear that mark.

Patrick was giddy at the notion of his son becoming a college man. Lucy was thrilled, and Kate was happy on Patrick's account. But no one came close to being as impressed as Junior himself. Earlier, he had developed a slightly patronizing manner when dealing with his family; he now became openly condescending.

Two years later, Junior announced at the dinner table that he had mastered every subject and was quite finished with school.

Unable to stand it, Kate asked him why such an expert as he had gotten such poor grades.

Junior grew so furious that he began to shake, and with his chins all a-wiggle, he sputtered that his teachers (every one of them) had been bitterly jealous and had had it in for him from the very beginning!

Patrick was appalled that college professors could be so petty, and vowed then and there to discontinue the generous annual donations he'd been making. It never

occurred to him that those donations were all that had kept
Junior from being bounced out on his ear in his first year.

Eileen surprised everyone by joining in the conversation (for normally, unless the conversation encompassed
movies, fashion, or boys, she remained aloof): "Oh, Junior,
does this mean that you're going to join up? You're old
enough now. Why, Marty Berry joined up last year, and
Brian O'Toole was drafted right after the Bay of Pigs. I
don't care what anyone says, I think they looked just
dreamy in their uniforms. You'd look real swell, too, Junior," she assured him, her golden eyes sparkling.

The room went silent.

Patrick set down his fork and slowly rose from the
table. For a moment, he stood speechless, his green eyes
burning with pride. A veteran of World War II, Patrick had
enlisted in spite of the fact that they'd had an infant son at
the time, and another child on the way.

"Son," he managed, his voice strained with emotion,
"son, I'm so proud—"

Junior was wild-eyed. He looked across the table at
Patrick, then, panicking, called on Lucy.

"Mo-om!" he cried, fear tightening his voice, render-
ing it as thin and high as a girl's. "Mom, tell him!"

Patrick turned to Lucy, who was staring intently at the
napkin on her lap.

"Lucy?" he asked. "Tell me what?"

"Patrick," she began, her voice barely audible, "Junior
received a draft notice in November."

"But—"

She raised her hand to silence him. "We just didn't
want to disappoint you." She looked away, unable to meet
her husband's eyes. "You remember the difficulty Junior
had in learning to walk." She met Kate's disbelieving stare
with an imploring gaze. "Well, Junior went to see those
specialists . . ." She paused, remembering his tears, and his
hysteria. She'd given in and told him the names of the
specialists. She took a deep breath. "Anyway, one of them
felt that his difficulty with walking stemmed from an inner-
ear problem. He felt it could impair Junior's ability to

perform as a soldier. Patrick, I'm sorry . . ." Her voice trailed off.

Patrick stood there for a moment, absorbing what she'd said. He then sat down heavily, and after a few minutes of utter silence, picked up his fork, stabbed a piece of meat, pointed it at Junior, and said, "Say, listen. Let those other lugs fight those commies. We need the boys with brains here at home. Besides, I could use a good man at my side. Sweeney and Son," he said, glancing around the table, enlisting their support. "It's got a ring to it. What d'ya say, Lucy?"

"It sounds wonderful, Patrick," she agreed, blinking back tears. "Excuse me," she said, pushing back her chair. "I seem to have something in my eye."

And so Junior went to work for Patrick. He was given his own office, which he arranged to have elaborately decorated. He kept his own hours, arriving after ten and leaving before three. After three months of exhaustive interviews with about two hundred pretty young girls, he hired a private secretary. And he was paid about twice the salary a top college graduate could have expected.

Not being completely stupid, he spent what time was necessary to learn the ropes. He met the key customers and learned impressive-sounding buzz words and statistics so that he could at least appear to be knowledgeable.

But the real work had already been done. Junior had no illusions of furthering his father's empire. Nor did he intend to be the sort of rich man's son who would send the family business into ruin the moment he gained control. He was perfectly capable of learning a routine and following it to the letter.

But he was not capable of playing second fiddle to his father—so he undercut him at every turn. He never relayed a message without giving Patrick a shot.

"The old man fought me on this one, but I insisted."

"The old man was confused, but I straightened him out."

"The old man almost blew the account, but I called and fixed things."

He corrected Patrick's grammar in the middle of meetings, rolling his eyes in open disdain. He was pompous, obnoxious, sneaky and vain, and in no time at all had earned a reputation for himself that would have broken his father's heart—had he known.

It was the height of irony that Patrick's son should despise him for lacking the privileges that he'd slaved his whole life to provide.

The other employees learned to work around Junior, calling him "Mr. Sweeney" to his face and "Mr. Sleazy" behind his back. In the entire company, Junior had only one ally; plump in all the right places, blond in the noticeable ones. Dimpled and juicy and overtly supportive, Bridget O'Rourke, private secretary to Junior, was his biggest, well, his only fan.

If Junior had ever once taken a minute to look past the blond fluff and dimples, he might have saved himself and everyone else a lot of trouble. But he didn't, and so he never noticed what no amount of artifice could conceal: the coldest, most calculating pair of baby blues this side of hell. Eyes as old and as sure as sin.

Bridget O'Rourke had hooked her fish. Now it was just a matter of reeling him in. She had no romantic illusions about Junior. In fact, Junior didn't matter to her in the least. What did matter was that he was Patrick Sweeney's only son and heir. Junior never really stood a chance.

They were married swiftly and quietly. And lo and behold, seven months later, to the delight of every finger-counting housewife on the southside, Patrick and Lucy became grandparents.

Three

Patrick and Lucy had always kept their socializing at a minimum. Lucy sat on a few boards over the years, and Patrick, through his business contacts, occasionally came home with invitations too good to pass up.

But now that Meg was thirteen and Eileen and Junior

were young adults, they were free to accept more invitations, and they found themselves very much in demand. They modestly assumed that their popularity had to do with Patrick's growing financial success and his prominence in the business community. The fact was, people genuinely enjoyed their company. They were bright, attractive, easy to be with, and fun to have along.

Before long, invitations were arriving in droves, and Lucy found herself spending hours each week just sorting through them. Not that it was a chore she objected to; she and Kate reveled in discussing the comparative merits of a black-tie dinner at the museum and a moonlight cocktail cruise to benefit the symphony. It was pretty heady stuff, they agreed, for a couple of gals from the old neighborhood. Of course, some invitations were more interesting than others—but no invitation was as thrilling to Patrick as the one he received at his office one July afternoon in 1961.

That evening he came bounding up the front steps, his eyes alight with enthusiasm, yelling at the top of his lungs for Lucy.

"You'll never guess who called!" he exclaimed as she came bustling from the kitchen, her cheeks flushed pink from the heat of the stove.

"Who?" she asked, intrigued.

"You'll never guess who invited us to have dinner at his club!" He was positively bursting at the seams.

"Then tell me."

"You won't believe it," he warned.

"Patrick . . ." She was losing patience. "If tonight's dinner is ruined . . ."

"Okay, okay, I'll tell you. Only Jim McBride, that's who!" he announced.

"Who?" she asked blankly.

"Whad'da-ya-mean, 'Who?' Jim McBride!"

"Patrick, I'm sorry, but who the devil is Jim McBride?"

"Oh, for Pete's sake, Lucy!"

She waited.

"Only the biggest developer in the whole city, that's all. I told you about him, Lucy. He's the one who gave me my start, bought those lots I gambled on years ago. Remember?"

"Oh, that Jim McBride!" She smiled, finally enlightened.

"Well, he and his wife have invited us to join them for dinner at their club."

Lucy had never seen Patrick so impressed and flattered. "Just the four of us?" she asked, suddenly apprehensive.

"That's right." Patrick nodded happily. "Imagine!"

By the time the appointed evening rolled around, Patrick was in such a frenzy that he couldn't think straight. He'd insisted that Lucy go out and buy a new dress, "and an expensive one." He'd gone out and bought himself a new shirt and tie.

It took him a solid hour to get dressed instead of his usual ten minutes, and he spent the entire time bemoaning the fact that he hadn't gone ahead and bought himself a new suit.

"Jim's the snappiest dresser you ever saw," he informed Lucy for the hundredth time that week.

When they arrived at the club, they were informed by a haughty-looking waiter that the McBrides were expecting them.

"Oh, Christ, Lucy, we're late," Patrick whispered out of the side of his mouth as he stepped back to let her pass. "Now he'll really think I'm a bum," he mumbled miserably.

Moira McBride was the loveliest creature Lucy had ever laid eyes on: long-limbed, elegant, and wonderfully poised. She was at least three inches taller than her husband, and Lucy thought she was closer in age to herself than to Jim. She had a deep, gravelly voice and a wonderfully husky laugh. Her mouth was wide and sensuous, her hair the rich golden color of honey, and her big glittering black eyes snapped and sparkled with a keen wit and penetrating intelligence.

Moira took one look at Lucy and burst out laughing. After overcoming her initial surprise, Lucy laughed, too.

While the two women were convulsed in laughter, their husbands stood stiffly by, staring helplessly at their wives.

Finally, Jim shrugged his shoulders at Patrick, rolled his eyes in his wife's direction, and grinned impishly—he clearly adored her. Patrick laughed out loud, and the ice was broken.

"And here I thought we'd have nothing in common," Moira gasped, breaking them up again.

For Lucy and Moira had worn identical dresses. Not subtly similar, but identical black cocktail dresses with yellow piping and polka dots. They were even carrying the same pocketbooks.

"Oh, but Moira," Lucy kidded, "I like your black shoes so much better than my black shoes. They really *make* the outfit!"

The couples got on famously, and by the time coffee was served, they were setting a date for their next dinner together. On that occasion, however, it wasn't long before Lucy noticed that Moira seemed somewhat upset and distracted, despite all the gaiety. As soon as the men were safely launched on a business discussion, she asked Moira if something was wrong.

Moira's dark eyes seemed to have lost their sparkle. "It's my son," she confided. "He informed us last night that he's asked his girlfriend to marry him."

"But, Moira," said Lucy, surprised, "what is it? Don't you like the girl?"

"Lucy, it's not that I don't like her. There is something off about this girl. I can't describe it well, but something's wrong. I feel it!"

"But then why would your son—" Lucy began.

"Oh, she's clever, Lucy, believe me. And she's gorgeous-looking. She has a figure that just won't quit, and does she know how to use it! She's got my son wrapped around her little finger, even though Luke's ten years older than she. You'd think he'd have more sense. He absolutely refuses to listen to anything I say regarding 'his Darleen'— her name is Darleen Madigan. You know how young men are. I'm telling you, though, there's something . . . If you met this girl tonight, you'd think she was absolutely charming. People are just captivated by her, especially men. But eventually you'd start noticing discrepancies, little things that don't mesh, stories that don't ring true. Lucy, last week I found her in our bedroom, going through my bureau drawers! When she turned and saw me, she just smiled pleasantly. It was eerie. I was actually frightened for a moment. Then she walked past me without a word! Lucy, forgive me for going on so. But I'm simply beside myself over the whole thing."

"Don't be silly, Moira," Lucy said reassuringly. "You've given me an idea."

"Really? What is it?" asked Moira.

"Well," Lucy began hesitantly, "my Eileen is seeing a young man I'm not too keen on . . ."

"What's wrong with him?" Moira asked.

"Now you'll think *I'm* crazy. It's hard to explain, really, but the fact is, I think he's as phony as a three-dollar bill. He's just a little too quick to open the door, or to run around the table and pull out my chair. He's a little too eager to help, if you know what I mean, and much too free with the compliments. 'Oh, Mrs. Sweeney!' " she mimicked him, " 'how lovely you look! You're a lucky man, Mr. Sweeney.' Now I ask you, Moira. Who is he to tell my husband that he's a lucky man? To tell you the truth, I think he's more interested in Patrick's money than he is in my daughter. Anyway," she continued, warming to her idea, "an older man is just what Eileen needs. Lord knows, she could use some direction—she certainly doesn't seem interested in college. How about it, Moira? What do you think of getting your Luke and my Eileen together?"

Lucy hadn't noticed that Jim and Patrick had stopped talking. All she knew was that they were now staring at her with their eyes bulging, and that Moira was looking at her with a similarly shocked expression. "Well, it was just a thought," she said defensively.

"A hell of a thought, too," said Jim, raising his martini to toast her. "Best damned idea I've heard in a long time."

"I'll drink to that," said Patrick. "I'm sick to death of that sissy buttering me up every time I turn around."

"But how would we do it?" asked Moira. "After all,

Luke's engaged and Eileen's involved. They'll never agree to a date."

After much discussion, they decided that the best approach would be a direct one. Patrick and Jim would simply come straight out and lie to their respective offspring. They would ask their son/daughter, as a great personal favor to them, to escort/be escorted by the son/daughter of a valued client to the Governor's Ball the following week.

The next evening, Patrick and Jim, slyly commiserating and archly sympathetic, extracted guilt-induced promises from their long-suffering children.

Later that night, Lucy called Moira, ecstatic. "Moira? It's me, Lucy Sweeney. Well?"

"Jim did it!" Moira whispered excitedly. "How about Patrick? Any luck?"

"Full steam ahead!" Lucy giggled. "Though you'd think Patrick was sending Eileen off to the convent, the way she's moping around here tonight. She says she'll 'just die' if Harry finds out. I'm thinking of telling him myself!"

They hung up laughing, pleased as Punch with their scheme. Neither woman suspected that their conversation had been overheard.

Darleen waited until she heard two clicks before replacing the receiver to the McBrides' kitchen extension. Just as she lifted her hand, Luke entered the room.

"Honey, where've you been?" he asked cheerfully. "I thought you were fixing us a snack."

"Oh, baby," she cooed in her most sugary voice, "I'm sorry! You know I'll give you anything you want." She walked across the kitchen and put her arms around his neck, pressing her breasts against his chest as if by accident.

"Anything at all . . ." she promised.

At twenty years old, Darleen Madigan was built like a dream—or a fantasy. Her measurements were 36-27-37, but by the time she finished dressing each day, they were 38-25-36. She wore her dark auburn hair parted on the side so that it fell seductively over one eye. Her full, pouting lips were painted the same deep shade of red favored by the young starlet, Marilyn Monroe. She plucked her heavy dark brows into come-hither arches, which she could raise and lower independently for effect. She wasn't beautiful, but she had sufficient confidence to convince men that she was.

But she couldn't hold a candle to Eileen Sweeney. Eileen, at nineteen, was a natural beauty of the first order, and no amount of artifice could compete with that.

Eileen's measurements were a more diminutive 35-22-34. Her russet hair was streaked with gold and fell shimmering past her shoulders. Her almond-shaped amber eyes had the same exotic upward tilt as her grandmother's and were rimmed with long, heavy black lashes. She had her late grandfather Jake Sweeney's smooth, golden skin. And while Darleen looked as though she might swallow a man whole, Eileen gave a man the feeling that she needed his protection.

To show his appreciation for the "tremendous favor" she was doing for him, Patrick had insisted that Eileen buy a new dress for the ball. Kate and Lucy accompanied her on the shopping expedition, and together they found the perfect dress. The satin was a creamy winter-white and contrasted beautifully with Eileen's golden skin. The gown was elegantly cut to follow the graceful lines of a woman's body and subtly revealed the perfection of Eileen's slim figure. Her only adornment would be Lucy's pearl-and-diamond choker, which they all agreed would be just right.

On the night of the ball, Lucy and Kate helped Eileen to dress. The finished result was so stunning that Lucy choked back tears of pride at her daughter's beauty.

Even Eileen, in spite of her earlier reluctance, couldn't help being excited by her appearance and the thrill of attending the Governor's Ball.

Lucy kept her upstairs, fussing in front of the mirror, until the doorbell rang. She wanted Luke McBride to be hit with the full impact of her daughter's beauty as she descended the stairs. "Let him get an eyeful of my Eileen coming toward him and then we'll see what he has to say about this Darleen Madigan person," she whispered to Kate.

Patrick greeted Luke at the door, assuring him that Eileen would be right down.

"You know how women are," he winked. "Ah! Here

she comes now," he said, turning to watch Eileen, who seemed to be floating down the stairs. She was followed by Lucy, who was grinning like an idiot, and by Kate, who was glowering suspiciously at Luke.

Patrick had been totally unprepared. What a vision his daughter had suddenly become!

If Patrick was awestruck at the sight of Eileen, Luke was positively dazzled. Never in his life had he imagined a girl as beautiful as this.

As for Eileen, it was love at first sight. Luke McBride was not only the most handsome man she'd ever laid eyes on, but to her nineteen years, his thirty seemed too thrilling to be true. Seeing him there at the foot of the stairs, tall and elegant in his tuxedo, with wavy auburn hair and warm hazel eyes, she felt her knees go weak. It was like a scene right out of the movies, and she and Luke were the stars.

Four

By the end of the first week, Luke was wondering how he would break it to her. Finally, after talking with his father, he realized that the only thing to do was to make a clean break of it.

He arrived at her door feeling guilt-ridden and miserable, and suggested they go for a drive.

"No, love." Darleen took him by the hand. "My parents are out for the evening. Come, see what I've done!"

She led him through the house and down the hall, finally arriving in the dining room. There she had created a romantic setting, complete with chilled champagne, candlelight, and flowers.

"Oh, Darleen," Luke said miserably, "we have to talk."

"Not now, honey," she cooed, attaching herself to him.

"Now!" he insisted, grabbing her firmly by the hand and leading her to the living-room couch. He sat her down and perched nervously beside her.

"Darleen, I don't know how to say this, so I suppose the best thing to do is to just come right out and tell you . . . Darleen, I've met someone else."

He was prepared for tears, he was prepared for pleading, he was prepared for anger and recrimination.

She looked up at him demurely through her black lashes. The expression on her face was unfathomable. She covered her eyes for a moment, as if to blot out tears, but he noticed, when she lowered her hands, that her eyes were dry.

"I'm sorry," she whispered.

Thinking that she had failed to understand him, he began to elaborate. "I swear, Darleen, I never meant—"

Delicately, she placed her finger on his lips. "Sshh. Hush now, Luke. It's not your fault."

"But Darleen, don't you understand? I'm breaking our engagement. I know it's awful—"

"Luke, I understand. It's okay, really. After all, you can't help falling in love . . . or out of it."

He couldn't believe what he was hearing. The woman was an angel! For a brief moment, he questioned whether he was doing the right thing in breaking up with her, but then he pictured his Eileen and his doubts evaporated.

"Darleen, you're a real friend . . ."

She flinched at his use of the word "friend," and he cursed himself for being insensitive.

"You're an amazing woman, Darleen," he told her sincerely. "I know you'll find someone who'll be a lot better for you than I ever was."

She rose with dignity and smiled down at him. Then she flipped her heavy dark hair back, squared her shoulders, and said, "Well, the important thing is that you're happy."

Full of admiration, he rose and stood beside her. She was staring out the window and seemed completely lost in thought, almost as if she'd forgotten his presence.

"Well, I guess I should be leaving. Darleen . . . Darleen?"

"Yes?" Her face was strangely blank. "Oh, yes, of course, you should be leaving."

She escorted him to the door. "Good-bye, Luke."

"You're the greatest, Darleen!"

She smiled an odd, distracted smile and kissed his cheek. "Remember, dear, it's not your fault," she whispered just before he turned and walked away, forever.

She watched until his car disappeared, then closed the door and walked slowly up the stairs. Her eyes had the strange, glassy look that always made her parents so uncomfortable. She entered her room and closed the door. "It's not your fault, darling." Her voice sounded strange in her ears, as though it was coming from a great distance. She walked to her dressing table and stared at her reflection. "People are weak, they just can't help it. It's human nature to make mistakes." Her tone was consoling, full of compassion, but the black eyes that stared back at her held no trace of emotion.

Months went by, and Luke and Eileen spent every possible moment in each other's company. They were like twin zombies, each wearing the perpetually dazed expression of youth in the thrall of a grand infatuation.

They instantly became "the couple of the hour" and were, without a doubt, the closest to movie-star celebrities the parish had ever seen.

But very little of the time they spent together was exclusive. They went to parties and balls, symphonies and plays, stepping into their roles as "glamorous young lovers" as though they'd been born to them.

They were young, they were beautiful, they were in love with being in love. It never occurred to either of them that for all of their declarations of adoration, and the tumultuous ecstasies of each other's touch, they barely knew each other.

They looked deep into the mirror of each other's eyes and discovered themselves anew—romanticized, idealized, fantasized—and for them, that was enough.

Their fathers were two of Chicago's most prominent businessmen. Eileen was as beautiful and delicate as any storybook princess, and Luke was the thirty-year-old heir to a fortune. He had served in Korea, where he had been decorated for bravery, and he was as handsome as Prince Charming.

It was manna from heaven for the Chicago society pages, and a day rarely went by without some detail appearing about Eileen and Luke's romance. One columnist even referred to them as the Windy City's "first couple" and drew parallels between them and the President and Mrs. Kennedy.

Four months after the Governor's Ball, the announcement everyone had been waiting for appeared. Luke and Eileen were engaged!

The wedding plans were hashed and rehashed in the papers, with columnists vying for details and correcting one another's "erroneous information," until finally they got it right.

"July wedding at the Cathedral; reception at the Drake; five hundred of their nearest and dearest. The couple will spend their wedding night at the McBride residence, leave the next day for Europe, London, Paris, Rome, Florence, Venice, Naples, Capri."

The wedding was the undisputed social event of the year. An invitation was the hottest ticket in town.

In a mindless rage, she threw the paper across the room, indifferent to where it landed. She lunged from the bed, picked up her reading lamp and sent it crashing against the wall. Shards of glass flew, and a few tiny splinters embedded themselves in the soft flesh of her cheek. She bent over to scoop up what remained of the lamp and hurl it once again. Her hands were shaking with unspent fury.

"Honey?" The door to her room swung open; her father stood there. "Honey, are you all right? I heard a crash."

She cursed under her breath, took a large gulp of air, then another, stood erect, and turned, a disarming, impish grin on her face.

"Oh, Daddy, I'm such a klutz! Look, I've knocked over my lovely reading lamp."

"Never mind the lamp, honey. Your face is bleeding!"

Her wide, dark eyes registered surprise. Her hand flew to her cheek. "Oh, it's nothing." She wrinkled her nose playfully. "Just a little scratch. But I'm afraid there's not much hope for me as a ballerina!"

When her father left, she retrieved the paper and studied the column again. One sentence seemed to jump out at her: "The couple will spend their wedding night at the McBride residence."

"How lovely," she whispered. "The McBrides are such nice people."

Everyone agreed that it was a magnificent wedding. Eileen's beauty brought tears to their eyes. As Luke watched her coming toward him down the aisle, his face seemed to be glowing.

As a little surprise at the reception, Jim and Moira gave the couple the honeymoon suite at the Drake. "We had an idea you'd be having too much fun to leave," Moira told them as she and Jim prepared to go home. "Your bags are already in the room. Have a wonderful trip!" she said, her voice breaking.

They all hugged one another, until finally Jim gently pried Moira and Eileen apart and led his wife out of the hotel.

As they walked up the steps to the front door, Moira asked Jim, for perhaps the hundredth time, "It really was beautiful, wasn't it, dear?"

He looked at her tenderly and opened his arms to his lovely Moira. In his eyes, she would forever remain his beautiful child bride. "It was magnificent," he assured her.

He turned his key. "Moira, is it possible that you forgot to lock the door this morning?"

"What! Me? As calm and unflustered and utterly relaxed as I was on the morning of my only child's wedding?"

They laughed together. In the state she'd been in, she would have forgotten her own head if it hadn't been attached.

"Let's go straight up," Jim suggested. "I'm exhausted."

"It's a bargain," Moira agreed. "I'm ready to drop, too."

They got word to Luke at six o'clock in the morning. He was gently stroking his bride's smooth back when he took the call. When he heard what had happened, he pulled his hand away as though he'd been burned.

Eileen conceived on her wedding night. There was never any doubt about that, for that was the last time her husband ever touched her. Just the thought of making love to her reminded him of his parents' death. The experts assured him that they had died of smoke inhalation long before the flames reached them, but he had a picture in his mind of his mother screaming, and he just couldn't make it go away.

They told him that the fire had started downstairs. The experts surmised that Jim had left one of his cigars burning in an ashtray and that somehow it had rolled to the floor and smoldered in the rug until around four in the morning. That was when the flames had first been sighted. There appeared to be a hot spot in the living room. What was strange was that there also appeared to be one in the dining room, and another in the den. But, after all, it was hard to be sure with a fire of this magnitude.

As it happened, Captain Shay had been on duty on the night of the fire, having left the reception early to begin his shift. He'd been one of the first men on the scene. Lucy overheard him arguing with Patrick over something to do with the fire, but she was so distracted with grief that she forgot to ask Patrick what they'd been fussing about.

Five

Luke McBride, once an athlete and honor student, then a war hero, then a carefree bachelor about town, was now a husband, soon to be a father, and the sole owner of a

multimillion-dollar company. The tragedy of his parents'
death had left him bleeding on the inside. But on the
outside, Luke appeared to be just fine.

He had dazzling good looks and the unmistakable
patina of wealth. He had charm and effortless style. But
what Luke had most of went beyond definition. It was that
unique, irresistible something called charisma. He had so
much of it that he could have bottled the stuff. It was in his
walk, the slope of his shoulders, the tilt of his head, his
contagious laughter. It was in his every unconscious gesture.

He was that rare being who could have anything he
wanted, anything at all—but he didn't know it. He didn't
even have an inkling.

And yet, Luke—beautiful, gifted Luke—had an invisi-
ble flaw. No matter where he was, who he was with, or what
he was doing, there was a part of him that was distracted—
in fact, tormented—by the thought that somewhere, someone was having a better time than he was. Somewhere the
real fun was happening, and he was missing it! As the
months went by, Luke became obsessed with visions of a
more glamorous, more exciting existence. He'd sit in his
newly decorated den with its hip, multicolored shag carpet-
ing, and he'd crank up Frank, and Dean, and Sammy on his
new stereo hi-fi to drown out the growling lawn mowers,
and the barking dogs, and the laughing children, and all of
the other suffocating sounds of suburban living.

He'd lie back with his eyes closed, listening to the boys,
and feel a longing so deep and piercing that to him it felt
like need for a world and a life that were going on without
him. For the rat pack and the jet set and the girls who let
you call them "chick." For places like Aspen and Vegas and
Beverly Hills, where the *real* fun was happening.

One day Luke realized that he couldn't live without it.
He arranged an invitation for himself and a few of his
friends to play in a golf tournament in Vegas, which led to
an invitation to a party in Tahoe, which led to another, and
another . . . and before he knew it, his dream was coming
true.

The "Chicago Boys" were like a fresh, wild wind blow-ing through. Rough edges and all, somehow they seemed more vivid and alive than the usual crowd. Luke and his friends, pals since grammar school, were tall and earthy and ruggedly handsome. All of them were married, too, but they didn't let that bother them. They were like a pack of hungry wolves circling around Luke, eager to snatch up any of his crumbs, ready to close in and take his place.

For Luke was the leader of the pack. He outshone "his gang," and though he was unaware of it, they were not, and they hated him for it. It was Luke who was fawned over. It was he whom people crowded around, wanting to "be seen" with him. And it was he who received the invitations. Without him, "his gang" would have been just another bunch of stiffs trying to get lucky, and they knew it.

Six months into marriage, Luke was leading a bizarre double life: he was an increasingly sullen and distant husband, and he was a glamorous Chicago playboy, jet-setter, and swinger.

He was pursued by starlets whom other men only fantasized about, and he partied aboard billionaires' yachts. He was living part-time in paradise, and he spent the rest of the time wishing he were there.

Not that he didn't think about Eileen. He did, at first. He thought about her a lot. He knew what he was doing to her; he could read it in her eyes. His guilt caused him many sleepless nights until he figured out a solution. It was simple, once he got to thinking about it. All he had to do was to blame her.

After all, was it his fault she was so . . . Midwestern? Did she have to be so hopelessly square? His inability to make love to her was due to the fact that she did so little to make herself desirable, even after he made suggestions. Couldn't she dye her hair blond or something? A push-up bra would have helped. Why didn't she have her makeup professionally done? The pros might have given her some ideas.

Before long, he was convinced that his transgressions were entirely her fault. He sent the message loud and clear that she was no longer attractive as a woman. Soon he had convinced her, too.

Of course she was as beautiful as ever, but she didn't

know it. She'd been coddled all of her life, admired and adored. She was utterly unprepared to cope with Luke's rejection. She lost the inner sparkle that had been so much a part of her. It was as though someone had pulled the plug on her and let all the joy escape. Desolate and alone, too proud to confide in anyone, Eileen waited for the birth of her child.

She lounged against a pile of fluffy white pillows. Her dark hair spilled down her shoulder, partially concealing one soft, round breast. The newspaper was propped against her knees.

Scanning the page, her eyes quickly found what she was looking for.

"Mr. and Mrs. Lucas J. McBride proudly announce the birth . . ."

Her grip tightened on the page. "Just as if I didn't exist," she said aloud. "As if nothing ever happened . . ."

She remembered the night so clearly; it seemed more like yesterday than nine months ago. She'd managed everything so perfectly . . . except that she'd made just one mistake, that was all.

She should never have stayed to watch the flames. She'd known it at the time, but oh, they were so spectacular! First the crackling, then the explosions, finally the deafening roar. She'd actually had to cross the street to escape the heat.

There, crouched in a hedge, she'd stayed to watch the blue inferno grow. That's where he had found her, the little monster, none other than Matthew Madigan. He'd heard the explosions from his bed (two blocks away!) and come out to investigate.

"Well, well," he'd said, looking down at her. "I see you can't sleep either."

"N-No," she'd stammered, faltering for barely an instant. "I just came out for a stroll, and then saw this horrible fire."

His eyes had reflected amusement. "Oh, right. I know, the house just spontaneously combusted, like in science class."

As he spoke, the night had filled with the sound of approaching sirens. Sweat had begun trickling from her brow and beading on her upper lip.

"We'd better leave, don't you think?" she'd asked, a little too eagerly. She'd struggled to instill calm into her voice, but she had begun to feel trapped. Her heart had been racing. The sirens were growing louder.

"Ya think," he'd asked, "that maybe we should just stay and explain to the firemen how the house just, ya know, combusted?" He'd grinned at her slyly, searching her face, enjoying her discomfort.

"But maybe you're right," he'd said finally. The sirens were drawing terrifyingly close. "Maybe we better skedaddle!"

He'd been tormenting her with those eyes ever since, enjoying the power he held over her. She'd stopped wondering why he didn't tell, because the answer had become obvious: he was having too much fun torturing her!

She came back to the present with a jolt. "Enough!" she said, her voice firm. "No more! No more mistakes, no more reminders!"

Six

She opened her eyes and came instantly awake. The sun had not yet risen, and the room was dark and still. The newspaper lay where she had placed it, inches from her hand. The sheets were smooth across her body, unrumpled, the pillows neat. Even in sleep, she remained in tight control, utterly disciplined.

Rising, she walked to the window. A faint mist hung in the air. The streets and sidewalks were damp, reflecting the still-lit streetlights. She breathed in the thick, spring air, then turned and dressed quickly, eager to walk the dark streets, too excited to remain inside, waiting.

She was almost out the door when an idea occurred to her. As happened so often, once she'd had the thought, she became almost consumed by it, compelled to act. She returned to her room, flipped through the directory, found the number she sought, and dialed.

"Mercy, can I help you?" a tired-sounding voice asked.

"Mrs. Eileen McBride's room, please. Maternity." She was expecting an argument about the earliness of the hour, but she was pleasantly surprised.

"I'll ring you through. Our new mothers just finished their early feeding."

She felt a thrill when the phone rang, and then Eileen came on.

"Hello?" Eileen sounded exhausted. "Hello, hello, is anyone there? Luke, is that you?"

She smiled, replaced the receiver, and went out into the night.

She walked the neighborhood for two hours. The adrenaline coursing through her veins made the minutes spin by like seconds. Despite the mist, the world seemed in sharper focus than ever before. She felt marvelous, strong and clear-headed.

She stood on the empty lot that nine months ago had been the McBride home. Only a pine tree remained. In its shadow, she held up her hands and stared at them: small white hands with crimson nails, capable of so much. She realized that the sun had risen.

It occurred to her that she could have taken the child by now. But no, there was a proper order to things that must be respected. Matt would be first.

She went back home and entered through the rear door. Of course, it was open. No one in this neighborhood ever locked their kitchen door; Pete's Dairy still delivered five mornings a week, just like in the old days. She slipped inside. There were dishes in the rack beside the sink, and cutlery as well . . . She heard a voice in the hallway.

"I'm really worried, Doctor. His fever is up to a hundred and three. Yes, he's soaking in a cool tub now, but he's so weak . . ."

She tiptoed up the stairs to the bathroom. The door was slightly ajar. Slowly, she pushed it open and peered in.

His eyes were closed, and he was submerged in water up to his neck. Still as pale and scrawny as ever, she thought. It was hard to believe how well things were working out!

She stepped into the room and stood over him.

"Mom?" he asked weakly.

"No, dear," she whispered. "It's me."

His eyes flew open at the sound of her voice. He opened his mouth to cry out, but she gripped his face in her powerful hands and forced him below the surface of the water.

He was so weak that he scarcely fought. She held him down until the bubbles stopped, and a little longer just for good measure.

"Good-bye, Matt," she said softly, then rose and left the house.

She experienced a letdown halfway to the hospital. Feeling suddenly spent, drained of energy, she stopped to rest on a bench at the corner of Ninety-fifty Street. After a while, the spell passed and she continued on.

Slipping unnoticed through a side entrance of Mercy Hospital, she felt a resurgence of strength and resolve. Locating the maternity floor was a simple task—the information was posted in the elevator.

She walked along the nearly empty corridor, smiling placidly at a young nurse hurrying by.

After trying three doors marked "Hospital Personnel Only," she found the nurses' locker room. She had hoped to find a spare uniform, but all the lockers were either padlocked or empty. Finally, beside a row of sinks, she found a laundry bin piled with used towels and dirty uniforms. She rummaged through them, settling upon the least soiled and wrinkled uniform of the lot. It was large enough to slip easily over her slim skirt and thin blouse.

She examined herself in the mirror. Her cheeks were flushed, and her dark eyes flashed, glittering with sudden, unexpected arousal. She felt a warm, tingling sensation between her legs. Her expression reflected her surprise. This was something new—unexplored territory—but she had no time to linger and enjoy it.

She left the locker room and followed the winding

corridor until she found the windowed nursery. Glancing over her shoulder, she entered.

There were no nurses there—only seven babies, swaddled in blankets and tucked in cribs. She walked directly to the third infant. She didn't really need to check the tag; she could feel that this was Luke's child. But she glanced down, just to be sure.

The tag read "Baby McBride."

"Hello, baby," she whispered, stroking the infant's flaming cap of hair. She spoke in a singsong voice, like someone reading a nursery rhyme. "You didn't know you were a mistake, did you? A very bad mistake. Poor, poor baby. Auntie will fix. You just weren't supposed to be, that's all." She reached for the child.

"Such a shame, Mr. McBride, missing the birth and all. But you men are always working, aren't you? In a way, though, maybe you're lucky . . . Your little one's three days old now, past that pinched look the newborns always have. I imagine your wife was thrilled to see you." The cheerful voice floated in through the open door.

Luke! Clutching the child to her breast, she searched wildly for a hiding place, but saw only bassinettes and flat white surfaces. She took a deep breath and forced herself to remain calm. There was only one thing to do.

She laid the infant back in its crib. "Another time," she promised, glancing down at the infant's face. She gasped, for the eyes were no longer closed, but wide open, staring at her as if in recognition. They were the greenest eyes she'd ever seen.

"Witch!" she whispered superstitiously.

She rushed from the room, averting her face from Luke's eyes, almost knocking into the elderly nun who stood beside him.

"Nurse," the old woman cried, "what in the world? Nurse!"

She walked briskly down the corridor, careful to keep her head down. She rounded a corner and found a stairwell almost immediately. How lucky she was! She should have located the stairs in the first place.

She shed the oversized uniform as she went and minutes later, emerged on the main floor in her simple skirt and blouse.

Crossing the lobby, she returned the flirtatious smile of a handsome young sailor and asked a uniformed security guard to direct her to the cafeteria.

There, after selecting a large Coke and a tuna fish sandwich, she slid into a booth and assessed her situation.

By the time she'd finished her food, she'd come to a decision. There was no avoiding it, she'd have to bide her time. Disappointing, but in the long run, for the best. In the meantime, she'd get on with the business of living her own life.

Seven

Take all the best of what the Sweeneys and the McBrides had to offer, roll it into one, and you had Farrell Moira McBride, Eileen and Luke's eight-pound, four-ounce baby girl. She had her mother's black lashes and brows. She had Great-grandma Kate's exotic tilt to her green eyes, and Kate's gold-and-copper hair, only brighter, like a sunburst. She was long-limbed like Moira, warmhearted like Lucy, clever like Patrick, direct like Jim, artistic like Meg. Plus that, she had her father's "presence."

For a while, her daughter seemed to be enough for Eileen. The baby provided an absorbing distraction from her heartbreak. But as the months wore on, and then a year, with Luke spending more and more time away on "business trips," the joy of motherhood lost its ability to dull her pain.

Eileen's drinking started on one dreary November evening when Farrell was eight months old. Luke was out of town again, the house felt damp and chilly, and Eileen was deeply depressed over the shocking news of the day: President John F. Kennedy had been assassinated. It started innocently enough, taking a drink to bed just to help her sleep. But by the time Farrell was three, Luke was absent for ninety percent of the time and Eileen was drunk by seven o'clock every evening. To Farrell, having no basis for comparison, Luke's absence seemed normal. What was frightening was never knowing which mommy she would encounter from one minute to the next. There was her happy, smiling mommy, or her angry, yelling mommy; there was the mommy who would look at her as though she didn't know her, and the one who scared her most of all—the sad mommy, who sat on the couch in the living room and cried and cried, until the pink-silk pillows were spotted dark with her tears.

Perhaps that's why Farrell was so vulnerable when the lady came.

It was a bright cold spring morning, and Farrell was outside, playing hopscotch in the driveway. She was immersed in the game, her breath forming vapor clouds and her long red-gold hair flying as she bounced from square to square.

She didn't see the lady walking toward her, didn't notice her standing so close, until the lady took another step and her shadow blocked the sun.

Farrell turned.

The lady wore a dark green cloak, and a hood that hung loosely around her face, casting her features in shadow. In spite of the hood, Farrell could tell that she was very pretty and that she had the biggest smile . . . The lady held out her hand.

"Do you want to play with me?" the child asked, appraising her hopefully.

"Of course I do," the lady said. "Come, Farrell. I know a much better game."

Just then the front door opened and Mommy called, "Farrell, are you out there without a coat?"

"But Mommy, the lady says she wants to play!" She turned to the lady . . . who was nowhere to be seen now.

"What lady? Farrell, stop telling stories and come inside. It's cold!"

After that, Farrell became even more shy and withdrawn than she'd been before. Her Aunt Meg, though unaware of Eileen's drinking, was very much concerned about her overly quiet niece. She arrived one day when

Farrell was four with an armload of art supplies, convinced that she could bring Farrell out of her shell by teaching her to express herself artistically.

At first Eileen protested Meg's expenditure, for Farrell's doting aunt had outfitted the child with an easel, a paintbox, brushes, palettes, canvas boards, oil paints, and watercolors. But eventually Eileen had to concede that Meg had been right. Farrell spent countless hours at her easel and showed remarkable talent for a child her age. She painted animals, and trees, and many portraits of "the lady," with a huge white smile and welcoming arms.

It never occurred to either Meg or Eileen that Farrell was using her painting as an escape. Of course Eileen minimized her drinking problem, and Meg was unaware of it. The idea that a child of four could have anything to escape from would have seemed absurd to both of them, had anyone suggested it.

And so, little Farrell McBride, blessed with so many natural gifts, painted away the moments of her childhood and spent countless lonely nights staring out at the cold black sky until it faded into dawn.

Eight

Finally, in 1970, when Farrell was seven, it was Meg's turn. After years—in fact, after a lifetime—of waiting and dreaming, she and Danny were getting married!

The waiting had been sheer torture as one friend after another had married, moved off campus and set up housekeeping—and now some of them already had children! But Danny had insisted on "doing it right."

"I won't have you struggling that way, Meg," he'd said on one of the many occasions when she had tried to convince him to elope. "Every one of those girls has had to drop out of school. And look at the apartments they're living in."

When she urged that "true love can't wait," he'd replied that "true love is worth waiting for." In the end, he won out by simply refusing to marry her until they each graduated. She didn't push it too far, because deep down, she wanted her wedding day to be special. After all, she'd been planning it since the first grade! And so they had waited, and if there was a love worth waiting for, it was theirs.

The Sweeney household was thrown into a tizzy of preparation. Patrick went on record that Danny was "ruining it for the rest of us men by carrying on so and acting as delirious as a bride." He instructed Danny to "look a little more mournful and reluctant, as is considered proper demeanor for a man about to be married." He was revving up to continue when he noticed the look Lucy was giving him and wisely decided to shut up instead.

Kate and Lucy were poised to throw themselves into the planning when Meg let it be known, in no uncertain terms, that she needed foot soldiers, not generals. She'd been planning this occasion for over a decade, and at twenty-two, she knew down to the smallest detail exactly what she wanted.

Hers would be an outdoor wedding on the rolling green lawns of Patrick's club. She knew what color linens they would use, the arrangement of the tables, and the kinds of flowers in the centerpieces. There was not a single detail that she hadn't already orchestrated.

She would wear flowers in her hair in lieu of a veil, and she knew just how her dress would look. All she had to do was to find it.

With Kate and Lucy, she spent literally hundreds of hours searching for "The Dress." Long after Kate and Lucy had despaired of finding anything that would please the "fanatic," as Kate called her, Meg walked into a store with a bedraggled Lucy and Kate in tow and found the dress of her dreams.

Danny was outraged when they refused to show it to him. "But that's crazy!" he insisted. "I have a right to see that dress. And besides, I have exquisite taste!"

Kate looked at him, shaking her head, and turned to Lucy. "Now I know he's lost his mind. A pity, too. He was such a nice boy."

Danny appealed to the Captain and Patrick for support. "Have you ever heard of anything so ridiculous?" he demanded. "They won't let me see my own fiancée's dress!"

Patrick gestured to the Captain, the Captain nodded, and they moved together, each grabbing an arm and leading Danny to the den.

"Come on, Danny," coaxed Patrick. "We'll have a little nip to calm your nerves."

"My nerves don't need calming!" Danny yelled.

"Well then, have a nip to calm mine!" the Captain roared.

Meg asked Eileen to be her matron of honor and Farrell to be her flower girl. The bride's joy was so infectious that soon Eileen appeared to be getting into the swing of things. For the first time in ages, she seemed to regain some of her old spark.

Farrell's transformation was even more drastic. It had happened so gradually that no one had noticed quite how somber and withdrawn the child had become—until they were presented with the contrast. Suddenly she was like a new person, carefree and bubbly, bursting with enthusiasm. She was fascinated with every aspect of the wedding, oohing and aahing over even the tiniest details. Eileen was shocked at the change in her daughter and began to realize how much Farrell was being affected by her mother's moods.

That summer's progression could be measured by the parties held in the couple's honor: brunches, cocktail parties, showers, and dinners. Danny and Meg reveled in the celebrations. They had waited for so long; now they intended to savor every single minute. Their shared love was so clearly stamped on them that it showed in their every look and gesture. It was like an energy field that encompassed only themselves, so real that even the worst cynics had to admit to feeling a little flutter at the sight of Danny and Meg together.

One week before the wedding, the Sweeneys' next-door neighbor, Dora Riley, gave a shower for Meg at her club. It was a lavish affair, attended by fifty women dressed to the teeth, and coiffed and bejeweled to the nines.

Meg, in handmade ecru lace, had never looked more beautiful. Her color was high, and her huge dark eyes sparkled as she moved among the guests, thanking them for their gifts. The ladies, pleasantly stuffed with crab salad, asparagus with hollandaise, sherbet and petits fours, were now table-hopping, sipping coffee and munching butter cookies.

The talk at one of the tables Meg was visiting was of the latest tragedy that had befallen the Madigan family.

"You remember them, Lucy," Shirley Haggerty insisted. "The daughter was engaged to Eileen's Luke years ago—stunning girl."

"Oh, yes." Lucy remembered how Moira had felt about her. "They moved away, didn't they, a few years ago?"

"After their son drowned, right in their own bathtub! Terrible how tragedy seems to follow some people. And now this."

"What happened?" Lucy asked, curiosity getting the better of her.

"Oh, it's terrible." Shirley was reveling in being "in the know." "Darleen's husband and new baby were killed in a fire. Apparently their home burned down—a mansion, I hear, somewhere in Texas. It was a miracle that she escaped. From what they say, he was as rich as sin—oil money." She *tsked* loudly. "A lot of good it'll do him now."

Just then Dora Riley, who was feeling extremely pleased with her successful hostessing, approached the group and interrupted their conversation. "So, Meg, dear," she asked, "are you enjoying your little party?"

Meg turned to her with a radiant smile and was about to answer, when suddenly the smile left her face and she gasped. Everyone turned to see what was wrong. She let out a scream, her face twisted.

"Oh, no!" she cried. "No! *Danny!*" She screamed his name only once, then turned, her eyes full of unspeakable grief, and sought Lucy. "Oh, Mom!" she wailed. "It's my Danny!"

Before Lucy could reach her, Meg had collapsed in a faint.

"Get a doctor!" Lucy screamed to Eileen and knelt at Meg's side, terrified at her pale face.

The ladies crowded around, whispering among themselves. They were unsure of how to react, struck somewhere between concern for Meg and dismay at her unheard-of outburst.

Lucy held Meg's head in her lap and prayed for the doctor to hurry. Kate made it through the crowd and knelt on the floor beside her.

"What do you think, Mom?" Lucy asked frantically. "What's wrong with her?"

Kate looked at her granddaughter's pale face and gently brushed her hair back from her forehead.

"I don't think there's anything wrong with her," she said, looking meaningfully at Lucy.

Just then Lucy heard her name being called. It was Patrick. Thank God, she thought, thank God he's here!

She looked up and saw him towering above the crowd of women, but one glance at his face drained the relief from her. Dread took its place. She had never, in all their thirty years together, seen her husband cry.

He stopped moving when their eyes met. He stood perfectly still, his arms hanging limply at his sides, tears streaming, oblivious to the staring women. "Ahhhh, Lucy," he said, weeping helplessly. "It's our Danny. He's gone."

"Gone?" Lucy asked, refusing to understand.

"He's dead, Lucy," Patrick cried. "Oh, God help us, he's dead."

The women, shocked, turned to one another, and in a matter of minutes, the room was buzzing with a single question. It wasn't "How did he die?" No, indeed. What they asked one another was "How did Meg know?"

There was something distinctly odd about Meg Sweeney. Amazingly, for many, that observation managed to overshadow the tragedy.

The Sweeney family was devastated by Danny's death. The house became a place of somber whispers, soundless footsteps, and eyes lowered to avoid the pain in others' faces.

An artery had burst in Danny's brain. He had had no

warning, had felt no pain. He was alive one instant, and dead the next. The doctors kept assuring everyone that it could have happened at any time, as though that was some sort of consolation. But what Meg wanted to do was to scream back at them, *"Why now? Why not in fifty years?"*

She withdrew completely. Her pain was so raw that to look at her was like a physical blow—it took your breath away. For months she remained in her darkened room, without energy or will. She responded only to Kate, and even to her, just barely.

Kate understood the depth of Meg's loss, and she alone had the strength to deal honestly with the tragedy. She offered no false cheer, empty promises, or assurances that "Things will be all right." Kate knew, and the knowledge broke her heart, that nothing would ever really be all right for Meg again.

There were no words that could give comfort; Kate knew this, and she offered none. She was simply there, stroking Meg's hair, holding her hand, or sitting beside her as she slept. As the months wore on, the heavy grief began to take its toll on Kate.

One bitter night in mid-November, Kate tucked an extra comforter around Meg's sleeping form and went to her room. She knelt, as she had every day of her life, by the side of her bed, her hands folded in prayer, her head bowed in devotion.

At eight-thirty the following morning, Lucy decided that she would take a peek just to see if Kate was all right, for usually she was up and about by six. Cautiously, she pushed the door open and peered in. Kate was so tiny that she barely made a mound in the blankets. Lucy tiptoed a little closer to the bed, and the moment she saw Kate's face, she knew.

Meg found Lucy an hour later, sitting on the edge of Kate's bed, tears streaming down her cheeks.

"Mom?" Meg whispered anxiously from the doorway.

Lucy turned to her. "It's silly," she said, wiping her eyes. "I had this feeling that if I just sat here and didn't say anything, it wouldn't be true."

Nine

Mrs. Elliot (Duke) Steager McCleary stood on the corner opposite the McBride home. She wore a Chanel suit from this year's spring showing. She'd flown to the showing aboard her late husband's Lear jet, accompanied by "the cream" of Texas society (i.e., the richest broads in the state). In Texas, bloodlines mattered only in discussing horses or cows. You could be an ex-hooker, or a dowager, darlin'. Money was all that mattered.

She wore glamorous dark sunglasses identical to the ones favored by Princess Grace. Her sleek dark hair was styled in an elegant chignon. With her newly reed-thin figure, her sense of style and poise, she would shine in any setting. Especially in the right one—like Washington, D.C. Yes, the seventies would be her decade to shine!

"Washington," she whispered. The mere sound of it was magic.

She'd gotten terribly sick of Texas: the homey, folksy, Texas twangs; the endless conversations about livestock and oil; and the barbecues, the goddamned barbecues! They could dress them up, serve the mess on crystal and bone china, in trumped-up Georgian palaces sprung from the dusty plains . . . but they were barbecues nonetheless.

God, but she'd been bored. Bored with the state, with their crowd, but mostly bored with Duke, with his doting smile and big pawing hands . . . and the baby! The brat had been the biggest bore of all.

Motherhood! She didn't know what all the fuss was about. She'd felt no tie whatsoever to the black-haired, reddish creature they'd placed in her arms. Nothing.

She hadn't felt anything on the night of the fire, either. No anticipatory thrill. Nothing. It was just a job, a necessary task to be performed in order to regain her freedom and get on with her life.

She studied the McBride house. She felt far more connected to the child who lived within those walls. A child who had twice defied her. There was the thrill she sought.

Not just a duty, but a mission. She was destined to correct the mistake that that young life represented.

But she must be patient. Now was not the time. With the family in mourning, the child was under constant supervision.

She'd be back. In the meantime, she had worlds to conquer—worlds where power and money went hand in hand. She'd been mistaken to think that money alone was enough to fill the void within her. It was a necessity of course, like air. But one didn't build one's life around it. Power was what she'd been missing. Real power would satisfy the longing that consumed her . . . and appease her silent fury.

Ten

Mrs. Patrick Sweeney, Jr. was furious! She slammed around the bedroom wearing her new too-tight pink-satin teddy—Bridget steadfastly refused to acknowledge her passage from a size twelve to a sixteen. Though the teddy made the most of her still magnificent breasts, it cupped her ample bottom so snugly that she had to keep tugging at it, which is why Junior had finally averted his eyes. He just couldn't bear the sight of her pulling on the damn thing one more time!

Assuming that his attention was riveted upon her, she pouted artfully into her Hollywood-style dressing mirror . . . and caught him in the act of ignoring her. With one clean stroke, she sent a thousand dollars' worth of oils, lotions, perfumes, and powders crashing to the floor.

"Aw, Bridgey!" Junior wailed. He inched his way to their canopied bed and ducked to snatch up his gray trousers just in time to escape being decapitated by the silver-backed hand mirror she catapulted in his direction.

"Oh, sweetie, look!" he cried. The mirror had crashed into the wall and splintered into a thousand tiny pieces. "Now you'll have bad luck!"

"Bad luck!" she screamed. "Bad luck! I've had nothing but bad luck since the day I met you, Junior Sweeney."

"Now, honey—"

"Don't you honey me, you simp! I hate you!" With that, she let fly the silver-handled hairbrush, missing his face by inches. "It's all your fault I missed my trip to Paris. All you care about is your stupid family!"

"Bridgey," he said, "I can't help it that my grandmother died. I wanted to go to Paris, too. But how would it look if we missed Grandma's funeral? The old man would never forgive me."

"All you Sweeneys do anymore is go to funerals!" she shrieked. "First that simpy Danny, who we hardly knew, and now your grandmother. For Christ's sake, Junior, the old lady was eighty if she was a day! I mean, it's not like it's a tragedy or anything." She took a moment to catch her breath and then added with a pout, "She never liked me anyway."

Junior couldn't argue with her there; Kate hadn't liked Bridget much. Not that the two of them had had much to do with Kate, or with the rest of the family, for that matter. He and Bridget had an active social life that revolved around their country club. They spent only as much time with the family as they considered necessary to "stay on the old man's good side," as Junior put it. Their two children, Kimberly and Patrick III, knew their paternal grandparents only slightly, and had met their aunts and cousin Farrell only when they'd joined the Sweeney family for Thanksgiving. Bridget considered it more civilized to have most of their holidays at the club.

Junior sat on the bed and reflected on the past months. It did seem like they did go to a lot of funerals lately. Danny's wake—what an ordeal! And the rumors! Meg had really managed to embarrass them this time, as he had always known she would. All the nonsense about her "being sensitive" and "having premonitions." He'd always known it would come out someday, and boy, had it ever!

The church had been so packed that people were waiting on the steps to get in. At first Junior had been amazed at how many friends Danny had. But when he had listened to what they were saying, he'd realized that most of these people weren't there to mourn, oh no! They were there to get the dope on Meg. The ladies at Dora Riley's shower had talked such a blue streak that by the time the wake took place, the stories were rampant and wild. Even Junior had been shocked.

In fact, he had become so preoccupied with worrying about how such talk would affect his social standing at the club that he'd failed to realize that Bridget was contributing enormously to the problem. She was busy spreading the rumors he was trying to squelch, revealing to anyone who would listen everything Junior had ever confided to her about Meg.

Junior brightened as he remembered his news. "You won't have to put up with my family much longer."

"Oh, right!" Bridget shot back sarcastically. "Only the rest of my life."

"No, really," he persisted. "Mom's decided she wants everyone to have a change of scenery. She's talked Dad into buying a second home in some godforsaken corner of the world called, believe it or not, the Village."

"The Village!" she screamed. "Are you talking about the Village in Michigan?"

"You've heard of it?" Junior asked, flabbergasted by her reaction.

"Heard of it? Junior, everyone who knows anything has heard of the Village. It is *the* place to go in the summer. My God! Colleen Berry and Franny Hennessey never shut up about the place. They act as though they invented it."

Bridget narrowed her eyes and pointed a stubby finger at her husband's nose. "Junior Sweeney! You listen to me! If anyone in this family is getting a house in the Village, it's me."

"But—"

"Listen to me, Junior! Does the name Bud Harrigan ring a bell?"

"Well, of course. But—"

"What about Pete McGuire?"

"Him, too?"

"Junior, I told you, everyone who is anyone has a house there. McGuire, Harrigan, even the Whalens!"

The Whalens did it. Junior now realized that he needed a house in the Village.

"But how will we do it, Bridge?" he asked anxiously. "Dad will expect me to mind the company, and we really can't afford another house."

"Don't be stupid, Junior. We don't move there permanently. I move up with the kids for the summer; you stay here and work during the week and drive up on weekends."

"I still don't see how we can afford it, not on what he pays me."

"Junior, we won't have to afford it. You just go to your father looking as heartbroken as you can manage and tell him how much you wish you could swing a place nearby, because—now listen carefully—in times like these, families should pull together. Got it?"

He repeated her words earnestly. "In times like these, families should pull together." He smiled appreciatively. "Sweetie, you're brilliant!"

He reached for her, but she slapped his hand away. "Don't muss me, Junior," she said primly.

Together, they finished dressing and departed for Kate's funeral.

Eleven

The Village lay like a sleeping child, cloaked in the cool, rose-filtered mist of almost-morning.

"The Village." Whether it was named carelessly, and with a rather shocking lack of creativity, or with a sublime sort of arrogance, implying that this, of course, was the only village worth mentioning, no one could recall. It was simply, had always been, "the Village."

From a purely aesthetic point of view, it was a miracle—surrounded on three sides by miles of ancient spruce and pine forests, and bordered on the fourth side by the white sand beaches and endless blue of Lake Michigan.

The Village nestled cozily, tucked up against the forests, its toes dipped languidly in the water.

Lucy had first heard of it from Moira McBride, whose family had rented a cottage there when Moira was a child. Lucy recalled Moira's loving description of the peaceful summertime community and decided to investigate.

The more she found out about it, the more convinced she became that this was a place where her grief-stricken husband and daughter could begin to heal. She summoned her considerable strength, set aside her own grief, and began the task of helping her loved ones to recover.

At first she had to force them to accompany her each Saturday on an excursion to the Village. But soon she started using other tactics. If she played them off of each other, she could distract them from their sorrow.

The weekend trips became a sort of therapy for all of them. Before long, the beauty of the Village had penetrated their ennui, and they began to look forward to Saturdays and the hours when they were forced to consider the future and stop dwelling in their memories.

At last they found the house, and asked only one question of the agent: "How much?" It was an elegant white-brick Georgian mansion with three-story-high pillars and an expansive veranda. It had its own swimming pool and eight acres of land, and overlooked the golf course, the wild In-Between, and the forests beyond.

Soon after they bought the house, Junior had a talk with his parents in which he discussed his desire to join them in purchasing "a little place" in the Village. Patrick had been moved almost to tears at this evidence of Junior's loyalty, but Lucy was more practical. "What about Bridget?" she asked doubtfully. "How would she feel about spending her summers away from your club?"

"She agrees with me completely," Junior assured them. "We believe that in times like these, families should pull together."

Patrick insisted on buying Junior's house for him. "After all," he explained to Lucy, "he's really doing this for us." Lucy had her doubts, but she wouldn't hurt Patrick by voicing them.

Before long, Patrick discovered a new pastime. It was called "buying up every lot he could get his hands on." With his eye for real estate, it hadn't taken him long to decide that the Village, with its unsurpassed natural beauty, its relative proximity to Chicago, and, most important, the limited extent of its land, would one day be a valuable investment.

What made his new hobby interesting was the fact that he had an anonymous competitor. Every lot he bid on was also bid on by someone who, for some reason, had established a blind trust. Patrick surmised that his adversary was a crooked politician or businessman who was hiding ill-gotten cash. His imagined scenario added spice to his hobby and made every victory that much sweeter and every defeat twice as bitter. In spite of his suspicions, Patrick respected his rival's business acumen and strategic sense, and the thrill of competition became far more important to him than the mere acquisition of land.

The only real estate that didn't interest Patrick was the lakefront. He'd never learned to swim and had a fear of the water. He found the sound of rolling waves ominous rather than peaceful, and the thought of houses hanging off hill-tops made him nervous. So he left the lakefront to his nameless antagonist.

Lucy was so pleased with the results of her strategy that she decided to apply the same tactics to Eileen. Though unaware of the seriousness of Eileen's drinking, Lucy found her depression obvious. She began calling her elder daughter and fretting about Meg's state of mind.

"She's not even painting!" she confided to Eileen in her fifth call that week. "Eileen, I know how busy you are," she lied, "but I wondered if you and Farrell could possibly visit for a few weeks, perhaps for a month? It would do Meg a world of good to have you near." It almost broke Lucy's heart to hear how eagerly Eileen accepted her suggestion.

If she could have, Eileen would have leaped right through the phone. She was desperately lonely. Luke had all but deserted her, and she was too ashamed to confide in anyone. The prospect of joining her family in Michigan was more of a lifeline than Lucy imagined.

* * *

As it turned out, it was Farrell who succeeded in getting through to Meg. Each day she would cart her supplies into her aunt's room, set herself up at the window, and begin to paint.

At first Meg would simply smile at her vacantly, then drift off again into a world of her own. But eventually the artist in her took over. Farrell was so talented, and had such remarkable powers of concentration, that Meg had to get involved. It began with a suggestion or two: "Try mixing a little gray in . . . that's it!" Or, "You might find it easier to work the sky with your palette knife."

Before long, Meg had her own easel set up beside Farrell's and was completely immersed in the process of teaching her niece everything she knew about painting. As the days went by, Meg's field of vision expanded beyond her own grief. She became concerned that her niece never went outside to play with other children. She encouraged her to make friends, but Farrell steadfastly refused. Meg realized that the child was laboring under some terrible burdens of her own and that, for some reason, she had chosen Meg to help her cope with them.

Meg began taking Farrell on little painting excursions. Initially they ventured only as far as their own property line. But eventually they began packing lunch, wearing swimsuits beneath their grubby painting clothes, and heading out for entire days of painting, swimming, and building sand castles on the beach.

Farrell took to the waves like a fish. In no time, she was effortlessly gliding past Meg, cutting the water with clean, sure strokes. Her smooth skin became burnished by the sun, and her long waves of copper hair glinted with golden highlights. She lost the pinched, sorrowful look she had arrived with. Though still a child, her features were beginning to blossom and sending out the unmistakable message that here were the beginnings of a great beauty.

Her exotic green eyes seemed almost luminescent in her finely sculpted, tawny face. At eight, she was slender and as long-limbed as a newborn filly. She carried herself with the unconscious grace of a natural athlete. And there was something else about Farrell—something more. Perhaps it was because she had borne the responsibility for adult emotions for so long. The men who watched her playing on the beach or splashing in the water didn't think about the child she was, but instead, dreamed of the woman she would one day become.

It was the best time of Farrell's young life. In addition to swimming and painting, she and Meg began taking long walks in the surrounding forests in search of interesting subjects to paint. Before long, it was apparent that Farrell had a special knack with animals. They seemed to sense that she was harmless. Meg was amazed at how close they would allow her to come to them, sometimes near enough to touch.

By the end of that first summer, Farrell had brought home and nursed to health a collection of ailing strays. She cared for the animals with a deftness and a natural instinct that amazed everyone around her. When at last one day she was confronted with a problem that she was unable to solve, she overcame her natural shyness and went for help.

When she arrived at Dr. Tenholm's residence with the injured bird in a shoe box, she didn't realize that she was calling on one of the country's most prominent cardiologists.

Jan Tenholm opened the door and recognized the stunning child she'd seen so often at the lake. Farrell's earnest expression fleetingly reminded her of her son, Max, when he was small. Seeing the protective way Farrell was cradling the shoe box, she immediately called for her husband.

Jan was a tall, large-boned woman with an air of breeding. One could imagine her at the helm of a sailboat, buffeted by winds and a salty spray, or having a quiet dinner at the White House. Her cinnamon-brown hair was pulled back casually and tied with a scarf, her skin was suntanned and glowed with aggressive good health, and her eyes were a startling, vivid blue.

She hunkered down and peered into the box.

"What's the trouble?" she asked kindly, her voice a warbling soprano.

"I think its wing is broken," Farrell answered, "but I don't know how to splint it. I haven't done that yet."

"Norman will know how."

"Norman will know how to do what?" asked her husband, appearing in the doorway.

"Splint the wing."

"Splint the what?"

"My robin's wing." Farrell held out the box. "I haven't learned how to do that."

Norman, quite accustomed to his lofty position, was shocked by the suggestion that he perform such a lowly task. He was on the verge of refusing when he looked at Farrell. Never had anyone appealed to him with such complete faith as this beautiful child on his doorstep. He turned hopefully to Jan, but she was clearly going to be of no help. She had her arms folded across her chest and a distinctly amused glint in her eye.

"But, I don't . . . birds aren't . . . Oh, bring it on in!"

Farrell followed him into the house and watched as he splinted the wing, questioning him constantly and memorizing his every move.

When the splinting was finished, Jan served lemonade, and the three of them sat and chatted for over an hour. By the time Farrell left, she had made two new friends, who insisted she visit as often as she liked. Norman, charmed out of his usual stuffiness, pressed upon Farrell a stack of medical journals that might have been suitable for a third-year medical student. Jan refrained from pointing out his error, as she didn't want to discourage him. Her husband was usually stiff and uncomfortable around children. Of course she attributed this to the fact that he'd never had any of his own, and that, sadly, he and Max had never overcome their mutual distrust. She thoroughly enjoyed seeing her husband loosen up a bit.

Eileen benefited from that summer in the Village as well. With Farrell occupied from morning till night, she was finally forced to confront the problems in her life head-on. She spent a great deal of time alone, sorting things out, and cut back on her drinking. As a result, for the first time in years, she began to face things as they were,

without the haze of alcohol softening the edges. It was a
difficult and painful process, but it was also something of
a relief to come to grips with herself and her future. By the
beginning of August, she had come to a decision. But it
took another two and a half weeks to summon the courage
to tell her family.

Junior, Bridget, Meg, the Captain, Patrick, and Lucy
were at the table when Eileen announced that she had
something important to discuss. Dinner had long since
been eaten, the dishes washed and put away. Farrell had
gone to check on her animals, and Kimberly and Pat III
were still off at summer camp.

After making her initial announcement, Eileen fid-
geted with her napkin for a moment, unsure of how to
begin. She was certain that her parents would be devastated
by what she was about to say, and she shrank from causing
them further pain.

Junior, aware of Eileen's discomfort, wriggled expectantly in his seat and gave Bridget a quick wink. He'd been
hoping for this, praying for it, really. If anything would
destroy her hold on their father, this was it. He crossed his
fingers beneath the table and waited.

What Eileen didn't realize was that her "announcement" was not going to surprise anyone. In her mind, no
one had a clue that there was anything wrong with her
marriage.

Finally she blurted it out.

"I don't know how to say this . . ." she began, and her
eyes filled with tears. "Things just haven't worked out, and
I, well, I can't seem to . . ." She placed her fingers over her
eyes and willed the tears to stop. "I'm asking Luke for a
divorce."

Junior had gotten his wish! He jumped up from his
seat, leaned across the table and wagged a pudgy finger in
Eileen's face. Blissfully certain that he was speaking for
Patrick, he began a scathing condemnation.

"How dare you?" he screamed, the soul of moral outrage. "How dare you disgrace this family? My God, Eileen,
have you no pride? No! Don't answer that; it's clear that you
don't. But has it occurred to you to ask what this will do to

Mother and Father? Did you ever stop and think about them? Did you ever stop and think about anyone but yourself?"

"*Shut up!*"

"Daa-aad!" Junior gasped.

"I said shut up, Junior!" Patrick repeated.

Junior's mouth, which was hanging open in disbelief, shut with a *clunk*. The rest of the family, including Lucy, looked on in shock. No one had ever heard Patrick use that tone of voice or those words with anyone.

"You listen to me," he continued. "In this family, right or wrong, we're on each other's side. You remember that, all of you. As long as I'm alive, no matter what, I'm on your side."

He turned to Eileen and took her hand. "If it's any help at all, I want you to know that I happen to think you're right about this."

Eileen looked gratefully at her father and was about to respond when the Captain broke the tension by grumbling, louder than he'd intended, "Of course she's right! The man's a bum!"

It was then that Farrell walked in, suntanned and smiling, to be greeted by an enormous, terrifying silence.

Eileen broke the news to her later that night in the privacy of Farrell's bedroom. Farrell listened to every word Eileen said, her eyes never straying from her mother's face, but she didn't make a sound. When Eileen had finished and asked if she understood, Farrell nodded, then lay back on her bed and closed her eyes.

As soon as the door closed behind her mother, she let the tears fall. The pain was like a piercing void. It wasn't the loss of her father. He'd never really been there anyway. It was the loss of hope. Now it would never be all right. No matter what she did, she couldn't fix what was wrong. She would never have the chance to make Luke love her too much to leave. She would never see her mother's smile reach her eyes. Her whole life she had dreamed of the day when they would all be happy, like a real family. Now she knew that day would never come.

Twelve

Ironically, Luke was genuinely surprised by the divorce. It had never occurred to him that Eileen would go that far. He didn't think she'd minded his absences that much. The other guys' wives didn't seem to. Oh sure, people in Hollywood and New York—places like that—split up all the time. But normal people didn't get divorced. Especially not Irish Catholics from Chicago's southside!

As shocked as he was, Luke had no intention of altering his life-style. And as selfish as he was, he wasn't intentionally cruel. He had never intended to hurt Eileen, and he wasn't about to compound his sins by holding her prisoner in an empty marriage. He agreed to the divorce, and when she asked for the child support and alimony in a staggering lump sum, he agreed to that, too, although he set the child support up in a trust, to be paid out periodically.

Still a beautiful young woman by anyone's standards, and now quite wealthy in her own right, Eileen decided that she'd played the role of housewife for far too long. She sold the house in the suburbs, bought a condo on Lake Shore Drive, enrolled Farrell in Chicago's exclusive Latin School, and asked Patrick for suggestions on finding a career.

Patrick, thrilled at the opportunity to do something constructive to help, sent out his feelers, called in a favor or two, and landed Eileen a job in a top advertising agency. She worked for the agency for six months, realized that advertising wasn't quite her thing, and took a job with a public relations firm. Almost immediately, her career was off and running.

At first, living in the city was a lark. Eileen and Farrell were equally impressed by the presence of a doorman. They found living on the twelfth floor thrilling, and their view of Lake Michigan was nothing short of spectacular. It didn't take them long to discover the joys of shopping on Chicago's Magnificent Mile and in the trendy, pricey boutiques along Oak Street.

Eileen coaxed Meg in from the country by convincing her that she couldn't decorate the condo without her. Meg arrived, color swatches in hand. In the fall of nineteen seventy-one, while every decorator in North America was busy assuring their clients that burnt orange, avocado, and harvest gold were "the absolute end," and teaching them to "see" the rusty shades as if for the very first time, Meg, with Farrell's enthusiastic support and Eileen's cringing assent, chose the soft sunset pastels of the Southwest, added deep terra cotta and navy blue for accent colors, and created a masterpiece.

The night before Meg was to return to the Village, Eileen informed her that she had something important to discuss. Meg turned down Eileen's offer of a drink and made herself a cup of tea. Eileen laughed at the look on her sister's face when Meg saw the amount of brandy Eileen had poured for herself.

"This is nothing!" she assured her. "Believe me, I could drink twice this amount and it wouldn't faze me."

"But do you think you should?" Meg pressed, uncomfortable with the subject. She studied Eileen's face with concern. "I mean, it can't be healthy."

Eileen stretched out on the butter-soft leather couch. "Don't start on me, Meg," she snapped irritably, then quickly regained her composure. "I want to discuss this with you before I say anything to Farrell," she said, her amber eyes glowing with excitement.

"Tell me!" Meg urged.

"Well, you know the Tenholms?"

"Norman and Jan? Of course. Farrell and I see them on the beach all the time. Jan's almost as crazy about the water as Farrell is. Why?"

"Well, evidently they're quite taken with Farrell."

Meg nodded. "They adore her. Jan told me that she's never seen Norman so smitten. You know, he's one of the top men in his field. It's quite an honor for Farrell, really."

"Well, they made me an offer."

Meg looked at her blankly. "An offer of what?" she asked.

"The lot next door to their house. They'll sell it to me if I'm interested. It's a full two acres."

"Two acres of lakefront property!" Meg whispered. "There is no lakefront property. Dad's mysterious rival bought it all."

"Not all." Eileen smiled. "What do you think?"

"Can you afford it?"

"Quite easily," Eileen assured her. "What do you think?" she persisted. "Should I buy it? Would you if you were me?"

"Would I!" Meg exclaimed. "You bet I would. Imagine having a house on the lake!"

"So I guess we don't concur with Dad's opinion about the lakefront."

"I guess not." Meg laughed. "Are you going to do it?"

"Well," Eileen said, "that depends on you."

"On me! Why?"

"First, I need to know what your plans are."

"What do you mean, 'my plans'? What plans?" Meg asked warily.

"I mean, what are you going to do?"

"You mean, like what am I going to do with the rest of my life?"

"Noooo . . ." Eileen answered hesitantly. "Not quite. But what are you going to do now, this year, next year? Where are you going to live? Are you going to remain alone in the Village all winter, or move back to the southside with Mom and Dad? Have you considered getting an apartment down here? You know . . . What are you doing?"

"Oh, God, Eileen!" Meg pretended to collapse on the floor. "I don't know what the hell I'm doing. I've really been taking things as they come." She sighed loudly. "You know that I really like the Village. It's kind of remote, especially now that everyone's gone for the winter, but I rather enjoy that. I work well there, and believe it or not, there are dozens of galleries nearby. The longer I stay, the more I like it."

"Perfect!" Eileen erupted.

"What are you talking about?"

"Meg, will you live in my house?"

"What?"

"Well, I can't very well go ahead and build a house and then leave it standing empty all year long. It would get run down in no time. I really want to do this. I think it will be a good investment, and I think it would be great for Farrell and me to have a place in the country. But I'm working full time now, and I'm just not going to be able to look after another residence. I need you to live in my house!"

"I don't know what to say."

"Say yes," Eileen prompted hopefully.

"Yes!" Meg cried.

"So it's a deal then." Eileen smiled, offering her hand.

"It's a deal," Meg agreed, blinking back tears. Ignoring the hand, she threw her arms around Eileen and hugged her.

Eileen was a natural at public relations. Her looks, her name, her upbeat personality all combined to make her a stunning success. She easily made the sort of contacts her colleagues were clamoring for, quickly establishing first-name relationships with every columnist, radio and television host in Chicago. She concentrated on making the major movies and their stars her area of expertise. She liked the glamour that this type of P.R. afforded her.

Of course, by concentrating on that arena, she committed herself to constant traveling from one coast to the other, and to working until the wee hours of the morning when celebrities were in town. But she adored it! She loved rubbing shoulders with the rich and famous. She enjoyed being admired and sought after. She made it her business to be seen at every important affair in Chicago, wearing the right gowns, mingling with the right people.

But while Eileen had developed a reputation for being inexhaustible, no one could have kept the kind of schedule she did without some help. She cut her drinking down, for she found that it dulled her senses, and in her business, she had to be sharp—razor sharp. So while she remained what she considered to be admirably sober, holding herself to only two or three drinks a night, she got the kick she needed from a little white powder called cocaine. She used it just to help out when the walls were closing in. She was far from addicted, she assured herself. And she just couldn't fathom how anyone could become dependent on it.

When people found out that she was raising a child by herself, they became even more impressed with her stamina.

"My God, Eileen! How do you manage?" they'd demand incredulously.

She would shrug modestly. "Oh, it's a joy, really; it's nothing."

The truth was, Farrell was left to fend for herself at least fifty percent of the time. When Eileen was in town, she spent most of her evenings at one function or another, or out on dates. When she did stay home, it was Farrell who prepared dinner and coaxed her mother to eat. It was Farrell who woke her in the morning with coffee and toast. And it was Farrell who talked her through her frequent and seemingly inexplicable bouts of paranoia and insecurity, assuring her that she was still beautiful, that she was wonderful at her job, that men would always find her attractive.

Finally, Eileen's absences became too much for Farrell. Overcome with loneliness, and secretly frightened of the long nights spent alone in their large apartment, she asked her mother to hire a housekeeper.

Eileen, though surprised by her request, consented, and ran an ad in a small Gold Coast newspaper.

Several women applied for the position, and the hiring process, which had to be arranged around Eileen's schedule, began. Eventually they settled on Trish Nelson, a slim, surprisingly chic-looking woman in her early thirties. They'd had several older applicants, and one considerably younger, but Farrell felt the most comfortable with a woman around her mother's age.

With Trish in residence, a period of stability set in for Farrell. Though Eileen's presence in the household diminished even further, Trish filled the void admirably. She became Farrell's confidante and friend, while still providing the guidance that eleven-year-old Farrell longed for. She prepared well-balanced meals, and saw that Farrell ate them. She made sure her school assignments were completed and correct. Farrell, though capable of fending for herself, reveled in the attention and the feeling of normalcy.

Normalcy, that is, except for her mother's frequent absences, and for her father's unique interpretation of parenthood.

Luke, having no concept of a schedule himself, never considered the possibility that his daughter might have one. Every few months she would receive an enthusiastic summons from him, declaring that he missed her pretty face.

Eileen, having decided on a policy of noninterference, never objected to the sporadic nature of his "fatherhood attacks," as she called them. And Trish was hardly in a position to object, even had she wanted to.

Not that Farrell was reluctant to go. His timing just made it difficult for her to establish herself, or to make any friends. But she adored her father, and trips with Luke were always an adventure. In some ways, she felt as though she was the adult and he the child. He was so enthusiastic, so delighted with each new experience.

Keeping up with Luke and his crowd was akin to trying to predict the newest fad. You never knew where they'd be headed next. They'd skip down to the Palm Bay Club, or to the Jockey Club in Florida. They skied Aspen, Vail, and the Italian Alps. They cruised the Greek islands, went to London for the theater, shopped in Paris and Rome, played in Tahoe and "Frisco," or just stayed in Beverly Hills and "hopped down" to Palm Springs or over to Vegas for weekends.

It was always a frenzied, wild good time. Luke tirelessly pursued his chosen life-style, convinced that if he had enough fun, he would eventually come out happy. He was always surrounded by an entourage. Not only the inevitable starlets and money groupies were in attendance, but his "buddies" as well, stroking his ego, drinking his booze, and sleeping with his castoffs. It never dawned on Luke that it might be upsetting for Farrell to see her "uncles" Pete and John and Brian cavorting with their mistresses when she

knew not only their wives, but their children, too. With a
quick wink and a finger to their lips, they made her a party
to their infidelities. While she was flattered that her father
trusted her with such big secrets, she was also torn by guilt
and confusion.

She didn't like keeping things from her mother, any
more than she liked it when Eileen made her promise not
to tell Luke (or the rest of the family) how much time she
spent away. She grew increasingly wary of relationships,
and of people in general. At school, though she was well
liked, she never became part of any particular group or
clique. Her looks alone would have assured her entrée into
any gathering, but she viewed her classmates with a mix-
ture of curiosity and envy. While they had the luxury of
leading the carefree existence of children, she was coping
with the terrible burden of her parents' secrets.

In time, Trish became an anchor in the turbulent sea
of her emotions. As months went by and Farrell slowly grew
to trust the woman, she began confiding larger and larger
portions of the many secrets she carried.

Trish listened quietly and attentively, nodding her
head encouragingly as Farrell unburdened herself. At first
Farrell felt guilty about her betrayal of her parents. But
since she trusted Trish implicitly, the relief she felt at opening up was too enormous to resist.

Then one morning Trish disappeared.

Farrell woke and realized that she'd overslept and was
already an hour late for school. She ran to Trish's room,
expecting to find her sleeping, but found instead that the
bed was empty and the room cleaned out. Everything was
gone: clothes, pictures, books, everything. It was as if Trish
had never been there at all.

Farrell ran through the apartment, refusing to believe
that Trish would abandon her. She became so desperate
that after searching all the rooms, she opened closets and
cupboards, calling Trish's name with tears steaming down
her cheeks.

It wasn't until that evening, when Eileen returned
from her business trip, that they discovered Trish had sto-
len more than Farrell's heart. She'd taken the best of Ei-

leen's jewelry, her sable coat, and all of the cash in the house.

The police were called in, Eileen ranted and raved, but in the end, nothing could be done. Trish had undoubtedly given a false name and address, the references were surely faked—it happened all the time. They warned Eileen not to hire through the paper: "Go with bonded agencies," they told her. "No tellin' what kind of nuts read the paper."

They didn't particularly notice the little redhead with the tear-swollen eyes.

Eileen turned to her after the officers had left. "Never mind, Farrell. We'll hire someone else."

Farrell shook her head. "No, Mom. I don't need anyone. I'm old enough now to be alone."

"Not alone, silly," Eileen insisted. "We have each other, right?"

Farrell looked up with red-rimmed eyes and met her mother's bright, golden gaze. "Right, Mom," she agreed in a hoarse monotone. "We have each other."

After that, her only refuge was the Village. There she was free to be herself. And there she had Meg, who had no secrets for her to keep and who understood, in spite of all evidence to the contrary, that Farrell was still a young girl who needed and deserved the opportunity to be treated like one. To be looked after, encouraged, and loved.

Thirteen

Eileen built her house. Perched on the edge of a wooded hilltop, it rose up majestically, an architectural triumph. The foundation had been sunk in bedrock to support the structure's uncanny, airy design. Embraced by stands of towering poplars, the exterior was stained the rich color of the tree bark so that the house blended with its surroundings and seemed more a work of nature than of man. It was encircled by wooden decks and walkways. Every room had a wall of glass that led out to a private balcony, each with a spectacular view of the lake. The mood of the house was always changing. On a clear, sunny day, it was serene and full of light. But on a stormy day, when the sky turned ominous and the lake changed from blue to an eerie, transparent green, its waves crashing violently against the shore, the house was a wild, dramatic place.

The moment it was habitable, Meg moved in to supervise the finishing touches. She had overcome Lucy's objections by telling her that she needed more room for her painting. Lucy was convinced that Meg would be lonely "rattlin' around in that construction site." She insisted that she and Patrick would be lost without Meg's cheery face in the morning. Meg smiled, appreciating their concern, but she knew that her parents would relish the opportunity to have their summer home to themselves. As for loneliness . . . after wintering in the Village, Meg seriously doubted that she would ever be lonely again.

Fall had been a melancholy time for her, as her family and all but a handful of residents had packed up and returned to the city. She'd spent her days in making sketches and taking long, aimless walks, reviewing her bittersweet memories.

Then one morning she'd awakened to find that the lake, which had gradually turned to a thick, steely gray slush, had completely frozen over. A heavy snow began to fall, and by evening, the fantastic moonscape of the glistening ice was totally blanketed.

The Village had been plunged into a silence so complete that the soft hush of wind through the bare trees and the occasional distant wail of a passing train were the only sounds.

Almost overnight, Meg had gone from a blissfully happy young woman, engaged to marry and engaged in life, to a solitary individual, unsure of her direction.

Slowly and painfully she had begun to adjust to her new life. Over that seemingly endless winter, she'd come to grips with her loss. She'd discovered new facets of herself as she turned to the frozen world around her, and to her art, for solace. She'd learned to appreciate the subtle, majestic beauty of the sleeping world, and eventually she had found peace and tranquillity in place of loneliness and pain.

Painting became her primary language, and the vivid images she created on canvas seemed to breathe with a life-force all their own.

By the time the Village came to life again in the spring, Meg had learned to accept herself and the new life she had created. No longer the radiant bride-to-be of yesterday, at twenty-three, she was a composed, introspective young woman.

The villagers, being southsiders, had heard the unsettling rumors about her. A few of them had been at Dora Riley's shower and had witnessed firsthand Meg's astonishing premonition, and later they had elaborated greatly on it. While they were pleasant to Meg's face and nodded politely at Sunday mass, their courtesy was more in deference to Patrick's position than out of any kindness or sympathetic feelings for Meg. An inbred, clannish group, they were highly suspicious of any irregularities, and they closed their ranks to Meg, but they did it almost imperceptibly, so that she was left to wonder if it was her own insecurity that made her feel snubbed and excluded.

If only someone had had the courage to confront her, or to simply ask for her side of the story. As it was, the rumors took on a life of their own. As years went by, it was no longer a matter of what someone had heard, but rather what everyone knew, had always known . . . like the fact that the world is round or the sky is blue.

If just once those stories had been held up to the light of day, they would have crumbled and turned to dust, rather than to gain in strength until they finally, inevitably, erupted in tragedy.

Fourteen

Farrell was thirteen when the house was completed. From that point on, she spent every free weekend and every summer with Meg.

Over the years, their friendship with the Tenholms deepened. Jan and Meg became each other's closest friend, the relationship strengthening as they discovered that they had more in common than they had realized.

For Jan suffered from a private, but terrible, guilt—as she painfully confided to Meg late one night—over what she considered her emotional abandonment of her son.

Max, now in his late teens, was the product of her first marriage. After his father's death, he'd been mourning deeply when Jan, heartbroken as well, had been pushed into marrying Norman.

In their first summer together, Max had begged to stay back East and attend summer camp rather than accompany them to Michigan. Jan, still struggling with her own loss, and emotionally drained from trying to bridge the gap between her new husband and her son, had agreed.

That summer had established a precedent—a terrible precedent, Jan had come to realize. The Village had become her and Norman's place, and Max, proud and resentful, had steadfastly refused her repeated invitations.

In spite of everything, Jan and Norman had made a good marriage. However, Max and Norman had never come to terms, although their relationship had finally settled into an uneasy truce.

Meg had listened to Jan with compassion, her wide black eyes reflecting her own unspoken regrets. She'd glanced in through the porch window at Farrell, who, cuddled up and sleeping on Jan's couch, looked vulnerable and small. "We all do the best we can, I guess." She'd sighed. "It's never enough."

The two women had looked at each other with perfect understanding.

"Never enough," Jan had agreed, shaking her head slowly.

Jan and Farrell shared a mutual passion for the water, and they spent half of their summers together happily submerged.

As for Norman, Farrell pumped him relentlessly for information and then hung on his every word. Though he would have died rather than admit it, he basked in her innocent hero worship.

The foursome frequently ate together, and they spent

countless evenings sharing conversations as they watched the sun set.

Not being Irish, and hailing from the East Coast rather than the Midwest, Jan found the Village's social politics endlessly amusing. She remorselessly picked Meg's brain in her attempt to understand the intricacies of the pecking order.

"What you have to understand," Meg explained patiently, "if you want to survive socially in this place, is that hating the right people is every bit as important as liking the wrong ones is deadly."

"What?" Jan asked. "What does that mean?"

"Forget it, Jan, really. It's too late for you, anyway. You became a social outcast the moment you befriended me. My advice to an outsider would be, keep your mouth shut, your nose clean, and God help you if you attend the wrong party!"

When she wasn't with the Tenholms, her grandparents, or Meg, Farrell spent her time painting, swimming, exploring the forest, and caring for stray and injured animals. Over time, people began to bring hurt creatures to her.

Though she kept to herself, she watched the lives of the villagers with unflagging interest, like a hungry child with its nose pressed against the candy-store window. She watched fathers return home each night to their families, and mothers spend afternoons on the beach playing with their children. Sometimes, when she was able to summon the courage, she would move her towel in close and pretend for a while that she was a part of a family.

Her favorite event was the annual lobster party. It was held on the second Saturday of August and was the high point of the season. Tickets were purchased six weeks in advance so that lobsters could be ordered and flown in from Maine.

It was an all-day event. Huge steamers were set up on the beach. The lobsters were steamed all afternoon; then fresh sweet corn was added. Beach fires were built, potatoes were roasted, and later everyone made gooey smores, that confection of toasted marshmallows, Hershey bars, and graham crackers. There were iced kegs of beer and soda pop, and huge vats of melted butter for the lobster and the corn. It was heaven!

Everyone came to the lobster roast—Patrick and Lucy, the Captain, Meg, the Tenholms, even Eileen whenever she could. On that one day every year, surrounded by her family, Farrell was able to feel that she really belonged.

Yet, as withdrawn as she was, and as engrossed in her solitary activities, it was impossible for her to go unnoticed. She grew more beautiful with the passing of each year. Wherever she went, she became the focus of attention.

By the time she was fifteen, she was breathtaking. From her long, shapely legs to her wavy, copper hair that glistened with golden highlights, she was perfection. Her flawless skin was smooth and tawny, her exotic eyes, rimmed with thick, black lashes, were the same translucent green as the curl of a wave on a stormy day. While a plainer child might have escaped notice, Farrell was the topic of endless discussion among the villagers, and everything she did added fuel to the fire. The sight of her riding the surf on days when most people wouldn't even dip a toe in the water was cause for comment. The fact that she was rarely seen without some animal sitting on her shoulder or nested in her arms was highly suspect.

The fact was, they would have found something wrong with anything Farrell did. Not only was her father a notorious playboy, but her mother was a social butterfly who was developing quite a reputation in some circles. If that wasn't enough, the girl lived with Meg Sweeney, and everyone knew about her!

Fifteen

One day in the fall of her sophomore year, Farrell sat at the breakfast table browsing through the morning papers. Because Eileen would be in New York until Friday, Farrell was, as usual, alone. She was scanning Kup's column when suddenly she froze, gasped in shock and inhaled a mouthful of cereal in the process. Choking painfully, her eyes streaming, she reread the paragraph, praying that it would somehow come out different. It didn't.

Luke had remarried! Farrell had known that he was seeing her, but she'd never actually met the woman. She knew who it was, of course. The whole country knew Tammy Evans. Or they ought to; they'd been watching her prance around on prime-time television for the past five years in a French-maid costume . . . cut down to her navel!

Luke had been dating her for at least six months. Since he'd met her, he had canceled Farrell's visits because "Tammy doesn't understand kids."

"You understand, don't you, babe?" Luke had pleaded. "I'll work on her, she'll come around, you'll see. She's really terrific. I know you two are just going to love each other! It's just that she's never been around any kids before."

That had been four months ago. She hadn't heard from him since, and now he was married! I'll probably never see him again, she thought morosely, beginning to wallow in misery.

After the wedding, a month passed before she heard from him. He called from Rome to let her know how blissful he was.

"I feel like a kid again!" he told her.

"Dad, when did you ever not feel like a kid?"

Luke laughed. "No, really, honey. Tammy's so terrific! She's a health nut. She's got me up jogging every morning, lifting weights, the whole thing! Imagine your old man up and jogging at six A.M.!"

Old man, thought Farrell. Since when? "Congratulations, Dad, but take it easy, okay? You know, I wish you had told me about the wedding."

"Well . . . it was kind of a spur-of-the-moment thing," he answered vaguely. "I knew you'd understand. Listen, I've got to run, babe. Talk to you tomorrow."

"I love you, Dad . . . Dad?"

Before the semester was out, the word was all over school: Farrell's dad had married Tammy Evans! The boys went wild with questions.

"Hey, Farrell, how about inviting me home for Thanksgiving?" "Farrell, any family reunions coming up?" "Whaddaya think, Farrell? Will you call her Tammy, or Fifi, or just plain old Mom?"

One afternoon during a study period, she sneaked into the art studio, ostensibly to work on a statue. She'd begun to be interested in sculpture, but today she wanted to escape her classmates' comments for a while. She was slumped on a stool, poking halfheartedly at some clay, when Jeff walked in.

Jeff Gibson and Farrell had discovered each other on Jeff's first day at Latin School, which had been in their freshman year. They had known right off the bat that they were going to be friends.

Jeff was a brilliant scholarship student from the west side who was enrolled in a unique, accelerated program that would enable him to complete his high-school requirements by the end of this year. He had already been granted a scholarship to Northwestern University. His ultimate goal was international law.

In spite of his remarkable intelligence, Jeff was an easy person to underestimate. He was perfectly aware of this discrepancy, and believed it would be a great asset to him in the future.

Jeff was six-one, but because he was so exceedingly thin, he looked much taller than that. He had dark, almost black hair and round, woeful black eyes. His skin was so pale that he was sickly looking, though he'd never had so much as a cold.

The total effect of his appearance was pathetic. He looked strung out and wasted. But when he opened his mouth, his features seemed to rearrange themselves as if by magic. And once you knew him well, he was beautiful.

"Red! What seems to be the problem?" he asked, nudging her with his bony hip in order to share her stool.

"I don't know what you're talking about," she answered, mashing the clay furiously, pretending to concentrate.

"Well then, perhaps you'll explain why you're trying to destroy that clay? And why you seem to cringe every time a certain starlet's name is mentioned? What is it? You can tell me. A little dash of an Electra complex, perhaps? Feeling like Daddy's replaced us?"

She looked him dead in the eye and burst out laughing.

"Hey!" he objected. "I take umbrage at your cavalier dismissal. It took me all morning to come up with that diagnosis. Seriously, Farrell, what is wrong? Don't you like her?"

"That's the problem!" she erupted. "I don't know if I like her or not. I've never met her. Jeff, I didn't know about their wedding until I read about it in the paper. Since he's been seeing her, he's canceled every one of our visits. He keeps saying that Tammy Poo's not used to kids. For God's sake! I'm almost sixteen years old! She's probably not much older than me!"

By the time she finished her outburst, she was literally shaking from head to foot.

"Aw, Red, I'm sorry . . ." He slung a comforting arm across her shoulders. "I didn't realize what was happening. Listen, give him time to become unbesotted. He'll come around."

"Unbesotted?" she challenged.

"Yeah, you know. Sort of like uninfatuated—only more befuddled."

"I don't know, Jeff," she teased. "Are you sure you're ready for Northwestern?"

"The question, my poor misguided child, is, is Northwestern ready for me?"

Luke called less and less frequently, until finally he stopped calling altogether. Farrell tried to reach him countless times, but somehow "Mr. McBride" was never home when she called. Occasionally he and Tammy were mentioned in the columns—for giving a particularly extravagant party, or for taking an exotic vacation. Once they had even appeared on the cover of a grocery-store rag. The caption had read: "Mr. and Mrs. Tammy Evans."

Farrell tried to talk to her mother about it, but Eileen dismissed her with a flippant wave of her well-manicured hand and a caustic, "That's men, honey. Out of sight, out of mind."

Eileen's drugs of choice had taken their toll. At thirty-eight, she'd already had two eye jobs and a face-lift. She still considered herself merely a social drinker, and still viewed her sporadic use of cocaine as harmless.

In truth, she was never obviously drunk, nor did she use cocaine daily, or even weekly. Not liking to pay for the drug, she waited for it to be offered, which, in her circles, happened frequently enough.

But years of steady drinking had dulled not only her once-spectacular beauty, but her ability to reason and function rationally.

The one area of her life that didn't suffer was her work. She was good at it, and single-mindedly devoted to her clients. She would have cut off her arm rather than lose ground in her career.

It was in Farrell's senior year, and on one of the rare nights when Eileen was home, that the call came. Farrell was in her room filling out college applications when she heard the phone ring. It stopped after two rings. Assuming that Eileen had picked it up, she continued working. She had her heart set on attending the Art Institute of Chicago, but she was applying to ten other schools just to cover her bases.

She was concentrating on her answers, her head bent low over her desk, so she didn't see Eileen enter. When she looked up, it was as if her mother had appeared out of nowhere.

"Mom, what's wrong? Are you all right?" she asked. Eileen was staring at her with intensity, her head cocked, her eyes glistening with unspent tears.

"It's Daddy, honey." Eileen hadn't called Luke "Daddy" since Farrell was a baby.

"On the phone?" Farrell jumped up and ran to her extension. "Dad's on the phone!" she cried ecstatically.

"Farrell! Stop!" Eileen shouted.

Farrell froze, then turned, beginning to feel frightened by her mother's behavior. "Mom, what's going on?"

Eileen walked to Farrell's bed, sat down, buried her face in her hands, and began to cry.

"Luke's dead!" she wailed. "That bitch killed him! She *killed* him!"

"What do you mean?" Farrell asked desperately. "What are you saying, Mom?"

"He was jogging, for Christ's sake!" Eileen sobbed. "Jogging! It was over a hundred degrees in L.A., and that fool was out jogging. Trying to keep up with that bimbo. And now he's dead!"

Eileen broke down completely. She rocked back and forth, her arms clenched around her body, sobbing and wailing; crying out in a tiny, childlike voice, "I always thought he would come back someday, Farrell. I always thought he'd come home!"

Farrell stood motionless. It was as if a mist had suddenly descended, throwing everything into a foggy half-reality. Her senses were cushioned by shock and the immediacy of her mother's need. She walked over to the bed and opened her arms. Eileen melted into them, sobbing, and Farrell rocked her mother gently, back and forth, staring out at the starless night and willing her own tears to fall silently.

Tammy's lawyer called on the following day, and the day after that. It seemed that Luke and Tammy had planned ahead. Their prenuptial agreements had included the understanding (well documented and legally binding) that in the event of the death of either one of the parties (provided they were still married to each other at the time), all of the deceased's worldly goods would pass to the surviving spouse. In other words, Luke hadn't left Farrell a dime.

In addition, Miss Evans wanted it understood that her late husband's funeral was to be a private affair, attended by only the couple's closest friends, and Eileen's cooperation would be appreciated.

"Are you telling me that my daughter, Luke's daughter, is not welcome at her father's funeral?" Eileen shrieked into the receiver.

"Miss Evans feels it would be best for all concerned."

Eileen was so outraged that she could barely speak.

Instead, she whispered, enunciating each word with excruciating care. "Now you listen to me, and listen very carefully. I'm going to hang up the phone now, and if I don't
hear from you in fifteen minutes, I'm going to call every
newspaper columnist, every rag sheet, every talk-show host,
and every radio interviewer from here to Hollywood with
the news that Tammy Evans is barring Luke's daughter
from his funeral."

"But surely, Mrs. McBride—"

Click.

Five minutes later, the phone rang. Eileen took her
time in picking it up.

"Yes?"

"Mrs. McBride, this is Reese Bender again, Miss Evans'
attorney."

"Yes?"

"I'm terribly sorry, Mrs. McBride. I made an inexcus-
able mistake. I don't know how I could have mixed things
up so completely. Miss Evans says she would be delighted
to have your daughter attend her hus—her late husband's
funeral."

"How big of her!" Eileen exclaimed ironically.

"Uh, yes, isn't it? So when can we expect the little
tyke?"

"Mr. Bender, my daughter is seventeen years old."

"Oh, I see. Well, in any case—"

"We'll make our own arrangements, Mr. Bender.
Good-bye."

Eileen called Patrick, fit to be tied. She wanted the
name of a lawyer. She wanted to sue Luke's estate. She
wanted to sue Tammy Evans. She wanted blood!

Patrick finally calmed her down.

"All you'll succeed in doing if you sue," he explained,
"is to drag Farrell's name through the papers and cause
her even more heartache. Leave it alone, honey," he said
gently. "We lost Luke a long time ago."

When he hung up, Patrick finished arranging the tray
of soup and crackers he'd prepared for Lucy.

Lucy had been fatigued of late, especially since her
birthday two months earlier. When Patrick voiced his con-

cern, she made a joke of it, insisting that "A body has a right to slow down a bit at my age. You're just grumbling because I'm not picking up your socks as quick as I used to!"

Lucy's eyes opened wide in astonishment at the sight of her husband, shuffling in with the tray, a sheepish grin on his face. She knew he was completely helpless in the kitchen.

"Patrick!" she cried. "You didn't!"

His smile took wings, even as he tried to appear casual. "Just a little soup," he muttered, like a small boy trying not to strut after hitting a home run.

"Oh, Patrick, how wonderful." Lucy tasted a spoonful. "Patrick? Ummm, did you happen to add any water?"

"Of course not!" he barked, indignant. "Why would I do a damned-fool thing like watering it down?"

"Never mind." Lucy winced. "It's perfect."

Patrick's expression grew concerned. "How are you feeling? Still weak? Were you able to rest all right?"

Lucy smiled reassuringly. "I'm fine, really. I'm feeling much better. I just have to remember that I'm not as young as I used to be." Then she added, "Patrick, who was on the phone?"

"It was Eileen. I think I talked her out of suing Luke's estate."

"Suing? Oh, no. The press would have a field day with that!"

"That's what I told her," Patrick agreed. "She *is* right about one thing, though. Farrell has been left without a penny. Nothing but that original child-support money doled out by the trust . . . Lucy!" he blurted suddenly. "I want to change our wills."

"Patrick! We settled that ages ago."

"I know, I know, but things were different then. After we're both gone, I want the estate divided four ways instead of three. I want Farrell to be taken care of, regardless of what happens."

"Fine," Lucy agreed softly.

"I know we agreed," Patrick went on, "but circumstances change, Lucy, and sometimes plans have to change . . . What did you say?"

"I said, fine, Patrick." Lucy smiled. "Whatever you think is best."

Patrick turned to her in amazement. This didn't sound like Lucy. She had already drifted off again, the corners of her mouth still turned up slightly, a faint echo of her smile.

Sixteen

Junior was so enraged that by the time he finally managed to dial his home number, his face was mottled with purple splotches and his breathing was ragged.

"Hello-oooo," Bridget said in her most silken voice, the one reserved exclusively for answering the telephone.

"You'renot gonnabelievewhathappened!" Junior bellowed.

"Junior, is that you?" she asked, switching to the exasperated tone that he knew best.

"Eileen's gotten Dad to change his will!" he sputtered, ignoring her tone. "She's convinced him to give Farrell an equal cut."

"What?" Bridget shrieked. "What are you saying?"

"You heard me, goddamn it! Dad just called me and told me what he was doing. He said that he didn't want to leave any surprises behind. I suppose he expects me to be grateful to him for telling me. Really, Bridget, this is just too much! It was bad enough when Meg and Eileen were getting an equal share. After all, I'm the one who's running the whole damned company! If it wasn't for me, the old man would have run the whole thing into the ground years ago . . ."

Bridget wondered sometimes if he had forgotten that she used to work for him and knew better, or if he had just been lying for so long that he'd really come to believe his own bullshit.

"Sweetie," she said softly, but he continued to rant. "Sweetie!" she snarled.

"What?"

"Can't you do something about it?"

"What do you mean?" he asked, startled.

"Well, I mean, after all, you're there."

Junior was beginning to catch her drift. "Oh! Uh, I'm not sure of exactly what you mean, but maybe something could be done."

"Oh, Junior, you're so clever! I knew you'd think of something."

"Bridge, wait. I'm not sure. It could get complicated. We'd have to plan."

"Don't fuss so, Junior," she demanded irritably. "We'll discuss it when you get home."

"Okay, Bridge. Gotta go. Bye!"

"Junior? Junior!" She stared in amazement at the disconnected receiver. It wasn't at all like Junior to hang up so abruptly.

She didn't let it worry her for long. She was far too excited to let anything bother her now. She'd worked it all out in her head years ago, ever since the day she discovered that Patrick was dividing the estate in three equal parts. She'd always assumed that Junior, being the boy, would get the lion's share. That not being the case, she'd done a little estate planning of her own. The only hitch had been Junior. She wasn't sure he'd go along. But now, now he'd be putty in her hands!

Junior slammed down the phone, looked up expectantly and licked his lips. Miss Patsy Thompkins, his private secretary, had just sauntered into his office and was, at that very moment, bending from the waist to search the lower drawer of a file cabinet.

Her bottom—her perfectly round, maddeningly firm, delightful pert bottom—was pointed directly at him, only inches away, within touching distance!

She let out a sigh—a long, slow, deliberate sigh—and shifted slightly, causing her derriere, which was encased in some stretchy, skintight material that clearly showed her panty lines, to jiggle invitingly.

Junior, unable to restrain himself, accepted the invitation. He reached out and stroked her protruding buttocks, ever so lightly, with the tips of his stubby fingers.

She quivered provocatively, causing her flesh to ripple visibly beneath the straining material. He stroked her again and again, until she was arching her back and gripping the drawer with both hands.

"Don't move!" he ordered gruffly. He rolled his chair over until he was seated directly behind her. Slowly he lifted her skirt and pulled her panties down around her thighs. He sat back and reveled in the sight of her plump, milky white, dimpled flesh; she was so pliant . . . so docile! He reached out and slapped her ass hard enough to make a perfect red handprint. She squealed.

"I told you not to wear panties," he scolded.

"Oh, Mr. Sweeney," she giggled coyly as she turned to face him, "I must have forgotten! Come on!" she insisted, pulling him up by the hand and leading him eagerly to the couch. "Time for lunch!"

"But, Bridgey!" Junior shouted, hopping into bed beside his wife. "You don't understand. Dad will never agree to this. He wants everything split equally!"

"Goddamn it, Junior! Are you deaf? Or are you just plain stupid?" She reached back and plumped her pillow. "For the tenth time, will you listen?"

As she attempted once again to explain her plan, his thoughts drifted from her cold-creamed face and rollered hair to the more piquant memories of his afternoon romp with Patsy.

Suddenly she interrupted herself. "What are you grinning about?" she demanded, scowling.

"I'm not grinning," he insisted. "I had something caught in my teeth. Go ahead, explain it to me again."

She continued through clenched jaws. "He'll allow it, Junior, because he won't know about it. On paper, it will be just as he expects. The estate will be divided into four equal parts. But in reality, Junior, the companies that Eileen, Meg, and that greedy little bitch, Farrell, inherit will be virtually worthless."

"Why?" Junior asked, beginning to feel lost again.

"Because, Junior, their assets will have been transferred to the companies that you and I are about to purchase outright."

"Bridget! We can't afford to purchase anything outright. We're up to our necks in bills right—"

"Shut up, Junior!" Bridget screamed. "We're not really going to buy the fucking companies. It's just going to
look like we bought them. I swear to God, if you start on me
about those bills again, I'm going to leave you! You know
perfectly well I don't spend half as much as some women.
What do you want me to do? Wear the same old outfits to
the club over and over again? You're the only one who
would look bad. Everyone would know how cheap you are."

Junior sighed. "Okay, Bridge, I guess you're right.
How do we do it?" he asked resignedly.

Bridget clapped her hands. "Oh, Junior, I knew you'd
come around! You'll see, it'll work just like a charm! Now
don't you worry about a thing. I've got it all figured out."
She patted the bald spot on the top of his head and flipped
over.

Junior lay staring at the ceiling for several minutes.
Finally he mustered the courage to speak up. "Uh, Bridge,
we could get in a lot of trouble doing something like this.
I mean, you know, if we got caught."

Bridget sighed indulgently. "That, Junior, is why we
musn't tell a soul or do anything stupid. Do you think you
can possibly manage that, dear?"

With that, she reached up, turned out the light and
slipped almost immediately into the deep, untroubled
sleep experienced only by the truly pure . . . or the purely
wicked.

Seventeen

One month before she was to begin at the Art Institute,
Farrell invited Jeff to the Village for two particularly auspi-
cious occasions. First, there was the lobster party. He'd
informed her last year in no uncertain terms that he would

no longer listen to her descriptions of the event, declaring them too painful to endure.

"If you want to talk about the damned party, you have two choices," he'd told her. "Either find someone who doesn't like lobster, or-rr-r"—he grinned mischievously and worked his thick brows up and down—"invite me."

The second occasion was Meg's annual one-woman show. Meg had begun exhibiting her work five years ago and had developed a good relationship with an outstanding gallery in the area. Although she now sold her work in galleries throughout Michigan, Indiana, Illinois, and Wisconsin, this annual show was her bread and butter, and the first exhibit of her most recent work.

Meg had persuaded Farrell to allow her to place a few of Farrell's pieces in the show. Farrell, initially horrified at the idea, had finally conceded when Meg convinced her that showing her work would help her to "grow" as an artist.

The day before the show, Farrell began having second thoughts.

"Jesus, Meg! I don't know how I ever let you talk me into this." She paced back and forth across the studio, wringing her hands like a madwoman. "Tell me, how am I going to manage to 'grow as an artist' if I drop dead of humiliation? Look at this, Meg. Jeff, tell her I'm not ready!" She gestured to the four pieces of hers that Meg had chosen to show.

Farrell had switched completely from painting to sculpture. The pieces were standing by the door, waiting to be transported to the gallery. Farrell's style was forceful and gutsy. Her subjects, usually wildlife in action, seemed to vibrate with energy and tension.

Utterly meticulous about her work, she studied anatomy as carefully as she did the techniques of sculpting. What gave her art its aggressive power was not some abstract interpretation of anatomy; rather, it was the startling precision with which the pieces were wrought, and her ability to "get inside" her subjects"—to understand them, and to make them true. All of her sculptures had one thing in common: they seemed to breathe. Meg had chosen a magnificent, fierce-looking eagle, swooping down upon a craggy cliff top; a lioness and her cub, curled together tenderly; a grinning dolphin dancing atop a glistening ocean wave; and a pair of wild stallions locked in deadly combat. The stallions' hooves were raised and clashing, their nostrils flared in rage, and their maddened eyes blazed with the taste of death in one, the knowledge of sure victory in the other.

"I can't show these in public. I'll be a laughingstock!"

"Jeff," Meg pleaded, "get her out of here! Please, do something with her. Take her to the beach. Buy her a lobster. Better yet, get her a beer!"

"A beer?" Jeff asked, surprised by the suggestion. "For Farrell?"

Meg winced at her gaff. "Right." Drinking was such an accepted part of Village culture that she'd slipped and forgotten that Farrell completely shunned alcohol.

"The lobster party!" Farrell cried. "I completely forgot about it! Come on, Jeff," she called over her shoulder as she ran from the room. "Let's get our suits on!"

Jeff turned to Meg, laughing. "Now I know how the survivors of that typhoon felt."

She nodded. "I've never seen her so keyed up."

They heard her call from the other end of the house, "Jeff! Are you coming?"

"See ya, Meg," Jeff said as he headed out the door. "I believe I'm being paged."

Later in the afternoon, Meg strolled down the beach with Norman and Jan. As they approached the crowd, Jan spotted Jeff. "There he is!" she announced. "Such a brilliant young man."

"A waste," Norman muttered.

Jan sighed. "Norman! Only you would consider the pursuit of international law 'a waste'."

"They're all crooks," he insisted.

"International lawyers?" Meg asked, incredulous.

"Lawyers, period," Norman proclaimed.

"I give up!" Meg laughed. "Norman, you are completely hopeless." She turned and squinted into the sun. "I don't see Farrell, do you?" she asked them.

"Just follow Jeff's gaze," Jan suggested.

"Oh, so you noticed that, too?" Meg asked.

"It's hard to miss," Jan told her. "Do you think she's at all interested?"

"I think she loves him like a brother," Meg said flatly.

"Poor schmuck," Norman sympathized.

"Kate, Jan, Doctor!" Farrell called. They turned toward the sound of her voice.

"Jan, come on! The water's perfect!" She was standing on a sandbar, waving both hands over her head.

Jan looked down at her beach cover-up, her towel, and her beach bag, then stared longingly at the water.

"Hand them over," Meg said, taking the bag out of Jan's hands.

"Thanks!" Jan said, handing over her towel and wrap. She turned and ran for the water, diving into the surf and splashing like a young girl.

"And you think I'm hopeless," Norman said. But the tenderness in his eyes as he followed Jan's every move belied his gruff tone.

It was the best lobster party that Farrell could remember. Patrick and Lucy arrived with the Captain at six-thirty. It made everyone's night to see Lucy, as she'd been feeling under the weather so often lately. Tonight, though, she was her old self, and she and Jeff hit it off immediately.

"Now I see where Farrell gets her looks!" Jeff had announced upon introduction.

"And I see why she keeps you around!" Lucy had responded without missing a beat.

"Ha!" Patrick laughed. "My Lucy knows when she's being buttered up."

"Butter away!" Lucy cried.

"Buttering, ma'am!" Jeff said, saluting her and laughing.

Eileen showed up around eight, and though Junior and his family had congregated on the opposite side of the bonfire, the Sweeney contingent was complete.

The Captain, who'd warily circled Jeff and openly cast suspicious glances in his direction, was slowly won over. He began to let down his guard when he realized that Jeff was willing to listen to his endless repertoire of stories (which everyone else had heard a few hundred times) and that he laughed appreciatively at his jokes. He was completely won over when Jeff admitted to knowing all of the words to "Danny Boy," "Irish Eyes," and countless obscure, old-country ballads. The unusual combination of Jeff's light tenor and the Captain's gravelly baritone made surprisingly lovely music.

"Ya never told me the lad was Irish!" the Captain scolded Farrell, an arm draped protectively around Jeff's shoulders.

Farrell, not anxious to send the Captain to an early grave, decided against telling him that Jeff was one-hundred-percent English.

It was well after one in the morning when Jeff and Farrell, among the last to leave, finally headed home. They walked hand in hand, barefoot in the moonlit surf, with a million stars winking in the black country sky.

"Your family is terrific," Jeff told her.

"Thanks, I agree. You'd better be careful, though," she warned, "or they'll have us married off. They were crazy about you."

He squeezed her hand and smiled. "It's tempting. Too bad you're not my type."

"Story of my life." She shrugged and looked up at him, smiling.

"I love you, Red," he told her.

"I know. I love you, too."

The doors opened at noon. By three-thirty Meg had sold a record number of paintings. She was high on success and the enormous satisfaction of having her year's efforts received favorably.

She stood alone for a moment to catch her breath, enjoying the sight of a gallery full of people examining her work, when the door swung open and a new crowd burst into the room.

She recognized them immediately. They were Chicago's elite, who had begun to discover the area. The invasion was inevitable, she supposed, and of course it would do wonders for property values, but still . . . She knew that things were bound to change. In fact, they were changing already.

For although the elite found the idea of going to the country "amusing," they insisted upon all of the comforts of home. As a result, condominium developments were increasing along the lakefront. There Chicago's coddled few could congregate, completely insulated against any possible interaction with nature, or with people not in their immediate circle.

Thank God the Village is protected, Meg thought as she watched them descend like locusts upon the room. Some of them she'd seen before, but most of them she recognized from their pictures in various gossip columns.

Without realizing what she was doing, she began rating their performance. She found their complete self-absorption astounding as they flitted among the other guests and their entourage of local groupies. They discussed only themselves, their clothes, their hair, their latest peccadillos. Not one of them so much as glanced at a painting.

She was ready to dismiss them all as ridiculous when she noticed Michael Payne. At thirty-three, his star was rising like a rocket. One of Chicago's hottest young attorneys, he'd recently pulled off the coup of a lifetime. He'd successfully defended a prominent judge accused of taking bribes. A total of seven judges had gone on trial, and Michael Payne's client had been the only one acquitted. The other six were doing time.

His career was made. If he did nothing else for the rest of his life, he would still have clients lined up outside his door. But Michael Payne wasn't about to rest. He was ambitious, and he was hungry. The publicity he had received since the trial, his subsequent entrée into the highest social circles, and his status as one of Chicago's most eligible bachelors had merely whetted his appetite.

Meg watched him as he circled the room. She ticked off his physical attributes as though she was taking inventory. Tall? check; dark wavy hair? check; probing blue eyes? check; cleft chin? check. He was perfect, right down to his

Fila sweater and Calvin Klein jeans—too perfect, she decided. He looked like a caricature of a handsome man, just a little too smooth. He worked the room like a pro, focusing completely on each individual for approximately ten seconds and then moving on. He had a definite and deliberate presence.

That man is scary, she decided, and no sooner had she formulated that thought than Eileen sidled up behind her and whispered, "Isn't he gorgeous?"

Meg turned to her in surprise. "Are you serious?" she asked.

"Hell, yes! Look at that body. Mmmm-mmmmm! I wish I were a few years younger."

"A few?" Meg demanded. "He can't be more than thirty-two or three."

"So what's six or seven years?" Eileen looked at Meg suggestively. "He's not too young for you."

"Eileen, are you crazy?" Meg exploded. "You already had one of those. Think! Who does he remind you of?"

Eileen sighed. "Luke," she conceded. "He's just like him."

"Not quite," Meg said. "Luke was like a little boy who didn't know his toy gun had been switched for the real thing. He had no idea of the effect he had on people. This Michael Payne is a completely different story. Look at him! His every movement is premeditated. He knows exactly what he's doing!"

"Well, whatever he's doing, it's working on Farrell," Eileen said, gesturing toward the door. "Look, she's leaving with him."

Meg watched dumbstruck as Farrell, laughing gaily at something Michael had said, went out.

"How could she?" Meg cried.

"Relax, Meg. They're probably just going out to get some air."

"That's not the point, Eileen. She invited Jeff to this opening. I can't believe that she'd just walk out with another man."

"Oh, that's right. I'd forgotten about Jeff," Eileen admitted.

"I don't see him anywhere, do you?"

Eileen shook her head.

"I don't understand it," Meg said unhappily. "Surely she's aware of how Jeff feels about her. It's not like Farrell to be so insensitive."

"Oh, forget it, Meg," Eileen said, growing bored with the subject. She spotted someone across the room and waved. "Besides, who can blame her? The man's a dream!"

Meg watched as her sister bustled away. She looks terrible, she thought; only threads of her beauty have survived.

Eileen's drinking, and more important, Farrell's exposure to it, had become an ever-increasing source of guilt for Meg. When Farrell was very young, it had been easy not to acknowledge the problem. But later, after the divorce, Eileen's alcoholism—yes, she had to admit that her sister was an alcoholic—had become impossible to ignore.

But ignore it she had. For though she'd come to recognize the damage Eileen was doing to herself and to her child, Meg hadn't had the strength to confront Eileen openly, or to take on the full-time responsibility of raising a child.

Across the room, Eileen had joined a particularly vacuous-looking group of V.I.P.'s. She's as impressed as any groupie, thought Meg, and just as intent upon cultivating fools.

Farrell returned about fifteen minutes later, looking flushed and excited. Meg caught sight of Jeff talking to an intense, scholarly looking young man. Jeff looked all right on the surface, but Meg was sure that he must be wounded by Farrell's blatant defection.

When the doors finally closed at six, Meg was more than ready to go home. Though it had been her most successful show to date, and two of Farrell's pieces had sold, she couldn't get over her disappointment in her niece, and she was frightened as well. Farrell's actions reminded Meg of Eileen, and she abhorred the thought. She was further dismayed when she learned that Jeff had decided to return to Chicago that evening. He was hitching a ride with the young man she had seen him talking with earlier.

"Thanks for everything, Meg," Jeff said, leaning down to kiss her on the cheek. "I had a terrific time."

He'd returned with them to the house to gather up his belongings. His "ride" was waiting in the driveway while they said their good-byes.

Meg searched his eyes for the hurt she knew he must be feeling, but he disguised it well. He looked as happy and carefree as ever. In fact, he seemed positively buoyant!

She watched as he lifted Farrell off the ground in a great bear hug. "I love ya, Red!" he enthused. "It was terrific!"

Meg and Farrell stood on the front steps waving as he climbed into the sports car and rode away.

"What a day!" Farrell exclaimed happily as she headed into the house. "Meg, aren't you thrilled?"

Meg followed her into the kitchen. "Farrell," she said angrily, "how can you be so insensitive?"

Farrell spun around and stared at her in shock. "What are you talking about?"

"I can't believe you don't know!" Meg cried.

"Don't know what, Meg? What happened?"

"What happened!" Meg repeated. "Farrell, are you completely unaware of Jeff's feelings?"

"Jeff's feelings? What about Jeff's feelings?" Farrell demanded.

"Farrell! This man is obviously crazy about you. How could you invite him to the show and then leave with another man?"

"Jeff? Crazy about me? Oh, my God! Meg, I think you better sit down," Farrell said, fighting to keep a straight face.

"Farrell, there's nothing funny about this," Meg insisted.

"Oh, yes there is." Farrell was unable to control her mirth. "Meg, if anyone deserves to be accused of taking off with someone, it's Jeff."

"What are you talking about?" Meg asked sharply.

"Meg, Jeff does love me, but not the way you think—"

"Oh, Farrell," Meg interrupted skeptically.

"Meg," Farrell continued, "Jeff is gay."

"What?"

"Jeff's gay," Farrell repeated. "Does that bother you?" she asked, unsure of Meg's reaction.

"Bother me? Of course not. Does it bother him?"

Farrell was surprised by her aunt's perception. "It did for a long time," she told her. "It was difficult for him to admit it to himself. And then it was a struggle for him to learn to accept himself and to feel comfortable with who he is."

Meg nodded in understanding, and then suddenly remembered her accusation.

"Oh, Farrell!" she cried. "I'm so sorry! I should have realized you'd never be that insensitive."

Farrell waved it off. "Forget it, Meg. How could you have known? God, now that I think of it, you must have died when I left with Michael. And speaking of Michael," she said, her eyes sparkling, "isn't he something? I can't believe he's interested in me!"

"He is?" Meg asked. Warning bells were sounding in her head.

"Well . . . he took my number," Farrell admitted. "God, I hope he calls."

"Isn't he a little old for you?" Meg suggested warily.

"No, thirty-three is just right," Farrell insisted.

"Well, do me a favor. If he does call, be careful with Michael Payne. That's a very fast crowd he's running with, and you know what it's done—" She stopped herself.

Farrell looked up sharply. "To my mother?" she asked.

Meg nodded. It was enormously painful for her to broach this subject. "I'm sorry, honey, but maybe it's time we talked about it." Her dark eyes searched Farrell's face. "I should have said something, done something, years ago."

Farrell took her hand. "You've been wonderful, Meg. Really." She looked away. She had never discussed her mother's drinking with anyone, except with Trish a long, long time ago. Now, coming this close to the problem gave rise to a tidal wave of emotions, all of them terrifying. She wanted desperately to change the subject. "Anyway," she said, "don't worry about Michael. I'm used to fast crowds. Don't forget who my father was. I was jet-setting when I was twelve, and that never affected me."

Meg opened her mouth to challenge her niece, but lost her nerve. "Well, just be careful."

"Oh, I will be," Farrell assured her, though she was barely listening. She was consumed with recalling every thrilling detail of the moments she had spent in Michael's company that afternoon.

Eighteen

Almost a month passed before he finally called.

Farrell had begun her classes at the Art Institute and had just about despaired of ever hearing from him again. She leaped at his invitation, so ecstatic at his interest that it never occurred to her to question why he was inviting her to a formal affair only two days in advance. She had no way of knowing that last-minute invitations were an integral part of the "Payne strategy." He liked to keep his women off balance, to let them "stew in their own juices," as he put it. If Farrell had declined his invitation, it would have been another two months before she heard from him again.

From the moment she entered the ballroom, she captured the attention of every man in the room. All were eager to discover the name of the gorgeous woman on Michael Payne's arm.

While she was oblivious to their admiration, aware only of Michael and his devasting good looks, Payne was not. He immediately spread the word that he and Farrell were in a "committed relationship." He hadn't given her much thought until he saw how other men reacted to her. He decided that night that he wanted her for himself, if only to keep anyone else from having her.

When Michael Payne wanted something, he went after it with everything he had, and he let nothing stand in his way. Farrell barely had time to come up for air before she found herself swept into the fast-paced world of a connected, ambitious Chicago attorney. It was an instant "relationship." They went from one date to total commitment. Michael called several times every day and insisted upon knowing everything she did, right down to who she had spoken to and what they had talked about.

He assumed that they'd go out every Friday and Saturday night, and instead of asking her first, he informed her of their plans. He resented every moment she spent with anyone but himself. He resented her art, her classes, anything that diverted her attention from him. Not that he wasn't busy; he kept a schedule that would have felled an Olympic athlete. He just didn't want her to be busy. He wanted her available at all times, just in case he needed her.

Farrell was enormously flattered by the overwhelming attention. No one had ever been so interested in her, and she was amazed and deliriously happy that a man like Michael Payne was focusing on her. He was so popular, so spectacularly handsome with his ice-blue eyes, dark hair, and cleft chin. The increasingly rare compliments that he doled out, as sparingly as precious jewels, were like a feast to her starving ego.

As the weeks went by, things began to change. Michael's treatment of her became confusing and erratic. He kept her constantly off balance by criticizing her for the smallest things. There was always something wrong, whether it was her makeup, her hairstyle, or her perfume. There was always some detail she had overlooked, or not known enough to notice in the first place.

Michael was everything she had ever wanted in a man. He was handsome, sophisticated, loaded with charisma . . . a little like her father, she thought. Believing that she had found the perfect man, she did everything in her power to please him. The more he criticized, the harder she tried, desperate for his crumbs of affection.

She dipped into her savings to buy dresses to wear to his numerous events. She cut classes to make herself more available to him. She made no new friends, and constantly broke dates with her old ones in order to be with him. Still, nothing she did seemed to be enough. She blamed herself entirely when things went wrong, feeling as though she was incapable of doing anything right. The strain of the relationship began to take its toll on her physically. She began to lose weight, and faint shadows appeared beneath her eyes.

Nineteen

It was a week before Thanksgiving, and Michael was out of town, working on a case. Eileen was in Omaha with a client, and Farrell was dozing in front of the television, the phone cradled in her lap, hoping that Michael would call.

When the phone did ring, startling her awake, she jumped six inches off the couch and knocked the receiver onto the floor.

"Hello, hello. Is anyone there?" Meg asked.

Farrell managed to keep the disappointment out of her voice. "Meg!" she said, surprised to hear from her, and guilty over the fact that she hadn't called her aunt in over a month. "What's up?"

"Farrell, I'm sorry to be calling so late. I'm afraid it's bad news."

Farrell realized suddenly that Meg was trying not to cry.

"Meg, what's wrong? What's happened?" she asked desperately. Deep inside she knew, even before Meg was able to collect herself enough to answer.

"It's Grandma. She died this evening," Meg told her. "She went to lie down after dinner. When Dad tried to wake her to watch the news, she was gone."

"Oh, no! Oh, poor Grandpa!" Farrell cried. "How is he, Meg?"

"He's heartbroken," Meg said, crying openly. "When they tried to take her, he wouldn't let them. He fought them all off—four ambulance attendants and the doctor. Thank God for the Captain. He finally talked Dad into letting the doctor give him a sedative."

"Oh, Meg!" Farrell sobbed. "I can't believe it! There's still so much I want to say."

"I know," Meg agreed softly.

They were silent for a moment. Then suddenly it occurred to Farrell that her mother didn't know.

"Meg, we have to tell my mom."

"I know. Is she there?"

"No, she's in Omaha. I have the name of the hotel. I can get the number."

"Do you want me to call her?" Meg offered.

"That's all right. I'll tell her."

"Are you sure?" Meg asked.

"Yes, I'm sure," Farrell said. She wanted to spare Meg the pain of retelling the whole story. After all, she reasoned, what could be worse than losing your mother? "Are you all right, Meg?" she asked.

"I'm not sure," Meg answered honestly. "I never realized until now how much Mom validated me. I can't stop wondering what the point of everything is if I can't talk it over with her, or show it to her. I feel like nothing's real if she can't see it. The world is really empty right now."

"Oh, Meg, I'm so sorry," Farrell said. She felt totally inadequate.

"I know, honey," Meg said gently. "Listen, I think we'd better let your mom know."

"I'll call her now," Farrell promised.

Eileen was working furiously. He was definitely not an easy man to deal with. Usually she enjoyed the preliminaries, but tonight, after half a bottle of Scotch and a gram of his excellent coke, she wanted it over with. Finally she heard a low, rumbling sound beginning deep inside his chest. She knew from past experience that this meant he was getting close.

His eyes were only half closed. He sat, rather precariously, on the side of the bed, watching. For him, half of the turn-on lay in seeing a woman, even a fairly old broad like Eileen, down on her knees before him.

She isn't bad, he thought dispassionately. And her technique . . . oh, Lord, her technique! They should give awards for a tongue like hers! She took him fully into her mouth, temporarily obliterating his ability to think. She maneuvered him expertly until he was screaming in ecstasy.

"Oh, yes! Oh, yes! Oh, yes! You fucking bitch! Yes!"

Finally, she thought, as he exploded inside her mouth. The phone was ringing. She rose, stumbled, recovered, and walked around the bed.

"Who is it?" she slurred irritably.

"Mom?" Farrell's voice was hesitant. "Is that you?"

"Farrell!" Eileen blurted, sobering slightly at the sound of her daughter's voice. "What's wrong? Why are you calling so late?"

He jumped at the mention of Farrell's name, then relaxed, chiding himself. It wasn't as if she could see him! He watched as Eileen's face registered shock, and then as she began to cry, on the verge of hysteria.

What a mess, he thought when she hung up and turned to face him. Her mascara had smeared halfway down her face.

"I have to leave," she cried. "My mother has died!" She jumped up, started pulling on her sweats, and stepped barefoot into her leather boots.

"You're not going anywhere tonight, babe," he told her, pulling back the curtains to reveal the blizzard that was howling outside. "Believe me, planes won't be taking off in this."

"Then I'll drive!" she shouted, stuffing her belongings into her suitcase.

"You can't drive, for Christ's sake! You drank almost a half-bottle of Scotch."

"Watch me!" she screamed as she pulled the door open, admitting a blast of frigid air and snow. "You know," she said, looking him up and down, "you're not bad looking, but you're borderline in bed, and you're a real pain in the ass, Michael Payne!" She strode out to the motel parking lot and her rental car.

"Suit yourself, you dumb slut," Michael said softly. He closed the door, climbed into bed, and had just about drifted off to sleep when a disturbing thought jolted him awake.

"Goddamn it!" he swore out loud. The wake and the funeral would probably be held over the weekend.

Farrell will expect me to spend my whole weekend with her at a fucking funeral home, he thought bitterly. But as he lay there frowning, a delightful alternative occurred to him.

Within fifteen minutes of leaving, Eileen was hopelessly lost. It was beginning to occur to her that driving home from Omaha was not the best idea. Snow was falling so heavily that it was impossible to tell where the highway ended and the shoulder began. The windshield wipers weren't even making a dent; she couldn't see more than two inches in front of her. She was tired and dizzy, and to top it all off, the heater didn't seem to be working.

It was hopeless, and she began to cry. Then suddenly she saw the welcoming light of an all-night restaurant. She turned toward the light, not realizing that she had crossed the median strip and was heading the wrong way down the road.

She tried to concentrate, aware that her light-headedness was growing worse. Eager to reach the restaurant, she pressed her foot on the accelerator just as she hit a patch of ice. The car began spinning out of control. Frantically she slammed on the brakes and spun the wheel, far too panicked and high to remember to turn into the skid, or to gently pump the brakes.

Terrified, too intoxicated to comprehend what was happening, she pressed herself against the seat and watched in horror as the blackness and the snow whirled by . . .

. . . Until the world exploded into light.

She threw her arms up to shield her eyes from the painful glare as the huge semi rose up like a monolith before her. She heard rather than saw the metal monster bearing down on her, and her final cry was lost in the futile, deafening blast of its horn.

"Luke!"

Amazingly, the truck was scarcely damaged. Its driver walked away with a sick heart, but hardly a scratch. The rental car was a different story. It crumpled like a tin can, and Eileen McBride never knew what hit her.

When Michael awoke on the following morning, he dialed his secretary's home number, walking her from a sound sleep.

"I'm flying out to California for a few days," he informed her, giving her a number where he could be reached. "Now listen, and listen good. Nobody, and I mean nobody, is to be given that number. Furthermore," he continued, "you are not to call me unless there is an emergency regarding a client. If anyone gets this number, if you call me for any other reason, you're fired. Got it?"

"Got it," she answered, yawning. Her boss's rudeness didn't faze her, any more than his constant intrigues did. As far as she was concerned, he was just another asshole lawyer, and she was quitting as soon as she got married, anyway.

In Omaha, last night's blizzard was just a memory. He took the first available flight to L.A., hopped a shuttle to Palm Springs, and was walking unannounced into Goldie's living room by two o'clock that afternoon.

He crossed the marble floor, slid open the glass doors, and headed straight for the pool. Sure enough, there was Goldie, stretched out on a chaise longue completely naked except for the thin gold chain that circled an impossibly slender waist. From the chain there hung a single charm. It was a solid-gold penis with two-carat diamond testicles.

Lying by Goldie's side was a dark, brutal-looking young man, equally naked, *sans* the gold chain.

Michael crept forward silently and slapped Goldie's bronzed bottom with all his might.

Goldie screamed and spun around. "Michael, you bastard! Don't you ever knock?"

Michael turned to Goldie's companion. "Get lost," he ordered.

"Hey!" The man jumped up and moved menacingly toward Michael. "Who the fuck—"

Goldie interrupted, "Go ahead, Vinnie. I'll call you later."

Vinnie marched sullenly away.

Michael looked Goldie up and down, drawing in his breath appreciatively. Goldie was magic, with eyes as clear and blue as the Caribbean, hair like spun white gold that hung down to the middle of that perfect ass. Skin as soft and smooth as a baby's, but the Indian heritage in Goldie's blood had left its mark in the color of Goldie's skin; it was a burnished golden-brown. Goldie, short for Golden Eagle, was part American Indian. But the only signs of it were in the color of Goldie's skin, the fabulous cheekbones, the unusual name, and the bank account. Goldie was a descendant of the Agua-Caliente Indians, the richest tribe in the country, for they owned the desert that the town of Palm Springs stood upon.

"You're magnificent," Michael whispered.

"And you are as impossible as ever," Goldie chided him. "I can't have it, Michael! You simply cannot continue to come barging in here whenever the mood takes you."

"Shut up!" Michael ordered, grabbing a handful of hair and forcing Goldie back onto the chaise. God, how Goldie turned him on, he thought, brutally kissing that perfect mouth. He rose and began stripping off his clothes.

"What happened to the nice young man you brought with you last time?" Goldie asked. "The young attorney, Joe Brown?"

"We had a difference of opinion," Michael answered vaguely. "By the way, you should congratulate me," he added. "I'm thinking of getting married."

"How could you?" Goldie shrieked. "You really are disgusting!"

"Seriously, Goldie," Michael said, lying down on the empty chaise. "You know that I'm planning to run for office. Well, there's a group that's willing to back me, provided I get myself a wife. They won't even consider a single candidate."

"Is your career that important to you?" Goldie asked, incredulous.

Michael spun around and grabbed hold of Goldie's

wrist. "My career is everything!" he said with frightening intensity. "Nothing else means a fucking thing."

"What about the girl?" asked Goldie. "I assume you have one picked out. Does she mean anything? Does she even know about you?"

"Are you nuts?" he asked "She's a nice little Irish virgin. She'll make the perfect wife for a Chicago-based politician."

"Do you think that's fair, Michael?" Goldie asked, appalled. "It's one thing for you to choose a life-style, but isn't this a little like playing God with someone else's life? Don't you realize that she has a right to know?"

"It's a good thing you were born rich, bitch, 'cause you'd never make it in the real world." He stood up and stretched lazily. "Come on, let's get out of the sun," he suggested.

"Why, Michael! Whatever do you have in mind?" Goldie teased.

"Don't play coy with me, you slut; you're as hard as I am."

Goldie looked up at Michael's erect penis, and then down at his own.

"So I am!" he agreed, smiling seductively, and then scampered playfully into the house.

Twenty

After completing thirty laps in her Olympic-sized swimming pool, Mrs. Charles Della Porta donned the terry-cloth robe that Maria held for her, cinched the belt snugly, and strode briskly to the terrace. Maria hurried at her heels.

There, under a pink-and-white umbrella, Mrs. Della Porta's breakfast awaited her. Her morning meal, like her evening meal (she ate only two meals a day), her laps, her massages—really every aspect of her life—were highly ritualized.

She lifted a sterling dome, chose a single piece of dry wheat toast, spread exactly one tablespoon of sugarless strawberry jam in an even swipe, and reached, without looking up, for her morning paper.

Maria, who held the tray on which an array of papers was arranged, glanced nervously down at her wares. Her warm brown eyes widened, like a doe pinned by advancing highbeams. "Dio mio!" she whispered. She craned her neck to search the walkway that led to the main house. "Carlos!" she called in a high, quavering voice. She turned and smiled ingratiatingly at her mistress.

"Oh, Maria." The woman's voice was as soft as wind through the trees.

Maria winced.

The striking woman's lush, newly blue-black hair swung and caught the early California sun. Her flawless, delicate tan glowed with perfect health. Her eyes searched Maria's; she arched one brow inquiringly.

"Señora!" a voice shouted from a distance.

Maria whirled around. "Carlos!"

"Señora!" The male voice drew closer. They heard the slap of leather soles against the flagstone walk.

Finally he appeared, dwarfed by the massive hedges that loomed on either side of the path. He waved his treasure high above his head.

"The boy was late, Señora!" He spoke in a rush, his voice inappropriately loud. "That boy is bad. I tell him, don't you be late again!"

While he spoke, he crisply folded in half the paper he'd brought and placed it on the tray. He turned to Maria, and with a loving look but a harsh tone, said, "Rosa needs you in the kitchen, Maria. Go now!" He took the tray from her before she turned and started toward the path.

Carlos watched her briefly, then bowed and presented the tray. "Your paper, Señora."

"Maria," the woman called softly, looking at the paper.

Maria froze.

"Carlos, Maria, I think you'll both be interested in this."

"Yes, Señora?" Carlos asked, a little too brightly.

She sipped her herb tea. "They've rounded up another group of those poor Mexicans. Wetbacks, I think they call them. It's a shame, really, the way they treat them. I understand that they keep them rotting in smelly cells for months sometimes before deporting them. Some of them even die. No better than dogs, really."

She looked up and smiled. "I thought you might be interested. You may leave me now."

Of course the front page of the *Chicago Tribune* held no such story. She scanned the paper with a well-practiced eye, enjoying all of it. Chicago! She savored the names of streets, stores, teams, even politicians—though God knew she'd had enough of those to last a lifetime! After all these years, Chicago was still "home." Though Charles insisted on reading all those other papers, for he had a born politician's need to know everything and anything that was happening, everywhere, she'd gotten in the habit lately of reading only the *Tribune.*

Poor Charles, she thought as she leafed back to the obituaries. He'd become even more obsessed with politics since his weak heart had forced him to retire. Charles Della Porta, the wealthy, once-distinguished senator from California, was now a shameless political groupie.

Ah well, Mrs. Della Porta sighed, he'd had his uses. But he was becoming an embarrassment, the way he fawned over the most insignificant local pols!

She scanned the obituaries. Almost immediately two names jumped out at her. She gasped aloud. Her emotions, for a rare moment, were clearly decipherable.

"Mrs. Lucy Sweeney." That wasn't so surprising; the woman must have been nearing her seventies . . . but Eileen!

She quickly read the article: ". . . the former wife of the late Luke McBride . . ." The blood drained from her face, and her heart fluttered wildly. How could this have happened, she wondered frantically, feeling a terrifying loss of control.

"Luke, dead?" she whispered. "How could I not have known? It must be a mistake, a mistake . . ." For God's sake, he was married to that Hollywood slut; it must have been news!

She scanned her memory for an explanation. I must have been in Washington, or in Europe. She'd spent a lot of time in Europe with Shane, during their brief dalliance . . .

She realized that she was sweating, that her heart rate was soaring. She took several deep breaths and closed her eyes. "It's all right," she said aloud. "It's all right."

She finished the article. "Survived by her daughter, Farrell Moira McBride."

Relief flooded through her. She'd waited far too long, she'd had to . . . but she could still rectify the past.

It was time to go home.

Twenty-one

Farrell stood in the gray morning light. The frigid mist prickled her cheeks, mingling with her tears. There was something perversely comforting about the stinging dampness. It gave substance to her pain.

She hadn't noticed when the priest had stopped talking, but suddenly they were lowering her mother, and then her grandmother, into the ground. Things seemed to fade in and out of focus; people moved in slow motion, and then fast forward. Even her emotions seemed somehow out of reach, beyond her control, as if someone else had taken over all of her senses and she was along just for the ride.

Everyone was walking away. Meg and the Captain were with Patrick, holding onto his arms, propping him up. He appeared to have shrunk to half his former height in just four days. He seemed so frail, so old, all of a sudden. It frightened her. Who would stand between her and the world now?

Junior walked arm in arm with Bridget and Kimberly. Young Patrick followed close behind, weeping into his palms. But Farrell stood rooted to the earth, staring blankly at the mounds of fresh black soil that marred the perfection of the cemetery lawns.

She felt Jeff's arms encircle her. "Come on, Red," he

said gently. "Time to go now." She let him lead her away, following his directions as docilely as a child.

He tucked her into the back of a waiting limousine. "I'll be right back," he promised as he closed the door.

Meg had just finished settling Patrick in another limousine. She turned, intending to seek Jeff out, and found him waiting for her.

"Oh, good," she said. "I was hoping to find you. Jeff, thank you so much for coming. I just didn't know what else to do. Dad insists on going back to the Village right away, and Farrell refuses to leave the city. I don't think she should be left alone. I hope you don't mind my calling you."

"Meg, she's my best friend! I'm glad you called me. I'd do anything for Farrell. Just between us, I want to ask you something. Where the hell is this miracle man, Michael Payne, for Christ's sake? All I've heard about for the past three months is how wonderful he is. Couldn't he manage to fit his girlfriend's tragedy into his busy schedule?"

"Jeff, you won't believe this, but Farrell hasn't heard from him since the day before my mother died."

"That's five days, Meg! Hasn't she called him?"

"She doesn't know where he is, and his secretary insists that he can't be reached. Farrell doesn't know this, but I tried calling him myself. I got the same story," Meg told him.

"Meg, I'm just a lousy college student, and I can't disappear for five days! You're telling me that the hottest attorney in Chicago goes away and doesn't call in for *messages?*"

"I know, Jeff," Meg agreed. "It's ridiculous, but apparently that's what Farrell wants to believe."

"It's bullshit, Meg! What is Farrell doing with this guy? She looks like hell. I've never seen her so thin; she barely returns my phone calls. What's going on?"

"She thinks she's in love with him, Jeff. You know, she doesn't have much of a basis for comparison. Her parents' marriage was a nightmare." Meg felt a familiar stab of guilt. "I just hope she can come out of this without getting seriously hurt. She could really use someone to lean on right now, but clearly, Michael Payne can't be depended on."

"What a bastard!" Jeff said bitterly. "Come on, Meg, you're getting drenched. Do you want to say good-bye to Farrell before you go?" She nodded and followed him to their limousine.

Meg hugged Farrell closely and was shocked at how bony she had become. The girl was soaked, and Meg could feel her shivering. Her lips had a slight bluish tinge.

"Is there a blanket in here?" Meg asked the driver, then found it herself before he had a chance to answer. She tucked it firmly around Farrell's trembling body.

"Are you going to be all right?" Meg asked. "I wish you'd change your mind and come with us." She searched Farrell's eyes for some sign of responsiveness, some indication that she was going to get through this. Meg and Farrell shared a secret: they'd made a pact never to tell anyone what the coroner had told them. They could see no good reason for Patrick to know that his beloved Eileen had been falling-down drunk and entirely responsible for the accident that had killed her. They certainly saw no reason to tell anyone else. But Meg wondered what the knowledge was doing to Farrell, how much guilt she was taking upon herself for being the one who had called Eileen.

"I'll be fine, Meg," Farrell insisted. "I don't want to leave. Michael may get home. He's going to be so upset when he hears what's happened."

Meg glanced over at Jeff. He looked as if he would like to explode, but he held his temper in check.

"I'll call you tonight," Meg promised as she climbed out of the car. Jeff got in, and the driver started the engine. Farrell drifted off to sleep. When her blanket slipped down, Jeff pulled it up and tucked it more firmly under her chin. The motion of the car as the driver expertly negotiated the kamikaze traffic on the Dan Ryan Expressway seemed to lull her. She continued to sleep.

His thoughts turned back to last August. Both of their lives had changed dramatically since that day at the gallery. Unfortunately, Farrell's had taken a turn for the worse, while his had unquestionably changed for the better. That

was when he'd met Joe, and Joe was the best thing that ever
happened to him. They had clicked from the word go, to
Jeff's utter astonishment. He couldn't believe that someone as good-looking, as worldly, as terrific as Joe Brown was
interested in him.

Joe was handsome in a scholarly, professorial sort of
way. He was an inch taller than Jeff, with curly, light-brown
hair, and soft brown eyes that seemed to look directly into
Jeff's heart. He dressed impeccably in soft tweeds, faded
denims, and flannel work shirts. He had graduated first in
his class, one year ago, from Northwestern Law School, and
that was what the two of them had in common: their brilliance. After being lonely on their rarified intellectual
planes for most of their lives, it was pure ecstasy to find
someone with whom they could communicate freely. When
they were together, they didn't have to stop and explain
what they were talking about, or curb their intelligence, or
explain their jokes. Each could move as fast as he was able
and find that the other was with him all the way.

In addition to their brilliance, they were both decent,
kindhearted people who were looking for commitment.
They handled the fact that they were gay accordingly. They
didn't advertise, and they didn't hide. If someone asked,
they answered honestly and without embarrassment. But
they didn't volunteer the information. Both of them were
private people, who considered their personal lives their
own business.

The limousine pulled up in front of Farrell's building.
Jeff hopped out, tipped the driver, and was helping Farrell
out of the car when a hand on his shoulder stopped him.

"I'll take care of her." Michael Payne stepped in front
of Jeff, almost knocking him over as he reached into the car
for Farrell.

"Michael!" she cried, flying into his arms. "Oh, Michael, where have you been?"

Jeff stood back, literally shaking with rage, willing
himself to calm down for Farrell's sake.

"I just flew in an hour ago. I came straight here from
the airport. I'm sorry about your grandmother. I was so

involved in a case that I lost touch. I just heard the news when I got in.''

"What about my mother?" Farrell asked, confused that he'd failed to mention her.

Michael froze, his mind racing. What was she talking about, he wondered. What about her mother? Had that bitch told her about him?

"Your mother?" he asked nervously.

"Michael, my mother was killed four days ago."

"*What?*" Michael roared. "Your mother! What the hell are you talking about?" He was shocked. But as he thought about it, he decided that the Fates had played into his hands. He'd wondered how Eileen was going to react when he told her of his intention to marry Farrell. She hadn't minded fooling around with her daughter's boyfriend, but her daughter's husband might have been a different story.

"Maybe we'd better get off the sidewalk," Jeff suggested.

Michael glared at him. "I can take it from here," he said in dismissal. Jeff turned to Farrell for a cue.

"I'll be all right," she told him. "Jeff, thanks for everything."

"That's what friends are for," he told her, staring at Payne. As Farrell headed into the lobby, he whispered sarcastically, "Nice tan, Michael."

"Isn't it?" Payne flashed a self-satisfied grin that incensed Jeff even further. Payne went into the building, leaving Jeff on the pavement, livid with fury.

They stood facing each other in the front hall of her apartment. Michael took the soggy coat from her shoulders and flung it carelessly across a table. He looked her up and down, his brow furrowed, and her heart skipped a beat at this evidence of his concern. He was so beautiful, his features so finely chiseled. His cool blue eyes were especially prominent now that he was tanned.

She couldn't know that his look was not one of concern, but rather, one of disgust. She was being compared, to her distinct disadvantage, to Goldie.

Here goes, he thought, preparing himself. Just think

of Goldie. Think of what you did to him! The memory of his last evening with Goldie was enough to get him aroused. It was worth it, he told himself for the hundredth time that day. And Goldie wouldn't dare press charges against him, lest his beloved auntie find out that her little golden boy was a fag!

Farrell looked about as appealing as a wet cat. Those green eyes were unnerving sometimes, but he knew that if he took her now, he'd have her forever. She would never be weaker, or more needy, and he was more than willing to take advantage of her condition.

He opened his arms and she went to him, reveling in his strength, in the warmth emanating from his body. Suddenly he reached down and scooped her up. Wordlessly, he carried her across the hall and headed toward her bedroom.

She was confused and frightened. He'd never pressured her before. Although she'd dreamed a hundred times of how it would someday be with Michael, this was not what she'd envisioned. She felt too raw, too exposed. She wanted to be held and comforted like a child, not challenged as a woman. But she was too afraid to tell him so. She didn't want to drive a wedge between them, or to make him think she wasn't interested.

He set her down lightly. He could see that she was frightened, and he liked that. Eventually he'd train her so that she'd always be frightened, always tremble before him. It wouldn't take long.

"Trust me, baby," he whispered, slowly unbuttoning her silk blouse and letting it flutter to the floor. He reached behind her and unfastened her skirt, then helped her to her feet so she could step out of it. He pulled her pantyhose down, unfastened her bra, and then stood back to examine her naked body.

She stood before him trembling with humiliation. She kept her eyes lowered and her hands clasped, inadequately, in front of her. He smiled at her helplessness; he'd never felt so powerful. In all his years, he'd never had a virgin, never even considered it. He would have thought it would be unbearably boring and mundane. Who would have thought it would be such a kick? He prided himself on his many conquests; the more frequent, the more pride. And the idea of sexually conquering both a mother and her daughter was proof positive of his virility.

Unfortunately, his picture of himself did not allow for his homosexual encounters. As a result, he was constantly struggling to make the reality fit the dream.

Goldie was easy. He looked so much like a woman that he hardly even counted. Other lovers were more difficult, but he managed it. They acted feminine, they had tiny, womanlike bodies, they talked like women. In a pinch, he could block entire episodes from his conscious mind.

It was so necessary to his self-image to be thought of, by himself and others, as a macho stud that he had learned to redefine his actions as he was committing them. What he never allowed to penetrate his conscious mind was the fact that no matter what sex his partner was, he was incapable of performing without inflicting some form of hurt or humiliation upon that partner.

For him, making love didn't exist. Sex was not a demonstration of love, or of caring. It was an act of hatred, domination, and, increasingly, of violence.

He ran his hands over her body, pausing to caress her breasts, then drifting down past her waist to her hips, and then lower. Again and again he stroked her, until she was leaning against his chest and moaning softly. He lifted her and laid her on the bed. He undressed himself, stopping every now and again to caress her, first with his hands, and then with his tongue. Her eyes, wide with fear and anticipation, never left his face. Her expression alone was enough to turn him on, her childlike terror an aphrodisiac.

"Turn over," he commanded her.

"Michael!" she objected.

He reached down and flipped her over, then climbed behind her and yanked her up by her hips so that she was kneeling on her hands and knees. She began to struggle, but he gripped her firmly, and she was no match for his strength. She was confused and terrified. It was happening so fast . . . what was he doing?

"Michael!" she cried as she fought him, but the more

she fought, the more turned on he became. He plunged into her with all his might, entering her from behind. She screamed in pain as he took her again and again, so brutally that it felt to her like he was tearing her apart.

It seemed to take forever, but finally he was finished. He collapsed on top of her, gasping for breath. She lay perfectly still, her hot tears soaking the pillow. In a few minutes he rolled off of her, and she could tell by his breathing that he was asleep.

She lay curled tightly on her side and looked through her tears at her bedroom. There were her white-eyelet curtains and bedspread, her princess furniture, all the pictures of the animals she had cherished, her ribbons and her dolls, her folded easel and paint box; and a long-ago picture of herself and Eileen and Luke, all of them smiling for the camera, their arms around each other—all of the mementos of her childhood.

The next thing she knew, Michael was kissing her awake, the radio beside her bed playing a soft, romantic tune.

"Come on, sleepy head! I'm starving!"

She looked up to see him smiling down on her, his eyes crinkling at the corners in the way she loved.

He could see that she'd been crying. He knew that he'd gone too far. He'd meant to take her gently, but he'd gotten turned on and had lost perspective. He cupped her chin, tilted her face up, and sweetly kissed the end of her nose.

"Don't worry, baby," he said tenderly. "It's always scary the first time. But I love you, and together we'll make it right."

"But, Michael—" she began.

"Shhh, quiet!" he ordered her sharply, tuning in to the sudden bulletin that had interrupted the music. He reached over her and turned up the volume. "Well, I'll be damned." He whistled softly. "Charlie Della Porta finally bought it! The old hack. Drowned in his own bathtub. Well, I always said he was in over his head."

He turned back to Farrell. "Now, little girl, I'm going

to fix you something good to eat." He bent and kissed the top of her head.

She watched him pad naked from the room, then heard him in the kitchen, banging pots and slamming the refrigerator door. The sounds were somehow comforting. They made her feel that they were really a couple, sharing a domestic moment.

He's right, she told herself. I was silly to be so upset. Michael loves me, and I'm behaving like a terrified virgin.

In this way she managed to stifle the voice within her that was screaming *"Run!"* She needed someone, he was there, and by God, she was going to make it work. In order to make him right, she learned to convince herself that she was wrong, time and time again. She did it so well that she didn't even know it was happening.

Twenty-two

Over the next few weeks, Farrell became entirely dependent on Michael. She stopped attending classes altogether and spent her days in a state of suspended animation while waiting for his phone calls.

The more subservient she became, the more ill-tempered and critical he grew. He treated her like an irritating pest, often talking down to her, and making her the brunt of his jokes when they were out in public. But she couldn't see it. She was so enthralled, and so empty, that a few kind words from him were enough to counteract days of ill-treatment.

The week before Christmas, they had their first argument. Farrell had been hoping that Michael would come to the Village so they could spend Christmas Eve with Meg, Patrick, and the Captain. Michael was appalled at the suggestion and informed her that he had made other plans for them.

"But, Michael! I always spend Christmas with my family," she explained.

"Yes, Farrell, when you were a child, but now you're an

adult, with adult responsibilities. What would you suggest I tell Frank Adler and his wife, who just happen to be my most important clients?" He didn't mention the fact that Frank Adler was also the man who was going to finance his political future. " 'Sorry, I can't come to your Christmas Eve party. I have to go to Michigan and sit around with my girlfriend's grandfather.' "

He spoke so sarcastically and made her feel so ridiculous that she gave in without a struggle.

On the evening of the twenty-third, Farrell was wrapping presents when the phone rang. She was amazed to hear the Captain's voice on the other end of the line.

"Captain!" she cried out. "Is anything wrong?" It was so unusual for him to call.

"You bet it is!" he roared. "Meg just informed me that you're not planning to spend Christmas with your grandfather!"

Farrell had never heard him so angry. "I wanted to, Captain, but Michael—"

"To hell with Michael!" he shouted. "Listen to me, girl. Meg tells me you think you're in love with this man. Well, bully for you! You go ahead and prove your love and your devotion some other time. This time, let the man prove his love for you."

"Captain—"

"I'm not done yet! Farrell, I know how much you love your grandfather, and I'm not going to let you make the biggest mistake of your life. I'm telling you this not to scare you, but because it's true. Your grandpa's fading. He's not going to snap out of it, so if you want to say your good-byes, you'd better come and do it now."

His somber words shocked Farrell to the core. For the first time in ages, she emerged from the fog she'd been living in and got her priorities straight.

"I'll be there tomorrow," she told him.

"That's my girl!" he cheered. "I'll tell your grandpa to be expecting you."

"Captain, thanks."

"For nothin'," he snapped, and hung up.

Farrell cradled the receiver slowly, deep in thought,

contemplating what the Captain had said. She hadn't heard Michael enter the apartment.

"You'll be where tomorrow?" he demanded furiously.

She spun around to face him. "God, Michael, you scared me! I didn't hear you come in."

"You'll be where tomorrow?" he repeated, his fury mounting.

"Michael, I have to go home," she pleaded.

"Home!" he jeered. "Home! Is this not home? What the hell are you talking about?"

"I mean I have to go to the Village. I'm sorry, but my grandfather isn't well."

"Your grandfather! What about me? What the hell am I supposed to do while you traipse off to Michigan to be with your fucking grandfather?"

Farrell stood staring at him as he carried on, and suddenly her nervousness dissipated. She remembered the Captain's words, "Let him prove his love for you." She'd been so busy trying to prove herself worthy of Michael that she'd never stopped to consider whether he was worthy of her. At that moment, and for the first time, she had grave doubts.

While he was ranting, she walked out of the room without a word. She went to her bedroom, closed the door, and picked up the phone. She needed to talk to a friend.

Her phone call interrupted the biggest fight Jeff and Joe had ever had. Jeff had been raging for close to an hour, and Joe was miserably trying to win his forgiveness.

"But how could you not tell me?" Jeff pleaded, needing to understand. "You knew she was my best friend! You knew how worried I was about her! How could you not say anything?"

"Jeff, I'm sorry. Please try to understand. I was disgusted with myself for being taken in by him. I was such a fool! I had no idea of what he was into. Michael Payne was like an idol to me; he was this awesome attorney. I didn't have a clue that he was such a sick bastard!"

"But you knew he was gay. Forget that he beat this Goldie within an inch of his life. Forget that he's a sadistic maniac. You knew he was gay, and you knew that my best friend was going out with him! *So why in God's name didn't you tell me?*"

Joe was crying now. "I'm sorry, Jeff. I'm so sorry. I just didn't want Michael Payne to be an issue between us. I should have told you. I wish to God I had."

"Tell me again what Goldie said about Payne running for office."

"He said that Payne has to get married in order to get backers. He told Goldie he'd found a nice little Irish virgin to fit the bill. He even told Goldie her name, and that he'd been screwing her mother for months."

Jeff buried his face in his hands. "God help me, how am I going to tell Farrell about him? It's going to break her heart. Jesus, Joe! How much can she take? How much can one person take?"

"He got carried away with Goldie the night before he left. He always liked it rough, but this time he went too far. He broke Goldie's arm in two places; he broke his collarbone; he cut him so bad he had to have sixty-seven stitches in his back. I think the man's losing his mind."

"I still don't understand why Goldie called you. Why doesn't he press charges against the bastard?"

"Goldie was raised by his father's sister. Apparently she's a one-in-a-million lady, and he'd rather die than hurt her. He says it would break her heart if she knew he was gay. He's not willing to take the chance of her finding out. But he said that he's been lying in his hospital bed worrying about the girl, and he wanted me to find her to tell her about Payne."

"Well, I see no reason for her to know about her mother and Payne. What did he want with Eileen, anyway?" Jeff asked, sickened by the thought. "Why did he have to sleep with Farrell's mother?"

"Publicity," Joe explained. "Don't forget, Eileen McBride was one of the best publicists in Chicago. According to Goldie, she came on to him initially, and we both know that Payne isn't the sort to look a gift horse in the mouth. She kept his name in the columns on a daily basis."

"Well, that explains his motives, but how about Farrell's mother's?"

Joe shook his head sadly. "From what I heard, Jeff, Eileen McBride was heavy into coke. We've both seen what that stuff can do to people."

"Jesus!" Jeff began, but he was interrupted by the phone ringing. He picked it up. "Farrell!" he blurted, shocked to hear her voice. "Hi!" He locked eyes with Joe. "Sure I can meet you. What time? No, an hour's fine. The Oak Treat? Great! See you then."

Michael was slumped on the living-room couch waiting for Farrell to come out. He could have kicked himself. He knew he had gone too far. He'd seen the way she'd looked at him. There hadn't been a trace of the usual doglike devotion in her expression. In fact, the look she had given him had bordered on contempt. He should have known better than to pit himself against her family. That had been a stupid mistake.

He reached in his pocket and pulled out the velvet box. Flipping open the lid, he sat contemplating the three-carat diamond he'd purchased that afternoon. Damn, he thought, it'll have to be tonight. He had intended to propose tomorrow night at the Adlers'. Sharing such an intimate moment would have further cemented his relationship with his chief backer.

"Shit!" he cursed out loud, rising from the couch. Someday he would make her pay for this inconvenience. He walked back to her room and knocked softly. When she didn't answer, he turned the knob and pushed the door open, but she was gone.

Farrell had slipped out the back way and gone down the service elevator. She just wasn't ready to face Michael, or to explain where she was going.

The welcoming atmosphere of the Oak Treat Café embraced her like an old friend. Prince's new album, *Purple Rain,* played in the background. She and Jeff had discovered the place years ago in their never-ending search for the perfect milkshake. The Oak Treat, with its cozy atmosphere and funky music, had fit the bill.

She saw Jeff's dark head poking above the back of an imitation-leather booth in a far corner of the restaurant—their usual spot.

"God, it's good to see you!" she said, sliding in across from him.

"Good to see you too, Red," he said, smiling wanly.

"Jeff, what's wrong?" She could see that he was upset. "Is everything all right with you and Joe?"

"Fine, Farrell. Everything's fine. Joe's fine, I'm fine." He stopped talking abruptly and stared at her. "Farrell, I have to tell you something, but it's so terrible that I don't know how I can say it."

"Jeff! What is it?" she asked, unable to imagine. To her horror, he started to cry, the tears running silently down his face.

"Oh, Jeff, what is it?" she asked tenderly.

"It's about Michael," he began.

"Michael!" That was the last thing she had expected him to say. "What about Michael?"

As gently as possible, he told her, leaving out the part about her mother. When he had finished, they sat in silence for several minutes while she digested what he had said. Finally she spoke.

"Well, I must say, Jeff, I would never have expected this from you."

"Expected what?" he asked, confused.

"This kind of jealousy. Apparently you can't handle the fact that I'm in love. What's wrong? Isn't Joe working out? I can see you pretending not to like Michael, but to accuse him of being bi! Of beating someone up! That's sick, Jeff. You know, you really need help!"

She was so upset that she was shaking. She couldn't believe the things Jeff had said; it couldn't be true! It couldn't be! She wasn't ready to admit it to herself, but part of what made the accusations so horrible was the fact that somewhere deep inside, a little bell was ringing and telling her that Jeff was right.

"Don't you think I'd know if Michael was planning on running for office? Well, he isn't, Jeff. And he hasn't asked me to marry him, either. So that blows that little lie, too!"

She rose from the table and threw some bills down in front of him. "It's on me, friend." She spoke so sarcastically that he winced at the venom in her voice. She spun around and stormed out. It wasn't until after the door had slammed shut that he realized she'd left her keys on the table.

She stood outside her apartment, still shaking with emotion. Michael opened the door and greeted her with open arms.

"Baby, I was so worried!" he cried. "Where were you?"

"I went for a walk," she told him.

"Come!" he urged, taking her by the hand and leading her to the living room. "I have a surprise. Voilà!" He gestured toward the coffee table, where he had placed a bottle of champagne and two fluted Waterford glasses.

Farrell felt a wave of fear wash over her. "What's this all about?" she asked.

He turned to her and reached in his pocket, pulling out the little velvet box. "Farrell McBride," he began formally, "will you do me the honor—"

"Oh, my God!" she cried. Her legs gave way and she fell back onto the couch. She put her head between her knees and began gasping for breath, convinced she was going to pass out.

"What the hell are you doing?" he shouted, stunned by her reaction. He was, for the first time in his life, completely at a loss. He took the ring out of the box and tried to slide it over her finger, but she balled her hand into a fist. "Don't," she whispered.

"What the hell is wrong with you?" No woman had ever rejected him, ever! He'd been expecting tears of joy and gratitude. What was happening?

She raised her head slowly and looked at him as though seeing him for the very first time.

"Michael, are you planning on running for a political office?" she asked quietly, staring at him. Her green eyes were like polar ice caps, frigid and unyielding.

He sucked in his breath. "What does that have to do with anything?" he shouted defensively. "It's none of your business." Who the hell has she been talking to, he wondered. Who told her?

"Michael," she asked quietly, "are you sleeping with

someone else? Are you gay, Michael?" She continued to stare at him.

He went cold. His eyes suddenly became wary, guarded, as if shutters had been drawn. He looked at her with unconcealed contempt. The bitch! The mewling cunt! He had to know who she'd been talking to. If this got out, it would ruin him! He'd do anything to stop that from happening, anything.

"What the fuck are you talking about?" he screamed, dangerously close to losing control.

"The truth, Michael. You've been using me all along. Gullible, needy Farrell, the perfect dupe. You never gave a damn about me. You didn't even show up when my mother died. She was killed in a goddamned car crash, Michael! And you didn't even show up for her funeral!"

"Your mother was a drunken slut," he screamed. "She was so smashed she couldn't even walk!"

Her head snapped back as though she'd been struck. His words had knocked the wind out of her. He hadn't meant to say it; he'd lost his temper and hadn't realized what he was saying. They remained motionless, staring at each another. He watched as the truth dawned in her fathomless green eyes.

"You were with her," she whispered. She suddenly remembered her mother's discomfort whenever she mentioned Michael's name. "You knew how drunk she was, how upset, and you let her drive? Get out, Michael, get out of here!"

"Like hell I will," he said, moving toward her. For the first time, it occurred to her to be afraid.

"You heard her. She said to get out."

They turned toward the voice.

"Jeff!" Farrell cried, running to him.

Michael stood his ground. He glared at Jeff with a murderous expression.

"Get the hell out of here, Payne!" Jeff shouted. "Unless you'd like to try to do a number on me. I warn you, though, I won't be as easy to beat as Goldie was."

The mention of Goldie's name shocked Michael into

motion. He stomped out of the apartment and slammed the door without a word.

Jeff drove Farrell to Michigan the following afternoon. They stopped and picked up Meg at four-thirty, then went directly to Patrick's. The Captain was already there, as he'd moved into the big house after Lucy passed away.

When they arrived, Patrick was seated in his favorite chair beside the fire. Farrell was shocked at his appearance. He'd lost so much weight since she'd last seen him that he seemed almost frail. His eyes were enormous in his drawn face.

Meg and Jeff went discreetly to join the Captain in the kitchen, leaving Farrell and her grandfather alone.

"Farrell," he said warmly, and opened his arms.

She crossed the room and hugged him close. "Grandpa, I've missed you!"

"Sit." He patted the chair beside him.

She obeyed, and looked up to return his loving gaze.

"We have the same eyes, you know," he said. "Same color, I mean. Yours are much prettier, thank God." He smiled. "I don't think I ever told you where we got 'em. My father had green eyes. As green as leaves, my mother used to say. He was a shameless drunk, and cruel to my mother to boot . . . but at least he gave us his eyes." He grinned and fell silent for a moment.

After a while, he continued. "Your grandmother loved you very much, Farrell."

Her eyes filled.

"We both loved you from the first minute we laid eyes on you in the hospital." He seemed to wander for a moment. "Did your mother ever tell you that someone tried to steal you from the hospital?"

Farrell was shocked by this revelation. "Tried to steal me?"

"Well, they thought so anyway. We never were sure. She was dressed like a nurse. Luke hired guards to watch the house for a while after it happened. Anyway, I'm losing my place. I want you to know that your grandmother and I took care of you in our wills."

"Oh, Grandpa, don't—"

He held up his hand to silence her. "No, Farrell, it's important. I want you to know that it isn't just because your mother died. Your grandmother and I made this decision years ago. Of course, initially everything passed to the surviving spouse." He smiled weakly. "I lost that lottery. But after I'm gone, the estate was to have been split four ways. Now it will be split three ways. We always wanted to take care of you."

Farrell rose and wrapped her arms around his broad, bony shoulders.

"Well now, isn't this a sight!" the Captain boomed. "When Irish eyes are smilin', indeed! I'm terrible sorry to interrupt, but dinner is served."

Jeff poked his head out of the kitchen. "Ta-da!" he cried, strutting into the room with a perfectly browned turkey.

Patrick rose and Farrell took his arm, Meg carried in the dressing, Jeff made several more frantic trips from the kitchen to the table, and finally they all sat down together.

After grace, they dug in and ate, the Captain said, "like a horde of wild, barbaric Englishmen!" Then they returned to the fire and spent a cozy evening there.

Once again the Captain coerced Jeff into joining him for multiple renditions of "Danny Boy," which, for some reason, struck Patrick as particularly hilarious.

The Captain finally gave up and accused Patrick of lacking the proper spirit. "And speaking of spirits," he said, brightening considerably, "I don't mind if I do!" He reached in his pocket and whisked out a flask and took a long, noisy swallow, which caused everyone to break into further fits of laughter.

Patrick Sweeney passed away in his sleep that Christmas Eve. When the Captain found him, after missing him at breakfast, Patrick was lying peacefully in his bed, a whisper of a smile softening his features. The Captain realized, as he pulled the sheet up over his friend's face, that the tears streaming down his cheeks were for himself and the loneliness left to him.

Patrick, he knew, was where he wanted to be. He had never fancied living in a world without his Lucy.

The funeral was the second biggest the southside had ever seen. The biggest, of course, had been when "The Mayor" had died a few years earlier, but Patrick would have been thrilled with the turnout.

Junior and his family had had to fly in from Acapulco. For once, Bridget hadn't complained a bit.

It took over eleven months for the estate to settle, and when it did, it was a bombshell! Farrell had inherited three companies, Meg and Junior had each inherited five. The net liquidated value of Farrell's inheritance was twenty-three thousand dollars—excluding, of course, the house her mother had left her. Meg's was twenty-five thousand dollars. And Junior's was in the neighborhood of fourteen million dollars. In addition, Junior inherited all of the Village properties.

At first Meg was too shocked to react. Then, driving home from the lawyer's office, she turned to Farrell. "Well," she reasoned, "I guess Dad just didn't think about his will. After all, he really wasn't the same after Mom died . . ."

"No, Meg," Farrell interrupted sharply. She recounted the conversation she'd had with Patrick the night before he died. "Grandpa knew exactly what he wanted. He gave a great deal of thought to his estate. God, Meg, don't you see? Junior and Bridget finagled this somehow. It was obvious! Didn't you see the looks on their faces?"

Meg swerved abruptly and pulled the car over to the curb.

"What are you doing?" Farrell asked, glancing around at the unfamiliar neighborhood.

"There's a phone." Meg pointed to a booth on the corner. "Call Jeff. Get the name of an attorney."

"Meg!"

Her dark eyes flashed. "Are you willing to take this lying down?"

Farrell held out her hand. "Do you have any change?" she asked.

Jeff directed them to Benjamin Stein, a leading probate expert and senior partner in the firm of Harper, Horwitz, O'Donnel, and Stein.

At their first meeting, as they explained their problem, Benjamin sat very still, absorbing every nuance of their story.

When they were finished, he cocked his large head, giving the illusion that his curling mass of steel-gray hair was a weight too heavy for his neck to manage. He tapped a pen against his upper lip and frowned, drawing his heavy, caterpillarlike brows together to form one solid black line.

"Sounds like you ladies have been hoodwinked," he said at last.

Meg sighed with relief. She'd been terrified that no one would believe them.

"I'll look into it." He rose to see them out.

"But—" Farrell objected.

"I'll call you when I have something worth billing you ladies for. From what you've just told me, neither of you can afford to sit in this office and chat."

Two weeks later his secretary called and set up a meeting. Once Meg and Farrell were seated, he got right down to business. He gestured to an array of papers spread across his desk.

"What you see before you are contracts, very legal and binding contracts, I might add. They represent, over the course of two years, the transfer of every valuable asset once held by the companies you ladies eventually inherited—all of those assets were methodically transferred into the now vastly valuable companies recently bestowed upon Mr. Patrick Sweeney, Jr."

"Then we can prove it!" Meg said excitedly.

He silenced her with a glance. "See that signature?" He pointed to the bottom of each page.

"It's my father's," Meg said.

"Your father signed each and every document." He came around the desk and sat on its edge, close to Meg and Farrell. "They were his own privately held companies. He had the right to do anything he wanted to with them. I'm afraid, short of proving coercion, there's absolutely nothing you can do about it."

"But he wouldn't have knowingly done such a thing!" Meg said.

"He didn't," Farrell insisted. "I told you what he said."

"And I believe you," Benjamin assured her. "Which is why I'm going to give these documents to you, and why I'm not going to charge you for my exorbitantly valuable time. You've been snookered, ladies, but short of a confession from Mr. Sweeney, Jr., you haven't got a case."

He scooped up the forms. "Hold on to these," he advised. "Who knows? Maybe someday something will turn up."

It was the perfect scam, no one the wiser. It was between Junior, Bridget, and God. Oh, and Miss Thompkins, of course. Junior told Patsy all of his secrets.

Part II

(Six Years Later)

Twenty-three

Farrell sprinted the last hundred yards. Dripping with sweat and panting, she ran between the stone walls, across the lawn, and directly to the faucet on the side of the house. Sighing with relief, she held the hose up and let the ice-cold water flow down the back of her neck.

It was just nine-thirty in the morning, but the temperature had already climbed past eighty degrees, and the humidity hadn't dipped below ninety in over two weeks.

She flipped her head back to begin soaking her hair . . . and screamed in fright at the sight of a pair of black eyes peering over the edge of the roof.

"Meg!" she shrieked. "What in God's name are you doing up there?"

"Patching the roof," Meg answered primly.

"Meg . . ." Farrell was dubious. "We are in the middle of the worst drought in history, and we're having the whole roof replaced right after the show. Now, what are you really doing up there?"

"Did I mention that Junior stopped by?" Meg asked, grinning.

"Oh-ho! Now I get it." Farrell burst out laughing.

"The old 'I can't talk now, Junior. I've got to fix the roof' routine!"

"Come around and hold the ladder for me, will you? We're about to have company."

Farrell held the ladder while Meg descended, holding a caulking gun in one hand and the rungs in the other.

"What do you mean by company?" Farrell asked just as a loud "yoo-hoo!" pierced the air.

"My God, it's Jan!" Farrell cried, utterly flabbergasted. "Meg, how did you know? It's been years since you've had a premonition."

Meg offered her best Mona Lisa smile, and then relented. "From the roof," she explained, "I could see her car pulling into her driveway. I knew she'd be walking over. Jan," she cried, "over here!" They hurried to the front of the house.

The three women greeted one other joyfully. Their last meeting had been four years earlier, and on the saddest of occasions. Norman had died quite unexpectedly, and Meg and Farrell had flown East for the services.

Since then, they had kept in touch through letters and phone calls, but Jan hadn't returned to the Village. Instead, she had spent her summers visiting the distant corners of the world. She had always longed to travel to exotic places, but Norman had considered Michigan "quite exotic enough, thank you" and had refused to budge.

Jan had begged Meg to join her on her excursions, knowing that Meg shared her passion for new horizons. But financial constraints and pride had kept Meg at home. Though she and Farrell made a reasonable living with their art, there was never a great deal of money left over, and Meg adamantly refused to accept the assistance Jan offered.

Finally the three friends broke apart and stood back to get a better look at one another. Jan was as straight and elegant as ever. At sixty-four, her suntanned, outdoorsy features were as glowing and vibrant as when she was a girl. Her shoulder-length hair was now silver, which, if anything, made her look even more sophisticated.

She turned fondly to Meg, her dear friend, now a

mature woman in her early forties. Meg's small face was still dominated by the huge, soulful black eyes that gave the impression of depth and penetrating vision. Her hair was cut in a short English-schoolboy style and had remained dark, except for the pure white streak that fell in a wave above her right eye.

Then Jan turned her attention to Farrell. At twenty-seven, Farrell was more beautiful than ever. Her tall, slim body, glowing with health, was golden from the sunlight and glistening with moisture. Her hair, still damp from the hose, curled around her face in shining wisps and fell in shimmering copper waves almost to her waist. Her full lips were parted in a smile that was as bright as the day, as welcoming as a breeze. Her green eyes sparkled with pleasure.

Jan, with a straight face, said to Meg, "You know, we look marvelous, but I happen to think it's indecent for a person to go around looking *that* good!" She gestured toward Farrell.

"Oh, right!" Farrell laughed self-consciously. She glanced down at her running shorts and cut-off T-shirt. "A true vision of loveliness!"

"Let's go into the house," Meg suggested. "The black-top is starting to bubble, and that's my cue to get out of the sun."

"Wait!" Jan cried. "I want to see what animals Farrell has collected this summer."

"I'll make lemonade while you two go," Meg offered as she escaped indoors.

Farrell and Jan walked to the pens that stood in a wooded corner of the yard. There, in the shade that caught the lake breeze, the animals remained fairly cool, even on the hottest of days.

"I haven't seen nearly as many animals as usual this summer," Farrell explained. "It's been so hot and dry. Not many bugs, either, which is nice . . . Oh, good! Timmy's here."

In a dark splotch of shade, a small boy sat cross-legged in the dirt, attempting to feed a black kitten with an eyedropper. He looked up as they approached, his blue eyes as big as saucers.

"I'm doing it!" he cried ecstatically. "He's eating it, just like you said."

"Great, Timmy!" Farrell squatted down beside him. "You're doing it just right."

"I already fed Trix," he told her, pointing to a rabbit with a broken leg. "I'll get to Bandit and Snowflake just as soon as I'm finished with Dark Star."

Farrell smiled up at Jan. "Timmy has named all the animals for me," she explained.

"So I gathered," Jan said, grinning. "Who's Bandit? Who's Snowflake?"

"Bandit's that baby raccoon right there," Timmy said, pointing to the tiny masked creature. "And Snowflake's the fluffy white kitten."

"Well," Jan said, "I'd say you have quite a flair for names, young man."

"Timmy, I'd like you to meet a friend of mine," Farrell began, but she was interrupted by a loud screeching from overhead.

"What in the world?" Jan said as a huge black bird descended on Farrell's shoulder.

"Raven!" cried Timmy. "Raven's back!"

"You've trained a raven?" Jan asked, incredulous.

"Actually, it's a crow," Farrell explained. "Timmy just thinks 'Raven' sounds neater. Right, Tim?"

"Right," he agreed happily.

"Raven smashed into the living-room window a few months ago and damaged his wing," Farrell explained. "Now he keeps coming back to visit. I guess he likes getting fed regularly."

"Amazing," Jan said, shaking her head in wonder. Then, "Listen, if you're ready, I wouldn't mind some of that lemonade."

"You're on," Farrell agreed, shooing the bird away. "Timmy, would you like to join us?"

"No, thanks," he answered, once again engrossed in feeding the kitten.

"He's adorable," Jan said as they headed across the yard.

"I know," Farrell agreed, looking back over her shoulder. "He worries me, though; he's so introverted. He has this little blue boat that he spends hours in, sailing back and forth along the buoys. He told me that when he grows up, he's going to sail around the world by himself."

Meg greeted them at the door with a pitcher of iced lemonade. "I see you've met Raven," she said, laughing at Jan's expression.

Jan flopped into a chair. "Nothing ever really changes," she declared, gratefully accepting a glass from Meg.

"That's for sure," Meg agreed. "Junior called while you two were out gallivanting around."

"Junior!" Farrell cried. "He just left! What does he want now?"

"Same old thing," said Meg.

"Don't tell me he's still after your house!" Jan exclaimed.

"You guessed it," Meg said.

"Now more than ever. He's obsessed with it," Farrell added.

"I don't get it," Jan said. "After all, he stole Patrick and Lucy's estate, and all that land. My God! I'd think that was enough for anyone."

"Well, first of all," explained Farrell, "Bridget has always been furious that this house wasn't included in the estate."

"Why would it be?" Jan asked, perplexed.

"Well, she assumed that because Grandpa had bought their house for them, he had also paid for this one. Somehow she had it in her head that this was going to belong to her."

"That woman is impossible!" Jan exploded.

"Secondly," Farrell continued, "you wouldn't believe what's happened to the value of lakefront property. It has absolutely gone through the roof. Of course you realize that there is virtually none to be had here in the Village. As a result, you'll be pleased to hear, having a house on the lake has become the height of chic.''

"And the golf course?'' Jan asked.

"Second best!'' Meg laughed gleefully. "It's driving Bridget crazy. Here she is, First Lady of the Village—''

"First *what?*'' Jan shrieked.

"Oh, ever since Junior was elected mayor, Bridget has declared herself First Lady.''

"God, I've missed this stuff,'' Jan said contentedly, scooting her chair in a little closer and fixing both elbows firmly on the table. "Go on,'' she prompted.

"Well,'' Meg continued, "here she is, First Lady, living over on the humble golf-course side while her eccentric, artsy, and—most unforgivable of all—poor relations, live in relative splendor, no pun intended, on the lake. And to further infuriate her, she can't find out who owns all of the blind-trust property. Jan, do you realize that whoever owns that land owns virtually the entire Village lakefront? They could name their price!''

"So basically what's happening,'' Jan said, "is that Bridget is torturing Junior into hassling you into selling?''

"Right,'' Meg agreed. "He absolutely refuses to give up. Unless, of course, I ask for help in repairing the roof,'' she added, laughing. "Then he runs like a bat out of hell.''

"The scoundrel!'' Jan exclaimed. "I really wish you had gotten another lawyer back before the estate settled. It drives me wild when I think of how Junior cheated you.''

"Oh, well,'' Meg sighed, "Benjamin Stein was first-rate. There really was nothing more to be done. Anyway, it's not worth going crazy over it.'' She brightened suddenly. "You haven't seen our work yet.''

"I was hoping you'd mention it,'' Jan said.

"I think I'll go for a swim,'' Farrell told them, rising quickly. "Jan, I'm so glad you're here.''

"Wait. Before you go, let me complete my true mission. I really came over to invite you both for dinner.''

"Great!'' Farrell agreed. "What time?''

"We'll start with cocktails around six,'' Jan told her as Farrell headed out the door. She turned to Meg with an amused smile. "I take it she still hates to be around when people view her work."

Meg nodded. "Unlike me, of course. I adore the attention."

"My God, Meg, she's absolutely breathtaking!"

"I know," Meg agreed. "She just keeps getting more and more beautiful."

"She still hasn't met anyone?" Jan asked.

"It's not that she doesn't meet them, or that they aren't interested. She just won't give an inch. They don't get any farther than the front steps. She's terrified, Jan."

Jan shook her head. "What's become of that horrible man, anyway?" she asked. "Do you ever hear anything about Michael Payne?"

"You don't want to know," Meg warned her. "He's thriving. He ran for state representative, then for state senator. Then, believe it or not, he ran for state's attorney, and won! I hear, though, that his wife had some sort of a breakdown."

"Small wonder, the poor thing," said Jan. "Imagine the hell he's put her through. What ever happened to 'what goes around comes around'?" she asked indignantly. "It really doesn't seem to be working out."

"No, it doesn't." Meg's tone was so dejected that Jan did a double take.

"Meg, what is it?" she asked. Something more than Michael Payne's success seemed to be troubling her.

"Oh, nothing," Meg demurred, and then changed her mind. "Actually, there is something," she confessed. "I'm just not sure what—"

"Hold on," Jan said. "You've lost me."

"It's hard to explain," Meg told her. "Something's wrong. I can feel it, but I'm not sure what it is. It's like a current has suddenly changed and become threatening. I feel it in the way people are acting, in the way they *look* at us all of a sudden. Even those who have been fairly friendly over the years are now drawing away from us, but I don't know why. Jan, you know how it was after Dad died and the estate was settled. We became less popular than ever. But there's always been a, oh, a frosty civility toward us. Now suddenly even that's gone."

Jan listened to her intently. Meg didn't have to convince her about her "feelings." Jan would never forget the morning Meg had called "just to check on her" because she'd had a feeling that Jan was in some sort of trouble. Jan had laughed off her concern and was still chuckling an hour later when Norman's best friend had arrived to tell her that Norman had died of cardiac arrest an hour before.

"Maybe it's Junior," Jan suggested. "Did it ever occur to you that he might be stirring things up somehow, to encourage you to sell?"

"I suppose that's possible," Meg said dubiously. She felt a chill run down her back and shivered in spite of the heat. "I'd really like to get to the bottom of it, though. It has me on edge."

"We'll work it out," Jan assured her. "Now come, show me your work."

"My God," Jan kept repeating as she walked around the studio, staring in awe at each painting, each piece of sculpture. "My God!"

Their work crowded the room, canvasses leaning against every wall, pieces of sculpture lining up in rows.

Meg's paintings were a celebration of texture, color, and light. They were joy, an indulgence, and easily an addiction. Whether they were of land or sky or seascape, when looking at them, one wanted nothing more than to enter that world, to leave this one behind.

Farrell's work was something else again. Her experiences had made her wiser, more introspective, and tougher. She had discovered something fierce within herself that could be released only through her art. She didn't sculpt as much as she attacked her medium. Her standards had become increasingly exacting, her work astoundingly vivid.

Jan stood gazing at one piece in particular. It was of a young man reaching for his woman. His face and his posture conveyed an agony of longing, while the woman pulled away, straining against the seduction of his need, the agony in her face equaling his, but within it there was determination and resolve. The tension in the piece was palpable.

Meg stood beside Jan. "It's magnificent," Jan said.

"Farrell's work is quite remarkable," Meg agreed.

"I'm speechless!" Jan exclaimed. "It's all remarkable. Both of you are long since ready for New York! Meg, is all of this just one year's work?"

Meg nodded. "This year has been unusual, though," she admitted. "Farrell and I really knocked ourselves out. The house needs some major repairs before winter sets in."

"I wish you two would let me help," Jan protested. "God knows, I have enough!"

"Don't be silly," Meg insisted, immediately regretting having mentioned finances. "We'll be in great shape after the show," she said. She hoped it was true.

"Well, it's here if you need it," Jan reminded her.

"I know, Jan," Meg said gratefully, embarrassed by the conversation. "And thanks . . ."

Twenty-four

Jan walked home along the trail that cut across their yards and wound through the acre of forest between their properties.

Once in her house, she pulled her clubs and golf shoes from the hall closet, tossed them into her golf cart and buzzed up to the club. As she drove, she made a mental note to thank the caretaker for doing such a splendid job; the cart had obviously been charged regularly.

At the club, she went directly to the pro shop to see about arranging for a locker for the season. Most of the villagers had arrived weeks before, so there were only a few undesirable lockers available. She settled for one crammed into a dark corner in the back row.

As she lugged her clubs down the aisle, berating herself for not calling ahead weeks ago, she decided to play a few holes. She propped her clubs up against a nearby locker and sat down on the narrow bench to change her shoes. As she leaned over, she heard the locker-room door swing open and two women enter, whispering excitedly.

Something in their tone captured her attention, and before she realized what she was doing, she found herself straining to overhear their conversation. What am I, the Village busybody, she chided herself, and immediately resolved to announce her presence by banging her locker door.

Just as she swung the door back, she heard one woman whisper in a scathing tone, "You mean you're *related* to Meg?"

Jan froze. Banishing all thoughts of social decorum, she resolved to listen to every word. Scarcely daring to breathe, she sat immobile on the bench as the women's voices drew nearer. For one horrifying moment, she thought they were coming all the way back, but luck was on her side and they stopped one row short.

"Well," the other woman responded defensively, "I'm not really related to her. She's Junior's sister."

It was Bridget, Jan realized, recognizing the transparently affected accent. Same old Bridget, she thought with disgust as she tried, unsuccessfully, to identify the second voice.

"Well, is it true?" the woman asked. "I mean, you of all people ought to know."

"Well—" Bridget began importantly.

"You do know what I'm talking about, don't you? You have heard what people are saying?"

"Of course," Bridget assured her. "You mean about the—"

To Jan's frustration, Bridget was interrupted by the arrival of two more women. "Are you two coming?" someone called.

"Over here!" Bridget answered in a loud whisper.

"What's up?" a new voice asked.

"Bridget was about to tell me about Meg Sweeney," the woman explained.

"Oh, her!" someone sneered.

"I want to know if the stories are true."

"What stories?" a fourth voice demanded.

"You know," the third voice insisted. "They live alone in that big house, just the two of them—"

"Oh, please. They're related!"

"So?" The voice was rife with innuendo.

"Come on, Bridget," the first woman prompted. "Is it true?"

Jan could tell from her tone that Bridget was relishing her role as expert.

"Well, all I know is what Junior has told me, and believe me, nothing would surprise me about either one of them. Do you know that when Meg was only two years old . . ."

Her voice trailed off as they left the locker room. Jan nearly fell off of the bench in her effort to catch the last words.

She jumped up, tossed her shoes and clubs into the locker, slammed the door, and ran from the locker room. Looking through the pro-shop window, she spotted a group of women on the lawn.

Bridget was among them; she was heavier than Jan remembered. Her rear end was now considerably wider than her shoulders. Her hair, bleached the same impossible shade of yellow that Jan recalled, was arranged in a French twist, with immobile sausage curls on either side of her pretty, round face. Aside from that, she'd aged well. Her face was smooth and unlined, and her claim to fame, those magnificent breasts, were still arresting.

Jan recognized most of the women, and as she strained to listen through the glass, she eventually was able to identify the owner of the first voice she had overheard.

The woman was far and away the most striking in the group. Tall, nicely built and solid-looking, she carried herself well and seemed to dominate the other women. She appeared to be in her mid- to late forties, although wearing her age spectacularly well. Her expertly dyed ash-blond hair was styled casually and fell in a blunt cut to just above her collar bone. She wore tinted aviator glasses, and her clothes were so simply and elegantly cut that Jan knew immediately they had cost the earth.

Jan could see that all the other women seemed to be

deferring to her. The conversation was directed to her, and eyes searched for her reaction. Even Bridget seemed to be vying for her attention.

Jan called to the teenager who ran the pro shop. "Young man, who is that woman?" She pointed her out.

"Oh! You mean Mrs. Laudin," he told her eagerly. "Darla Laudin. Her husband is Victor, you know, Victor Laudin . . . Laudin Industries. My dad says he's one of the richest men in America. They're renting the Marlin estate."

Well, thought Jan, now I know why the ladies are so impressed. She breezed out the door and presented herself to the women.

"Hello, ladies!" she sang out gaily. "Hello, Bridget! You're looking wonderful, as always."

"Jan Tenholm!" Bridget cried with ill grace, casting an anxious glance toward Darla. She wasn't at all sure of how this was going to go over. Why did Jan have to single her out?

"Did you say Tenholm?" Darla cried excitedly, spinning around to face Jan.

"She did indeed," Jan answered, curious. What could her name mean to this woman? "It's Jan Tenholm."

Bridget was wondering the same thing. Why was Darla even speaking to Jan Tenholm? After all, she was just a peripheral person.

"Oh, Jan!" The woman seemed beside herself with joy. "Tell me, is that your fabulous Cape Cod on the lake?"

"Well, actually it is," Jan admitted. "Thank you."

It's the damn house, thought Bridget. Just because she's on the goddamned lake!

Darla continued, "I've walked by your house a hundred times just to look at it. It's adorable!"

Jan thanked her again.

"Jan . . . oh, my God! We haven't even been introduced, have we?" She glanced reproachfully at Bridget. "I'm Darla Laudin." She extended her hand formally.

"It's a pleasure, Darla," Jan said politely, shaking her hand. "Welcome to the Village."

"Listen, Jan," Darla said. "Victor and I are having a

casual little get-together Saturday evening. Will you come?"

Bridget could hardly believe her ears. Here she'd gotten the nod only yesterday, and Jan Tenholm gets herself invited right off the bat!

"I'd love to," Jan accepted graciously. She didn't miss the satisfied smile on Darla's face.

"Wonderful! Until then . . ." Darla said dismissively.

Jan watched as Darla turned her attention back to her flock. Bridget was drooping conspicuously. Her little round mouth was stretched out into a livid pink line.

"Bridget," Darla bubbled, "what do you say we get those big old husbands of ours to take us out to dinner? Just the four of us," she added.

Bridget was instantly transformed. "Oh, that sounds wonderful!" she gushed.

Jan rode home so immersed in thought that she whirred past the stop sign without so much as a curtsy. Her usually clear blue eyes were clouded as she struggled to make sense of what she'd heard.

It's too bizarre, she decided. No one in their right mind would believe that sort of nonsense!

But even as she scoffed, she remembered what Meg had told her about people acting strangely and drawing away. She remembered the vindictive whispers she had overheard, and how the women had relished each morsel of hurtful gossip. She pictured their faces. Some of them were bright and friendly, but others were bored and resentful, the perpetually disappointed faces of women endowed with enough intelligence to realize that somehow, somewhere along the way, they'd been cheated. They'd raised their children—and their husbands, for that matter; they were reasonably devout, they'd done good works, they'd followed the rules, goddamnit! And still, they knew that something was missing from their lives. But they lacked the drive or the initiative to find out what it was. So instead, their boundless energy was channeled toward insatiable materialism and bitter rivalry.

One thing is certain, Jan decided. Somebody is doing

a hell of a job in stirring things up. She shuddered at the thought of such malignant slander.

She was already pulling into her driveway when she remembered that she'd meant to play a round of golf.

Twenty-five

Jan sat at her dressing table absently brushing her gleaming silver hair. She'd been dressed and ready to go for half an hour, but she couldn't quite get herself to move.

Instead, she kept reviewing the evening she'd spent barbecuing with Meg and Farrell. They'd sat out on her screen porch long after darkness had descended, sipping wine and iced tea, telling tales, rediscovering the pleasure of one another's company. And all the while, through the laughter and the shared memories, Jan had been utterly consumed with guilt. For she had decided not to tell them about the conversation she had overheard.

After all, she reasoned, what possible good could come of telling them now, when she knew so little? The only thing gained would be hurt feelings.

When they told her that they would be spending the weekend in the city shopping for art supplies, she decided to carry her deception a little farther and not mention the Laudins' party.

She felt vile, as if she were betraying them somehow. But she reminded herself that she wasn't going to the party for the purpose of enjoying herself. Lord knows, I'd rather stay home with a book, she thought. I'm going for information, not for a good time. Someone's out to cause trouble, and I'm going to find out who!

She willed herself to get up from the dressing table and walk out the door, pausing briefly to give one last, longing look at the book she'd begun that afternoon.

As she pulled into the drive of the Marlin estate, she congratulated herself on having guessed that Darla Laudin's concept of a "casual little get-together" would be closer to most people's idea of a black-tie affair. Her first clue that she'd done the right thing in wearing her Yves Saint Laurent cocktail dress was when one of a half-dozen uniformed valets took her car.

A canopied awning led to the back of the house, where an elaborate tent had been erected. The party was in full swing. Against the background music, provided by a seventeen-piece band, over a hundred guests mingled amid tables draped with pale pink linen. Exotic flowers scented the soft evening air, and the scene was lit seductively by hundreds of flickering candles and torches. There were long buffet tables manned by smiling chefs who deftly carved everything from roast tenderloin of beef to smoked salmon, and others who were busy sauteeing delicacies from crepes to saganaki. There were bars dotted here and there for those too impatient to wait for the uniformed attendants who took drink orders and passed enormous trays of piping-hot hors d'oeuvres.

Well, well, Jan thought approvingly, the Laudins certainly know how to throw a party! As she searched among the guests for Darla, she spotted a few unfortunate individuals who had taken the "casual invitation" to heart. She finally caught sight of her hostess, escorting Junior and Bridget into the tent.

As Jan advanced to greet Darla, she overheard Bridget complaining. "But you said casual," Bridget whined, looking around in dismay. "You told me!" she insisted, looking at Darla's elegant silver sheath. It was impossible not to be amused by Bridget's predicament. Both she and Junior were dressed for a backyard picnic. The only indication that she'd made any effort about her appearance was her elaborately made-up face and the enormous, unrecognizable flower that she had squashed into the top of her French twist.

She was fit to be tied, but at the same time, she was at a complete loss as to whom to blame. She could hardly vent her wrath on Darla, the very person she'd spent weeks trying to cultivate. She was still in the midst of grappling with her irritation when Jan approached in her impeccable little black dress and shattered her anew.

Darla used Jan's arrival as an opportunity to disentangle herself from Bridget. After briefly assuring Bridget that she looked "adorable," she took Jan by the arm and led her off in search of the party's host.

Bridget shot Jan a look so childishly menacing that Jan bit back a laugh as they walked away. Darla, on the other hand, seemed completely oblivious to Bridget's fury. She directed her considerable charm toward making Jan feel comfortable.

Victor Laudin was a terrible disappointment. Jan had been expecting a worldly dynamo, with looks to match his wife's. But instead, she was confronted with a portly, dull-looking man at least twenty years his wife's senior.

He greeted Jan politely, if a trifle absently. There was no question as to who called the shots in this marriage. He seemed positively flattered by Darla's fleeting attention. His gaze barely brushed Jan before it went back to Darla, where it fixed adoringly until she sent him off to fetch drinks.

No sooner had he departed than Bridget scurried up, a malicious gleam in her eye. Clearly, she was up to no good.

"So, Jan," she began sweetly, "how are your good friends Meg and Farrell? I know how close you all are." She smugly searched Darla's face, certain that this bombshell would put Darla off Jan Tenholm once and for all.

"Why, they're fine, Bridget," Jan answered pleasantly. "How thoughtful of you to ask."

Bridget looked confused.

"Oh, yes," said Darla, "I've heard about them. I understand they're quite, uhm, unusual in some ways."

Jan was wary now, unsure of how to proceed. After all, she reminded herself, she was here for information. She wanted to get them talking freely in front of her, so she surprised Bridget with her answer.

"Oh, they're unusual all right!" she agreed gaily, feeling like a total rat. She gave a pointed little laugh. "Being their neighbor can be quite an adventure!"

"What do you mean?" Bridget demanded, completely thrown by her attitude.

"Oh, come now, Bridget," Darla admonished her.

"We all know what's being said. The question is, what are we going to do about it?"

It was Jan's turn to be shocked. "Do?" she asked. "What do you mean 'do about it'?"

"Well, clearly they're unhinged!" Darla answered impatiently. "Frankly, I think it's disgusting. It's like one of those stories you hear where the whole town knows that something's going on, but everyone sits idly by until it's too late. Honestly, far be it from me to pry into my neighbors' private lives . . . but this, this has gone beyond the boundaries of common decency!"

Jan was shocked. "What are you suggesting?" she demanded, unable to restrain herself. "What exactly are you accusing them of?"

Darla arched one perfect brow meaningfully. "My dear, I certainly am not the one who accused them—"

"Not to mention the animals," Bridget interrupted.

"What?" Jan asked.

"You know, Farrell's animals," Bridget answered. "I mean, what happens to all those animals she collects?"

"She cures them!" Jan almost shouted. "She cures them and lets them go."

"That's what she says," Bridget said skeptically.

"Did I hear you mention Farrell?" Two more women joined the group: Shirley Benatta and Peg Malloy.

"You won't believe what Mary Dooley told me this afternoon," Shirley offered. "Her son Timmy helps Farrell take care of those animals—"

"I wouldn't let my kids near that house," Peg announced virtuously.

"Well, she won't either, not anymore," Shirley said. "Guess what Farrell has now? A black raven! Tell me that's not creepy."

"It's a crow," Jan informed them. "They just call it Raven."

The women looked at her as though she'd said something crazy.

"Well, I don't know about ravens," Peg announced, "but I did read an article last week about this quaint little hamlet over in England. It seems that the townspeople kept finding goat carcasses all over the countryside. Finally they put it together and discovered a whole sect of witches! Unfortunately, they didn't find them until after they had kidnapped and murdered four children!"

"Coven of witches," Darla corrected her.

"Is that what you're talking about?" Jan demanded. "Are you accusing them of practicing witchcraft?"

"Don't be ridiculous," Darla insisted.

"What was that about goats?" Maureen Sheridan asked.

The cluster of women was growing, and the conversation was getting louder and more animated by the minute. Everyone seemed to have a gruesome tale to relate, each of them insisting that her story was true.

Jan listened in amazement. She no longer doubted that people would believe this utter nonsense . . . they were eating it up! It thrilled them every bit as much as it repelled them. Here was something wicked and bizarre, happening right in their own backyards. The question was, what was it? Were Meg and Farrell being accused of sexual deviancy, or of practicing witchcraft, or what?

For the first time in her life, Jan fully understood mob mentality and the use of a scapegoat. She'd never seen the villagers so excited. What she didn't understand was what it was all for. And who was behind it.

"No, they use goats," someone insisted. "I'll bring the magazine over tomorrow if you don't believe me."

It was too much. Jan moved away from the group and walked over to a bar. "Vodka tonic, please," she said. "Make it a stiff one."

"I'm afraid we've upset you," said Darla, appearing suddenly at Jan's side.

"It's vicious slander," Jan answered.

"Well, of course, they're your neighbors," Darla said.

Jan lifted her glass and took a healthy gulp of her drink. "I'm afraid I have to leave," she said, setting her glass down on the bar.

"But you haven't eaten!" Darla protested.

"Somehow I seem to have lost my appetite," Jan said. "Thank Victor for me. Good night."

Bridget, watching her go, wore an expression of such profound enjoyment that it almost concealed the venom in her stare.

Jan tossed and turned for almost two hours before finally giving up and switching on her bedside light.

It's so insidious, she thought. How do you combat something like this? It's like fighting smoke. The more she thought about it, the more hopeless it seemed. Finally, at dawn, she decided that she needed help.

She picked up the phone and dialed. She allowed the phone to ring seventeen times, secure in the knowledge that eventually it would be answered. When it finally was, she was confronted with silence on the other end of the line.

"Max?" she asked. "Max, is that you? *Max!*" Still nothing but silence greeted her.

"Max, I know you're not delighted to hear from me just now, but I must talk to you . . . Max, stop it! Max, I need you!"

Someone groaned deeply on the other end. "All my life I've waited to hear those words," a man said wistfully. "Simple words, really, yet somehow so compelling. 'I need you,' " he mimicked. "Wonderful. But Mother, *why must you need me at five A.M.?*"

"It's important, Max," Jan said in a slightly wounded tone.

Max Rosen sighed. A wise man, he knew when he was beaten. He ran a callused hand through his close-cropped, silver-tipped brown hair, stretched his rangy body, and groaned loudly again into the receiver. In spite of himself, he grinned. His clear blue eyes, so like his mother's, glinted in amusement. He rubbed them with the back of his hands, reached behind his head to plump up the pillows, and waited.

"How's Vermont?" Jan asked.

"Vermont is fine," he answered.

"How's the book coming?" she asked.

"It's coming, Mother. What's wrong? Something is wrong, isn't it?"

"I'm afraid it is," she told him. "And I haven't got a clue as to what to do about it. I've mentioned my friends Meg and Farrell? Well, something terrible is happening to them." She went on to relate everything that had happened. She told him of the innuendos, the open accusations, the distortion of innocent facts, and the growing hostility.

"The thing is," she concluded, "I'm convinced that someone is behind all this. After all, this campaign didn't get started on its own. I think that somebody is directing these rumors, but I can't think why.

"Anyway, it occurred to me that you might have some ideas. What with all of the research you do on crazy people for your thrillers . . . Well, it was just a thought." Her voice trailed off. "Max, are you there?"

"I'm here. I'm just thinking. It seems to me there are two possibilities," he said. "One is that your friends are the target of some unusually vicious and, I must say, creative gossip. If that community is as rigidly conventional as you've described"—a tinge of resentment crept into his voice. Though he and Jan had made their peace, the Village was still something of a sore spot—"then it makes a twisted sort of sense that your friends would attract a certain amount of ill will. Two women alone may seem vulnerable to you, but to someone else, they might be enormously threatening. After all, they're independent, creative, able to survive without men. Historically, that's reason enough to burn them at the stake. It certainly might be infuriating to some people. In other words, they're not playing by the rules. To someone who is imprisoned by those rules, that might be tremendously upsetting."

"Sort of a misery-loves-company situation?" Jan suggested.

"More of a misery-demands-company situation, I would think," Max said.

"I don't know," Jan mused skeptically. "I can think of several people who might be threatened by them and capable of petty gossip, one in particular, but this seems more serious to me. There's something so deliberate about this, so evil . . ." Her voice trailed off again. "What's the other possibility?" she asked. "You said there were two."

"Well, the second one is less attractive," he warned her. "If in fact there is a crazy, as you so delicately put it, who's orchestrating this slander, your friends could be in trouble."

"What do you mean?"

"Well, if someone is deliberately planting these rumors with malice aforethought, as the saying goes, then it's possible that that someone really is a psycho, who will eventually grow bored with idle talk."

"And then what?" Jan demanded.

"And then I don't know. It depends on how crazy she—or he—is," Max answered.

"Max, I have a bad feeling about all this. Do you think I should tell them?"

"Why don't you wait a bit?" he suggested. "Maybe people will get tired of them and find something else to talk about. If not, they'll find out soon enough."

"I suppose you're right. Well, I'll let you get some sleep now."

"Oh, right!" He laughed.

Just like his father, Jan thought lovingly as she hung up the receiver.

Her thoughts drifted back to when she was a headstrong young girl, madly, passionately, in love with David Rosen. It hadn't mattered to her in the least that he was an inventor and destined to be poor. She didn't care at all that he was fifteen years her senior. The fact that he was Jewish simply was a non-issue. None of this had meant a thing to her, but it had mattered enormously to her family, one of the oldest and wealthiest in Boston.

On the day she turned eighteen, she ran away and married David Rosen. Her family had disowned her, as his had disowned him, but in spite of this, or perhaps because of it, they were the closest and happiest of couples.

A year later, to their joy, their son Max was born. And six months later, David had a breakthrough. Jan thought he had lost his mind when he danced and sang around their apartment like a madman.

"I've done it!" he cried. "I've done it, love!"

Another year passed before his patent was finally approved, but as it turned out, he had "done it" indeed.

David had invented a little round disk that fit inside a faucet—any faucet—and made it operate more smoothly. Within a few years, there were no faucets manufactured that didn't contain David's little disk.

When his headaches began several years later, he dealt with them by pretending they didn't exist. But after three weeks, the pain overwhelmed him. The cancer was swift and sure, and Jan's beloved David was dead within two months.

He left behind a staggeringly wealthy widow and a hollow-eyed young boy, both of them crippled by the enormity of their grief.

Jan's parents had arrived on the scene and taken their daughter home, barely tolerating her "foreign-looking" son, who, they said, looked "so unfortunately" like his father.

A year later they had pointed her at a former suitor, now a brilliant young doctor, and had pushed hard. She hadn't had the strength to resist.

Norman had been a kind and loving husband. He had never asked for more than she was willing to give. His one fault was his inability to open his heart to David Rosen's son. To Norman, Max would always be a living reminder of his wife's true love.

In a way, Norman was right, for in Max, Jan would forever see the ghost of David. He had his father's height, his wavy, soft brown hair. He had his rugged body, his wiry strength, even the habit of cocking his head just so when he was listening.

Max had turned to writing when he was still a boy, to keep himself company. Before long, he found that it had become as necessary to him as breathing. He'd published his first book at twenty-eight, had his first bestseller at thirty-three, and now, at thirty-seven, was known and read around the world.

Though both Meg and Farrell knew of Max's existence, and had a vague awareness that he wrote for a living, they had no idea that Jan's son was the well-known author, Max Rosen. He'd been in Hong Kong when Norman had died, and so had missed the services. And Jan, still riddled with guilt over her own shortcomings as a mother, felt that she had no right to brag about him.

She decided, as she headed to the kitchen to make a pot of coffee, without really knowing why, that she would keep quiet about Max for just a while longer.

Twenty-six

Meg and Farrell pulled into the driveway late Sunday afternoon. They were exhausted from their trip, but exhilarated by their many purchases. For them, new art supplies were akin to buried treasure, or to a shopping spree at Bloomingdales. Pure bliss.

After unloading the car, they carried the supplies into the studio and sat cross-legged on the floor, unwrapping packages like kids on Christmas morning.

"We have about one month left till the show," Farrell said as she fumbled with the brown paper and string on a particularly well-wrapped package, "so let's assume that we're about done, give or take a piece or two. Do you think we'll make enough for the new roof?"

Meg looked around at the huge volume of work they had produced. "Honestly, I'm not sure, though God knows, we've been productive."

Farrell laughed at the understatement.

"I think so," Meg decided. "We won't be living high, but I think we'll make it." She turned to Farrell, now hopelessly entangled in wrapping paper and string, and realized that Farrell wasn't listening to a word she was saying. "Of course," she continued mischievously, "we could always sell the house, move somewhere away from the lake, be safe . . . secure . . . sensible."

"*What?*" Farrell cried when the words penetrated. She stared wide-eyed at Meg, who was laughing at her, and realized she'd been had.

"You were doing your Michael Jordan imitation again," Meg told her, referring to Farrell's habit of sticking out her tongue and biting on it when she was concentrating.

"I was not!"

Meg held up her hand, laughing. "I swear."

"God, I hate that! Why do I do it?"

"It's kind of cute," Meg told her. "Really."

"In your unbiased opinion," Farrell said ironically. She stood up in one fluid motion. "I think I'll go check on the animals. I want to make sure Timmy left enough food and water for them. Then I'm going for a swim. I'll stop at Jan's on the way back and see if she'll share that Uno's pizza we brought back with us."

Meg squinted out the windows. "The light's still good," she decided. "I think I'll work for a while."

Farrell changed into her suit and then cut across the lawn to the pens. After carefully checking on each animal, she saw that Timmy hadn't kept his promise after all. In every case, the food was completely gone and the water was extremely low.

Farrell was baffled; it was unlike Timmy to be so irresponsible. She wondered, as she fed and watered the animals, gently stroking them and talking softly to them as she worked, whether he was sick. That seemed the only reasonable explanation. She decided that Trix—she smiled at the name Timmy had given the little rabbit—would be ready to be on his own in another week. When she had finished tending to the animals, she started off for the beach.

She sprinted down the steep sand dune, airborne with every leaping stride. By the time she reached the bottom, she'd gained so much momentum that she had to keep running almost to the waterline. It was after five, and the beach was nearly empty. The lifeguard was storing the last of the buoys beneath his aluminum rowboat. A few die-hard sunbathers were gathering their belongings.

Down the beach was Timmy, dragging his little blue sailboat up into the reeds, where it would be safe from the rising tide.

"Timmy!" she called. "Wait up! I'll give you a hand."

She saw him pause at the sound of her voice, and she started running toward him, smiling, but when she got close enough to see the expression on his face, she stopped dead.

"Timmy, what's wrong?" she asked, checking over her shoulder to see if there was something frightening going on behind her.

"What is it, Tim?" she asked, still puzzled, and then to her horror, he began to back away from her. "Timmy?" she asked softly. It was beginning to dawn on her that it was her he was afraid of.

"No!" he cried suddenly. His little face crumpled, and tears poured down his cheeks. "Stay away from me!" he squeaked. Then he turned and ran as fast as his little legs could carry him.

Shaken to the core by the terror she had seen in his eyes, she watched him disappear beyond the dune. She stood motionless for a long time, staring at the spot where he had vanished.

Finally she turned and walked down to the shore, where she plunged into the cold, glassy surface and swam with swift, sure strokes toward the horizon. About half a mile out, she stopped swimming and turned to float effortlessly on her back, forgetting everything for a while, everything but the sky above, the warming sun, and the water lapping gently at the floating island.

Twenty-seven

She brought the car skidding to a stop in the dusty gravel drive, her heart beating furiously. Pressing her fingers to her temples, she made an effort to quiet herself by breathing deeply and evenly.

She was finding it increasingly difficult to preserve her usual calm. Now that she was so close, it seemed to require an ever greater effort of will to maintain the perfect control that was so essential to her.

Like a weathered rope stretched taut for far too long, she was beginning to unravel.

What had begun as a simple chore had consumed her entire morning in telephoning, and the second half of the day in driving down endless country roads, getting stuck behind crawling tractors and dilapidated pickup trucks, asking for directions from simpleminded morons who scratched their heads and looked utterly blank. The final insult came when she was handed a speeding ticket for going thirty-five miles per hour. Thirty-five! But at least the pathetic cop had known how to get here, she conceded. Besides, it was too good an opportunity to miss.

All that nonsense about goats the other night had given her the idea. It's truly amazing, she thought, placing her hand in the center of the steering wheel, how easily people are led. She sounded the horn.

An old man appeared in the black rectangular doorway of the dilapidated barn. He wore ancient denim overalls and a once-colorful cotton shirt, now tissue-thin and faded from countless washings and days in the sun. He advanced tentatively. His face, brown and puckered like a raisin, creased into a shy but welcoming smile. His eyes, the same washed-out blue as his overalls, disappeared in folds of weathered, leathery skin.

"You are da lady what called?" he asked hopefully.

She was unable to place his accent. She flung the door open and was instantly assaulted by a blast of hot air. In the Village, even on the hottest of days, you could count on a breeze off the lake. Here in this godforsaken nowhere, the heat shimmered in waves above the white-hot gravel, and the air was deathly still.

The old man jumped back with surprising agility to avoid being struck by the car door. He was taken aback by the woman's carelessness and looked questioningly at her.

"I spoke to your wife," she said briskly. God, the farm was a run-down wreck!

"Ya, Mama says show you. So come on." He turned and headed for the barn. He was shamed by her obvious contempt for his poverty. Once, a long time ago, this farm had been a showplace. But that was when he was still young and strong enough to keep it up, and before his son had died.

The barn was dark and smelled of hay and sweat and fresh manure. She thought it would be cooler, but the heat was even worse in here. He leaned over the latched half-door of a stall.

"Here, baby. Here, little baby, come!" he called sweetly to the little animal, which cocked its head in response and blinked its huge brown eyes. He smiled tenderly and turned to the lady. "He is so cute! Yes?" he beamed.

"Adorable," she said sarcastically. The creature was disgusting. "How much?"

He caught her look. Suddenly he decided he didn't like this lady, not at all.

"I don't know if we sell," he said evasively. "I'm not sure. I must talk to Mama."

She spun on him in sudden fury, her features contorted. He stepped back quickly, horrified by the change in her. The skin on her face had retracted, her lips drawn back to expose the uniform perfection of her sharp white teeth.

"I'm afraid you're mistaken," she hissed, and shoved him backward with both hands, catching him off balance and knocking him onto the mud floor.

She unlatched the stall door and reached down to grab the kid, but it ducked away. Infuriated, she kicked it in the side, sending it sprawling against the wall, then grabbed it roughly and slung it under her arm.

She stepped out of the stall and grinned down at the old man. Reaching into her pocket, she withdrew a hundred-dollar bill and threw it on his chest.

"That should satisfy Mama," she mocked him.

The old man searched her eyes, then quickly looked away in terror and recognition. Unconsciously he shifted his gaze to his forearm, where the numbers had been burned into his flesh so long ago . . . by a man with eyes just like this lady's, eyes that had no soul.

She followed his gaze, saw the numbers, and laughed.

The old man spoke. "What for you really want this baby?" he asked solemnly.

"Just like I told Mama," she taunted him. "The goat will be a present for a little girl. A wonderful surprise!"

She turned, once again utterly composed, and left him lying in the dirt.

Twenty-eight

They sat out on the wooden deck in ancient wicker chairs of different shapes and sizes. The steady breeze was a soft caress against their cheeks and bare brown shoulders . . . barely strong enough to ruffle their hair.

The sun, already lost beneath the depths, had gone down amidst a vivid spectacle of colors, faded now to muted shades of rose and heather, backed by a darkening golden glow.

Overhead, the sky was black enough for stars, and the dark was slowly bleeding down. In minutes, the faint colors would be swallowed up when the inky night met the horizon.

The women, each immersed in her own anxious thoughts, watched wordlessly as darkness fell . . . waiting, as though the spell of silence would be lifted in the night.

Meg sat with her feet pulled up and her arms locked around her knees. She stared out at the lake, seeing nothing, aware only of the nameless dread that filled her. It was coming back. The gift, as her Grandmother Kate had called it, was coming back.

It had stopped after Danny died. As if a black curtain had been drawn over a window, where once there was vision, suddenly there'd been nothing at all. The most sensitive part of her had simply shut down.

Then, four years ago, on the day that Norman died, she'd had a glimmer of the old feeling, just a hint, but enough to prompt her to call Jan and check on her.

This was different. It was coming on strong, filling her—like an old war wound that aches when the storm clouds gather.

Farrell still felt the sting of Timmy's fear, and with it,

the awakening of an awareness that up until now, she'd
been fighting to suppress. No longer could she dismiss
the villagers' shuttered glances and sudden silences as
unimportant. Clearly, something was being whispered
about her, something cruel enough to frighten away a
child.

Jan was brooding about her certain knowledge of the
rumors that were spreading. Unsure of how to proceed,
and frustrated by her helplessness, she struggled with her
decision to keep silent.

Minutes passed, and then an hour, and the darkness
was complete.

Meg shifted in her chair, and the creaking of the
wicker sounded as loud and as shrill as a siren after so
much quiet. The women, brought back to the present,
became uncomfortably aware of their unnatural silence.

"Marvelous sunset," Meg ventured lamely.

"Fabulous!" "Terrific!" Jan and Farrell agreed desperately.

The silence crowded in again, insolating them.

"Well . . ." Jan began.

Meg and Farrell leaned in hopefully, eagerly.

"I think I'll head on home," Jan said, sensing that she
was letting them down. "I didn't get much sleep last
night," she told them honestly.

Farrell expelled her breath, unaware that she'd been
holding it.

"Oh, yes," Meg agreed inanely. "It must be getting
late." She instantly regretted her comment. They knew
perfectly well that it was barely ten o'clock.

They rose and walked to the front door. There they
turned and faced one another. There was a moment then
when they were on the verge of speech. The words, suppressed for hours, rose up and teetered on the tips of their
tongues . . . but the moment passed.

"Good night!" they called to one another, until Jan
disappeared into the night.

Twenty-nine

It was dusk when she passed through the Village gate. Risky entering before dark, but she was tired of waiting. When at last she pulled into her garage and closed the heavy door behind her, she could feel the adrenaline coursing through her veins. And this, she promised herself, is only the beginning!

In the house, she poured herself a double shot of bourbon and sat back to wait. She was too keyed up to contemplate food. Her husband was in the city, thank God, so there would be no interruptions.

She'd waited years for this . . . She stopped. "Years?" she asked aloud, disoriented for a moment. "How can it be years? Eileen is still young . . ." She shook herself. "It's Farrell, Farrell, Farrell, Farrell. Eileen is dead, and Luke is dead. Of course they are." She laughed off this lapse, refusing to acknowledge such brief bouts of confusion as important. It was just the excitement, she was sure of it. These disoriented moments had come over her a few times recently . . . but stress did terrible things to people.

Soon it would be over, and this time everything would turn out just as she planned; even better now that Jan Tenholm had arrived. At first she'd been thrown by Jan's presence, and furious at the unexpected intrusion. Then she'd realized what an asset Jan could be; an ally, really. She laughed out loud at the irony of that.

She let her thoughts drift delightfully to the task at hand and began to plan her movements for the evening, step by step. She felt herself beginning to grow warm. It happened every time she thought about it! Soon her skin was damp and glowing, her breathing ragged. She wouldn't even have to touch herself, just thinking was enough. She started writhing in her chair, her eyes rolled back, and as her ecstasy mounted, deep moans escaped her. She whimpered as her passion built, aching for release, her hands clenched into fists, her fingernails slicing into the softly padded flesh of her moist palms. She bit her lower lip until, finally, she tasted blood. As the tinny sweetness filled her mouth, she stiffened and convulsed. Then, explosively, she came. She slept after that.

She awoke in total darkness. As always, she was instantly awake, with no groggy lag between sleep and total consciousness. She checked the glowing digits on her watch. It was nearly one A.M. The Village would be as quiet as a tomb.

She could smell herself, the odor of stale sweat with a hint of Joy. Switching on a light, she glanced briefly in a mirror and was shocked at her reflection. Her silk blouse and linen slacks were wrinkled in accordion pleats. Her hair was a tumbled mess, and her makeup was smudged beyond repair. How odd, she thought; she must have been thrashing about in her sleep. Normally she didn't stir at all.

She went into the garage and peered into the car. The baby goat was curled up, sleeping, on the back seat. She opened the car door and choked on the sickening stench. How could she have forgotten something so obvious? The goat had defecated all over the backseat. She willed herself to tune out the smell, and climbed into the car.

She drove through the sleeping village, then pulled up soundlessly behind high stone walls. Bending down she felt underneath the seat for the coil of twine and the crowbar. She climbed out, placed the crowbar on the roof and reached back to tie the twine around the goat's neck, then pulled the little animal roughly from the car. The Village was silent.

She reached over and lifted the goat's spindly right front leg onto the floorboard. With one hand, she held the leg in place. She raised the crowbar in the other hand, high over her head, and kept it there, poised to strike, prolonging the moment.

She closed her eyes and pictured Luke's face, then Eileen's . . . and after a moment, the two faces merged and became one: Farrell's. She brought her arm down with all her might, slamming the steel bar down against the stiffened leg. She heard the bone splinter and the animal shriek in pain, and for the second time that night, she came.

At the same moment, Meg woke screaming in her bed,

her heart pounding violently, shaking with fear at the unspeakable terror that had awakened her. Her face and her pillow were soaked with tears; the only memory that lingered was the awareness of evil and sudden, sharp, unbearable pain.

Outside, she heard Meg scream and felt a prick of apprehension. She lifted the limp animal in her arms and ran silently to the front steps. There she untied the rope and laid the kid down on the front porch, then turned, ran to her car, and was gone.

Farrell rose just after dawn. Still groggy from sleep, she stepped into her swimsuit and padded silently through the house. Carefully, so as not to wake Meg, she eased the front door open and slipped outside. She was so intent on keeping quiet that she almost tripped over the limp creature that lay curled on the front porch.

"What's this?" she whispered, squatting down beside the kid. She placed her hand on its chest and felt the quick beating of its heart. Then she noticed its foreleg. It was clotted with dried blood and bent at an impossible angle.

"Oh, my God!" she cried. She reached out and gently touched the leg. Instantly the goat awakened, its huge brown eyes wide with panic. It made a pathetic and clearly excruciating effort to escape.

Farrell spoke soothingly, and gently stroked its back. When its trembling had abated slightly, she rose and ran back into the house.

"Meg! Wake up!" Farrell shook her urgently.

"What's happened?" Meg asked, sitting up in bed. "What's wrong?"

"I need your help!" Farrell told her. "There's a baby goat outside with a broken leg. It's a bad break. We'll have to take it to the vet. Will you drive so I can hold it?"

"Where did it come from?" Meg asked.

"I don't know, Meg. Hurry! It's really bad."

"Give me two minutes," Meg promised, "and Farrell, you might want to throw something on, as well."

Farrell looked down at her bathing suit and ran to her room to change.

Two hours later, they left the vet. The goat's leg had been splinted and the animal lay sedated, its little head in Farrell's lap. The Village was just beginning to stir as they drove along the quiet streets. They approached the Sweeney estate, and there, lined up along the drive, was a platoon of golf carts. And marching toward them down the driveway, clutching styrofoam cups of coffee and the remains of sweet rolls, were several of the lady golfers.

"Oh, God, look!" Bridget whispered to Darla Laudin. "It's Meg and Farrell!"

"Introduce me," Darla demanded excitedly. "I've never met them."

"Oh, Me-eg! Faa-Rrell!" Bridget bellowed importantly. "Hello-oo."

Farrell turned to Meg. "You'll have to stop," she said.

"I know, I know," Meg said regretfully as she put her foot on the brake.

The ladies converged around the car.

"How are you, Bridget?" Farrell asked politely.

"Just fine, Farrell, fine." Bridget spoke in the clipped, patronizing tone she reserved for those whom she considered her social inferiors.

She stuck her bubble head through the open window. "I want you both to meet a dear friend of mine." She turned. "Darla," she called. Then slowly she turned back to Farrell.

"What is that?" she cried, pointing at the kid.

"Oh, it's a goat," Farrell said casually.

"*A goat!*" Bridget squealed, leaping back from the car.

"A goat!" the golfers screamed, leaning in to get a closer look.

"It's just a baby," Farrell explained, confused by their reaction.

The women backed away, looking horrified. All except for one, who looked quite pleased.

"What's going on?" Farrell asked Meg.

"Who knows?" Meg shrugged as she shifted into drive and pulled away. "I wonder who Bridget wanted us to meet."

"I don't know," Farrell said, "but that's a first."

The phone was ringing when they pulled into the drive. Meg ran to the house, leaving Farrell to tend to the goat, and caught it on the fifth ring.

"I was about to hang up," Jan told her.

"We just got home," Meg explained.

"Listen, Meg, about last night . . . we have to talk."

Meg said, "Why don't you come over for coffee? We've had some excitement here this morning. Farrell has a new animal to take care of."

"Just so it's not a goat," Jan said without thinking. Slowly she became aware of the silence on the other end of the line. "Meg, are you there?" she asked.

"Jan, why did you say that?" Meg asked.

Suddenly Jan felt weak. "It *is* a goat!" she exclaimed.

"Yes," Meg told her, sounding baffled, "it is. Someone left it on the front porch last night. Its leg is badly broken."

"I'll be right over," Jan promised, "as soon as I make a phone call."

Jan was so frantic that it took her three tries before she got the number.

"Come on, answer!" she yelled into the receiver.

Max laid his hang-up bag in the backseat and put his duffel bag in the front. He patted his pockets, checking for keys, tickets, and his wallet. Once he was sure he had everything, he walked back to his cabin to slam the door, but weakened at the last minute and picked up the phone.

"Max! Thank God!" Jan's relief was overwhelming.

"Mother! What's happened?" he asked.

"Max! You were right. You know, the second choice. They got tired of idle gossip!"

"Mother, calm down if you can and tell me what's happened."

She told him about the goat. "Don't you see?" she cried. "They were all talking about goats the other night. Someone is doing this, Max!"

"Mother, take it easy." He spoke soothingly. "I'm on my way. The more I thought about it, the less I liked the idea of you in the middle of something so twisted. Now listen, I'm going to fly into O'Hare this afternoon. I'd like to wait a couple of days before arriving in the Village. That will give you time to pave my way."

"Oh, Max!" Jan was overcome. "You're really coming?"

"I'm on my way."

"What do you want me to do?" Jan asked.

"Does anyone there know that I'm your son?"

"Not really. Meg and Farrell know that my son Max is a writer. But they have no idea that he and Max Rosen are one and the same."

"Very flattering, Mother."

"Max, I explained it to you before . . ."

"I know. I'm just kidding. Actually, I'm glad. It'll work much better this way. I want you to spread the word that you have a houseguest coming. Emphasize the famous-author bit and don't mention that I'm your son. I'll do much better at snooping if I'm a free agent. You'd be amazed at how welcome an unattached bachelor is in a small community."

"Shall I tell Meg and Farrell?" Jan asked.

"Why don't you wait a bit on that? Now I've got to run or I'll miss my plane."

"Max."

"Yes?"

"Thank you, Max."

"Sure, Mom."

They sat at the table sipping coffee and trying to digest what Jan had been telling them.

"Well, what are you saying?" Farrell asked, incredulous.

Meg was staring at Jan with a devastated expression on her face.

"I mean," Farrell continued, "are they saying we're gay," her voice trembled, "or crazy . . . or what?" Her voice cracked, and tears streamed down her face. "And who's saying it anyway . . . and what does any of it have to do with goats?"

Jan shrugged helplessly.

"It's insane," Meg said quietly.

"That's just it," said Jan. "It *is* insane, and I think it's dangerous."

"What do you mean, dangerous?" Farrell asked.

"Farrell," Meg said, "has it occurred to you that some-one broke that animal's leg on purpose?"

Farrell stared at her. The thought had never crossed her mind. "Oh, my God!" she cried, sickened by the possi-bility.

"The question is," said Jan, "who would do such a thing?"

"Do you have any ideas?" Meg asked.

"There's only one person I can think of," said Jan, reluctant to say the name.

"Bridget!" Meg and Farrell said in unison.

"Exactly," Jan agreed.

"The next question is, what do we do about it?" said Meg.

"Well, actually," Jan said, "I thought I'd do some snooping. You see, I'm about to become very popular here in the Village."

"Oh, really?" Meg teased. "And to what do you attrib-ute your sudden rise in favor?"

"To my houseguest!" Jan announced. "Max Rosen is coming for a visit. He'll be staying in my coach house."

"The author?" Meg asked.

"The same," Jan answered, gratified that Meg had recognized his name. "And not only is he well known, he's also single and quite presentable. I'm willing to bet that the combination will prove irresistible to Village hostesses."

"In other words," Farrell teased, "you're going to use your unsuspecting houseguest to gain entrée into people's homes."

"Precisely!" Jan agreed. "And now I have just enough time to get to the clubhouse before the ladies leave the course. I'm going to spread the word about my guest!"

"Wait, Jan," Meg said. "I have one last thought on the subject."

They turned to her, curious.

"What if it isn't Bridget?" she asked.

But neither of them had an answer.

Thirty

The Village hadn't been this entertained in years. Sure, everyone played the role of horrified and outraged citizen. They spoke of nothing but the moral threat that Meg and Farrell posed to their righteous community. But oh! . . . it was thrilling!

Just the thought of such perversion was enough to send titillating shivers down their collective spine. It really hadn't taken much, just a well-placed suggestion here and there—and, of course, the goat—to send the bored community into a virtual feeding frenzy.

Meg and Farrell had ascended into the realms of evildom like rockets. They were practicing everything from lesbianism to witchcraft, from devil worship to God only knew what other obscene blasphemies—with heavy, even hopeful, emphasis on the "obscene."

And something else was happening, too. Though no one mentioned it, all were aware of it. The fact was, everyone was getting along beautifully this summer! Here it was, the first week in July . . . and everyone was still speaking. Being united against a common foe not only made them feel virtuous and smug, it brought them all together.

The latest high point, of course, had been yesterday's sighting of the goat. And hadn't they just been talking about goats? If there had been any doubts still lingering in anyone's mind, the goat had put an end to them.

And then, just when it seemed that things couldn't get any wilder, Jan Tenholm announces that a famous author is coming to stay in the Village. Well!

By the time Max actually arrived, "facts" about him had been invented, disseminated, and elaborated upon with gleeful abandon and an impressive flair for the dramatic.

He was no longer just a bachelor, but a rake and a womanizer of the first order. He wasn't a quiet writer, but an artist driven by dangerous passions. Imagine what urges boiled beneath his deceptively calm surface!

Within five minutes of his passing through the gate,

word spread that he had arrived. There wasn't a woman in the Village who could keep her legs crossed, or a man who didn't want to "punch the little creep's lights out."

Unsuspecting Max, driving a cherry-red Mercedes (Jan had felt that a Mercedes would give him "credibility"), idled along the shaded Village streets, taking in the playground, the golf course, the tennis courts, and the lavish homes. He couldn't help but feel a welling up of the old anger that had been the constant companion of his youth. He watched as a pack of whooping boys ran across a huge expanse of lawn, shooting each other with semiautomatic water guns.

He shook his anger off as he drove past them, reminding himself that he'd been largely to blame for what had happened. He'd been, he now realized, a stubborn, intransigent brat, preferring his own misery to the essentially harmless company of his stepfather.

Continuing along, he admitted to himself that he liked what he saw, very much indeed. The homes were well spaced, there were lots and lots of trees. With the forest on three sides and the lake on the fourth, he could understand why Jan loved the place so much.

As he drove along the lakefront road, a woman flew out of her front door, spun around to get a look at him, spun back around and began walking away from his approaching car, ostentatiously pretending that she hadn't noticed him. He drove on.

Susan Renatti kept walking. Her neck was stiff from craning it out the window; her head was sore where she had bashed it on the window frame when she had finally spotted his car. She'd been dressed since eight o'clock this morning, in the sexiest outfit she owned. And she had damn near broken her ankle running down the stairs two at a time.

She was strolling as nonchalantly as was possible for someone wearing four-inch heels, and staring avidly at some indeterminate point in the sky, when Max pulled up beside her.

"Excuse me," he called, slowing to match her pace.

She whipped her head around in a gesture that might

have been effective had she had long hair to flip. Instead, she looked dangerously close to dislocating her scrawny neck.

"Yeeessss," she cooed in a throaty whisper.

Max jumped. The woman is hissing at me, he thought, horrified. He looked on in amazement as her right eyebrow started bobbing up and down, independently of the left one. It was terrifying. It's a nervous tic, he assured himself, that's all, just a nervous tic.

"Excuse me, could you direct me to Jan Tenholm's residence?" he asked politely.

She leaned into his window, displaying her breasts at a particularly revealing angle.

"I'm SSSuusssaann," she began.

She *is* hissing! Max thought wildly. "Never mind!" he cried, pulling away. "I'll find it."

"Well!" Susan thought approvingly. "He is a shy one."

Jan's house looked like a little bit of home. It was a typical eastern-seaboard house, with the sprawling, yet casual look of comfortable old money. The smoke-gray shingles were properly weathered, the window frames were fresh and white, and the shutters were a vivid periwinkle blue.

He walked in, calling her name, remembering at the last minute not to call her "Mom."

"I'll be right down!" she yelled from upstairs. "Welcome! Make yourself at home."

He walked around the house, peering from windows, admiring the views. He had circled back and was once again in the living room, when he heard her come down the stairs and walk up beside him. He spoke without turning.

"I must say that so far, this Village is everything you said, and more!" His voice was slightly sarcastic.

"What do you mean?" she asked defensively.

"Well, I've been here for a grand total of about fifteen minutes, and in that time I've encountered one woman having some sort of nervous breakdown on the main street and now, even as we speak, there is, running past that window, an astonishingly beautiful woman . . . with a bird on her head!"

Jan peered out the window. "Oh, that's just Farrell," she said, as though that explained everything.

"That's Farrell?" Max shouted.

"Oh, Max," Jan said reproachfully, "don't you start, too!" She explained, "She saved the bird, and now it thinks she's its mother or something. It's really no big deal."

"Mother!" he began.

"Jan," she corrected him.

"Jan!" he yelled in frustration. "I don't care if she is the bird's mother. That is the most gorgeous woman I've ever seen!"

"Oh. Do you think so?" Jan asked evasively.

"I think so," he echoed.

"Well, forget it," Jan told him. "She isn't interested."

Max broke up laughing, shaking his head. He followed her out to the screened porch.

"And I wonder why I'm insecure," he teased.

Jan laughed with him as they sat down.

"Well, be attracted if you must, but I warn you—" she waved a finger at him "—hurt that girl and you'll have me to answer to!"

"Whose side are you on?" he kidded.

"Hers," she answered instantly. "You can take care of yourself."

"She looked pretty capable to me," he said.

"Oh, Max," Jan chided him. "Surely you, of all people, realize that we hurt the most in the places that don't show."

Max took her hand in his. "Mother," he said soberly, "remember me? Your son, Max? I'm one of the good guys, remember? I'm not here to hurt anybody. Okay?"

She patted his hand and looked up at him, chagrined. "Oh, don't pay any attention to me. I'm being overprotective. This has all turned into such a nightmare, it has me half nuts. Max, do you realize how impossible it is to defend yourself against a rumor, or to convince someone that you're not crazy if they want to believe that you are? Everything you do is suddenly suspect. It's just horrible!"

"What have you told people about me?" he asked.

"Oh, you're a mini-sensation in your own right. I've told everyone that you're coming here to soak up atmosphere for your next novel."

"Perfect." He nodded.

"Well . . . actually, I've said a little more than that," she confessed, looking guilty.

"Yes?" he asked warily.

"Well, I told them that your novel is going to be about a wildly passionate woman of a certain age, who possesses the soul of an adventuress and the heart of a seductress."

Max groaned.

"Now, this woman," Jan continued unperturbed, "has been trapped by life and circumstance, and through no fault of her own, in a small, Midwestern community, married to a dull, plodding man who has no couth or understanding—"

"Noooo!" Max pleaded. "You didn't really do this!"

"I also added a detail or two about your sex life."

"What!"

"Just to spice it up a bit," she assured him.

"Mother, you are perverse!"

Jan laughed, delighted with herself. "They'll be lining up outside your door to audition for the role."

"Oh, my God!" Max cried, slapping himself on the forehead. "I think I've already had my first audition." He described the scene on the street. "I think she said her name was SSSuussaann."

"Susan Renatti!" Jan exclaimed. "She's the Village vamp."

"God help the Village," Max said.

"She doesn't really do anything. But she gets a lot of mileage out of acting sexy and talking dirty."

"Isn't it a bit late in the day for her to be playing the delinquent?" Max asked.

"It must have worked for her back in high school," Jan surmised. "Some people never get over a success. Anyway, Max, you're sure to be in demand in no time at all. Meanwhile, I've invited Meg and Farrell to dinner tonight so you can become acquainted."

They sat together for another hour while Jan filled him in on all the details. Max listened intently, interrupting only when it was necessary to ask a question. When she had finished, he was more disturbed than ever. He rose and walked to the edge of the deck. "My God!" he said, looking down at the jutting rocks that protruded through the sand like enormous daggers from the beach below. "The slope to the beach is so gentle everywhere else; why is it so eroded beneath your deck?

Jan rose and stood beside him. "The spring storms do most of the damage," she explained. "The waves crash the melting ice floes against the dunes, then pull the sand away. I'm having several loads dumped the first week in September. I couldn't get anyone to come before then. It's rather dramatic though, don't you think?"

"Unsettling." He shivered. "You'd break your neck if you fell."

He left her to settle himself in the coach house, promising to return for cocktails at six-thirty. The house was quite large and comfortable. The bedroom had a balcony that fronted on the lake. The sitting room had a large picture window that looked down over the sun-dappled path that led in one direction to Meg and Farrell's house and in the other direction to the forest. There was a large, sunny kitchen; and the bathroom had a double sink and an enormous and elaborate shower stall.

After unpacking his clothes, he decided to go for a run. He'd been cooling his heels in Chicago for three days and was feeling lazy and sluggish. As he stripped down and pulled on his shorts, he assured himself that his decision to run had nothing whatsoever to do with the fact that Farrell was out there somewhere.

He'd gone about two miles when he spotted her. She was standing perfectly still in a small clearing, staring intently into the forest. Max stopped and followed her gaze, but since he saw nothing unusual, he took advantage of the opportunity to study Farrell.

She stood in profile to him; she was alert, ready to spring. She looked to him as though she belonged to the forest, the way he imagined Indians once did. She seemed a part of things, not an intruder.

The sun caught the golden highlights in her hair. Her skin was smooth and honey-colored. Her legs . . . her legs were magnificent. He studied the strong line of her jaw, her high, prominent cheekbones, the slight, exotic tilt of her large eyes. But it wasn't until he took a step and she turned on him, her clear, green eyes flashing in anger, that he was lost . . . instantly and totally lost.

He heard, rather than saw, what he had done. The family of deer turned and fled, hurtling through the forest at the sound of his approach.

"I'm sorry!" he apologized, shrugging as he approached her. "I didn't see them," he explained. "Clumsy of me."

"Yes, it was," she answered through her teeth, irritated by his blundering intrusion. It had been ages since she had seen deer in these woods!

He was so delighted by the silken cadence of her voice that he was already grinning from ear to ear when her answer sank in. Before he could react, she darted past him down the path, running back toward the Village without a word.

He was still grinning when she disappeared from view.

As she ran the last two miles, she assured herself that it was anger that was causing her heart to pound so loudly. Anger, and of course, the exercise. It had absolutely nothing to do with that huge, gangly oaf with those smiling blue eyes, and that sheepish grin, and that wavy, soft, silver-tipped brown hair.

Thirty-one

Jan eyed Farrell from across the table. Farrell was twisting a lock of hair around her finger, clearly a million miles away. She hadn't been herself all evening, not since the strangely awkward moment when Jan had first introduced her to Max.

Farrell had mumbled something under her breath, ducked her head shyly, and then proceeded to blush from her collarbone right up to her forehead. Max, for some reason, had seemed inordinately pleased with himself.

In fact, Farrell had been mortified when she realized that the stranger in the woods was none other than Jan's celebrated guest. Max, on the other hand, had been delighted to see that she had the good grace to be ashamed of her rudeness, and he was further captivated by her tendency to blush. Since then, Farrell had been unusually quiet, while Max had been at his most expansive—obnoxiously so, in Jan's opinion.

He's making a perfect ass of himself, Jan thought, irritated that he had somehow managed to alienate Farrell within one minute of meeting her. She glared at him.

He caught her look, gave her a wink, and turned his attention back to Meg. He knew he was irritating his mother, but as far as he was concerned, Farrell had cooked her own goose, and furthermore, he much preferred her present discomfort to her earlier dismissal.

"I'm sorry," he prompted Meg. "What was that?"

"I was wondering about something in your last book. You said that many serial killers have certain traits in common."

"Oh, yes. I said that a startling number of them were detectable as children. They have certain behavioral characteristics in common. For one thing, they're drawn to fires, and often set them. It's an entirely different disorder than pyromania, however. For another, many of them torture and kill animals."

"How horrible!" Jan shuddered, momentarily forgetting her anger at Max.

"When I was growing up," Meg reflected, "there was an older girl . . . oh, five or six years older, which of course, at the time, was an eternity. She was considered a great beauty in our parish . . . In fact," Meg recalled suddenly, "she was engaged to your father for a while, Farrell."

Farrell jumped at the sound of her name. "What?" she asked, completely off guard.

Meg suppressed a laugh. Farrell had clearly been away in her own world.

"Darleen Madigan!" Meg said, gratified that she'd been able to dredge up the name. "She was engaged to Luke until he met your mother."

"Really!" Farrell exclaimed. "I never knew he'd been engaged before Mom."

"Well, he broke it off as soon as he met Eileen, and then there was some sort of tragedy and the Madigan family moved away. Anyway, the reason I brought her up is because there were horrible stories about her along the lines Max was just discussing."

"Such as?" Max asked.

"She tortured animals," Meg said. "You see, she lived on the same block as Danny . . . he was my fiancé," she explained to Max. "One day Danny and his little brother were taking a shortcut through her yard and they saw her. She had a cat staked out and tied, and she skinned it . . . alive. Danny told me she was smiling and humming softly to herself the entire time."

"My father was engaged to her?" Farrell cried out, appalled.

"Well, as I said," Meg explained, "she was extremely beautiful, and I'm sure she was very charming when she chose to be. There were other stories, but that's the only one I know for sure is true."

"Were any of the stories about fires?" Max asked.

"Not that I recall," Meg said.

"My grandparents were killed in a fire," Farrell volunteered, misunderstanding the question.

"Oh, but that had nothing to do with—" Meg paused as a horrible thought occurred to her. She dismissed it from her mind. "That was an accident," she explained.

But Max had seen the look that had crossed her face.

"These were Luke's parents?" he asked casually.

"That's right," Meg nodded. "Jim and Moira McBride."

"They died before Luke married Farrell's mother?" Max persisted, making sure to keep his voice even and his face expressionless.

"Actually," said Meg, shifting uncomfortably in her chair, "they died on the night of the wedding. Luke and Eileen would have been killed, too, if Jim hadn't surprised them with the honeymoon suite . . ." Her voice trailed off, and she suddenly looked ill.

"Meg! What's wrong?" Farrell asked.

Meg smiled weakly and rose. "Nothing. I'm fine," she insisted. "I just need a little air."

"Good idea!" Jan agreed, jumping up. "Let's go out on the porch," she suggested. "I'll bring a tray of coffee and join you in a minute. Max"—she impaled him with her eyes—"perhaps you'd like to help me."

"I'll help," Farrell offered.

"No," Jan insisted, more forcefully than she'd intended. She wanted Max alone for a minute. "I'm sure Max won't mind a bit."

"Delighted," he said, and trailed her into the kitchen.

What's wrong with everybody, Farrell wondered as she followed Meg out to the porch. Why was Jan ordering Max Rosen into the kitchen? And what had come over Meg? What is everybody talking about?

Jan carefully closed the kitchen door, and then exploded. "What are you doing?" she cried. "Don't you think they have enough on their minds at the moment without worrying about a fire that occurred over twenty-five years ago? Can't you talk about current events, like a normal person? What's wrong with Saddam Hussein taking Kuwait, for God's sake! And what did you do to Farrell? How on earth did you manage to get her to hate you in twenty-seven seconds flat?"

Max had to laugh. "Whoa!" he cried, holding up his hands in surrender. "She doesn't hate me yet, for Pete's sake, and you have to admit it was pretty interesting the way that story developed."

"Max!" she cried, exasperated.

"Okay, okay. I'll forget about it," he lied. "Now, where's the coffee?"

"Never mind the coffee," she ordered. "Go out there and be charming!"

Farrell was waiting for him. She'd had enough bizarre

behavior for one evening and had decided to take matters in hand. Her own rudeness now seemed insignificant in comparison to everyone else's.

"Max, I wondered if you'd like to join me?" she asked. "I have to run home and check on Chevo. I thought you might like to come."

"Chevo?" he repeated blankly.

"He's a baby goat," she explained. "A kid. His leg is broken. I just thought . . ." Suddenly she felt ridiculous. What am I thinking of, she wondered; inviting a famous author to come look at a goat! "It was just a thought," she added lamely. Her cheeks were flaming red.

"Farrell," he said softly and gently placed a hand on her shoulder.

She looked up and saw that his eyes were smiling down into hers. She smiled back without even knowing why.

"I'd love to join you," he assured her. Her heart gave a little leap. Surprised by her own response, she turned away and headed for the door. "Well, come on, then," she said crisply, breaking the spell of intimacy that had gripped both of them so unexpectedly.

He followed her down the path, hurrying to keep up in the darkness. She moved just as he'd expected, silently and swiftly, sensing rather than seeing her way through the night.

Max was overwhelmed at sight of the house, its beautiful lines stark in the moonlight. "I've never seen anything like it!" he exclaimed. "It's magnificent!"

"Thanks," she said proudly. "My mother designed it."

"I love it," he told her. "It's a dream house."

She led him down to the living room, where Chevo was curled in the padded box she had built. The little goat's splintered leg stuck out at an awkward angle, and he had continued to lose rather than gain weight.

She knelt down and gently stroked his side. "He's not doing very well," she told Max.

"I'm sorry," Max said. He'd heard the slight catch in her voice, and his heart had turned over.

She looked up at him, surprised by his concern. For a moment, she let down her defenses.

"Someone broke his leg on purpose," she told him.

He'd known, of course. Jan had filled him in on everything, but somehow, hearing it from Farrell made it worse.
All of the horror of those words was reflected in her eyes.
He ached with the desire to wrap his arms around her and
comfort her.

He knelt down beside her and stroked the sleeping
kid. His touch was as light as hers had been; she found it
strangely comforting that a hand as large and rugged could
be so gentle.

Thirty-two

Bridget was displeased. "You're in my sun, Junior!" she
snapped. He shuffled sideways six inches and entered the
pool. She was sprawled in a chaise longue, her knees
propped up to support the yellow legal pad that she was
frowning over.

She wore a Hawaiian-print bikini, from which her
abundant flesh billowed a bit too much like buttered
dough. She held her pen gingerly as she added and crossed
out names, vainly attempting to keep the suntan oil on her
fingers from soaking through the paper.

"Damn!" she erupted in a fury, causing Junior, who
was now floating on an inner tube, to flip over backward
into the water. As he came sputtering to the surface, she
addressed him bitterly.

"Well, that's it! There's just no way around it." Her
tone clearly implied that whatever was wrong, Junior was
solely to blame. "We're going to have to invite Jan Tenholm if we want to get Max Rosen."

"Bridge," Junior argued reasonably, fingering his
bald spot to check for tenderness, "I don't really see the
problem. After all, we've had two hundred people for the
last five years. What's one more?"

"That's not the point, Junior," she said in disgust. "It's
not the number of people, it's the caliber. Jan Tenholm is
a nothing!"

It was Bridget's worst insult.

"Well, then, don't have Max Rosen," Junior naively suggested.

"Don't have Max Rosen?" she shrieked. "Junior, do you think it would be possible, for just once in your life, to consider someone besides yourself? Just once? First of all, we'd be a laughingstock if we didn't have Max Rosen. Everybody is having Max Rosen. Second of all . . . did it ever occur to you that he'd be perfect for our Kimmy?"

Junior was shocked. "Bridget! He's Jewish!"

"I don't care if he's Hare Krishna! He's handsome, wealthy, and successful. And Kimmy's turning thirty next month, for Christ's sake!"

"Kimmy's a career woman," Junior argued.

"Junior! You know as well as I do that she hasn't stepped foot inside that office for at least three months."

"That may be so," Junior conceded. "But everyone at work just loved her," he added irrelevantly. "I'm not sure I like the idea, Bridget."

"Oh, go soak your head!" she snapped, disappearing behind her yellow pad.

He floated off to the deep end. Junior had his own problems to sort out. His mistress had threatened to leave him. She was demanding a new condo, though Junior couldn't imagine why she thought she needed two extra bedrooms. But Patsy was adamant. It was the condo . . . or nothing.

It wasn't that Junior minded spending the money. God knows, he had enough for a dozen condos. It was getting the money without Bridget noticing that was the problem. She watched the bank and brokerage statements like a hawk. The only way he could do it would be to sell another of Dad's lots to that blind land trust. The broker who handled the trust was always willing to pay cash . . . and to settle quickly. But he just hated to keep selling off that land; it was becoming so valuable. He'd already sold seventeen of the twenty-two lots he'd inherited, just keeping Patsy in the style to which she demanded to become accustomed.

He peered at Bridget from beneath his eyebrows.

She'd abandoned the list for the moment and was splayed out on the lounge, dozing. Even in recline, her breasts were majestic, massive, ripe. They'd remained firm, and round. His eyes traveled down her body. Her belly was still admirably taut and appealing . . . Suddenly she let out a snort and started in her sleep, causing the flaccid flesh on her bottom and thighs to ripple and roll like the goo inside a lava lamp.

Junior sighed and looked away. He'd sell the lot first thing Monday morning.

He looked back when a car came screeching to a halt in the driveway. His face was instantly transformed at the sight of Kimmy, now fighting her way out of her newest sports car.

"Sunshine!" he cried. "You're home!"

"Oh, hello, Daddy," she called, not bothering to look at him. She'd learned quite young that Daddy wasn't to be taken seriously. She ran to her mother, grabbed her hands, and tried to pull her out of the lounge.

"Mother, get up! You won't believe what I just saw!"

"What! What!" Bridget squawked, struggling to her feet.

"Where are the binoculars?" Kimmy demanded.

"In the cabinet behind the bar," cried Bridget, infected by Kimmy's excitement.

"Got 'em! Come on!"

Junior watched as they raced to the far end of the pool, which overlooked the golf course and the In-Between. Bridget and Kimmy looked startlingly alike, although Kimmy's eyes were brown instead of blue. From beind, it was almost impossible to tell them apart. Kimmy's hair was bleached slightly lighter than Bridget's, but the two were built almost identically, although Kimmy's breasts were even bigger than her mothers'. They had the same broad bottoms and comparatively small waists. It was almost eerie to look at them standing side by side that way.

"There!" Kimmy cried, pointing. She handed Bridget the binoculars.

"What am I looking at?" Bridget demanded. "I don't see a thing."

"Over there!" Kimmy adjusted her mother's stance.

"What! I still don't . . . *ooohhh, myyyy Goddd!*" she cried, dragging each word out to its fullest.

"What I want to know," Kimmy said, "is, who is the guy? I mean, he's some kind of cute! And what is he doing with Farrell?"

"Who is the guy?" Bridget exploded. "You want to know who the guy is?" she screamed. "I'll tell you who the guy is! He's only the reason I told you to come up here, that's all. He's only the whole point of having a party. Only the bestselling, rich, single author Max Rosen, that's who the guy is. Junior!" she screamed, "I hope you're happy! Our guest is out jogging with your niece!"

Kimmy slipped the binoculars out of Bridget's hands.

"Our guest!" exclaimed Junior. "Bridget, we've met the man only a half-dozen times or so, at other people's homes. How does that make him our guest? Personally, I don't see what you two are getting so excited about."

Bridget and Kimmy exchanged a look. Bridget rolled her eyes; Kimmy nodded and giggled.

"Mother," Kimmy said, "just look at what Farrell's wearing. She's such a slob!"

Bridget took the binoculars again and focused on Farrell's flat brown midriff. She wore a cut-off white T-shirt and a pair of faded-blue running shorts. "Ugh! do you believe it?" Bridget gloated.

"And she's got almost no boobs," Kimmy added. "Besides, men don't like athletic women . . . do they, Daddy?" She preened.

Junior looked adoringly at his baby. "No, Sunshine," he assured her. "They like girls just like you."

She rewarded him by dimpling for a split second. "See, Mother?"

"You're right," Bridget nodded. "She's a nothing."

Thirty-three

"Hey!" Max called. "Hey, slow down!"

Farrell looked back, smiling. "Too much for you, huh?"

"You're damned right," he panted. "I've had it." He stopped dead in his tracks, folded his arms across his chest, and waited.

Unaware that he had stopped, Farrell disappeared around a bend in the trail. Max stood his ground as a minute passed, and then two. Finally, she reappeared.

"You're serious!" she cried in amazement.

"Yes, I'm serious," he told her. "We've run four miles, it's at least a hundred and fifty degrees, it's as humid as hell! Enough is enough. Don't you ever get tired?"

"Sure," she admitted, "but I don't stop until I'm done."

"You've got heart, McBride," he told her, shaking his head.

She smiled at the compliment.

"So this is the In-Between?" he said, looking around as they headed back to the shore. "I must say, you Midwesterners have a real knack for naming things—The Village, the In-Between."

Farrell laughed.

"I like it here, though," he told her. "It has a primeval feel to it, and it's so quiet."

"I know. It's a little bit eerie . . . like you've just walked off the planet. There's something so peaceful about it. I guess it's because no one but me ever comes out here."

Max didn't take his eyes off her. He'd grown to love the sound of her voice. Since he'd arrived, he'd spent as much time in observing Farrell as he had in trying to resolve her and Meg's troubles. He found himself resenting the time he had to spend away from her, going to parties, socializing. As Jan had predicted, he had become the focal point of the season.

"Tell me about the Village," he asked her. "Give me an insider's perspective."

She laughed ruefully at his use of the word "insider." Since her first summer here with Meg and her grandparents, this had always been the one place in the world where she felt at home. Though she knew that the villagers considered her different somehow, and an outsider, she had always longed for their acceptance. Now, more than ever, she felt the pain of their rejection. She shuddered at the thought of Max finding out just how disliked she was in the Village. Eventually, she told herself, he's bound to start wondering why we're never invited to any of the parties. She sighed, not bothering to analyze why what he thought mattered so much to her.

"Well," she began, "let's see . . . how can I describe the Village? I know! I'll tell you about the battle of the In-Between."

"The what?" he asked.

"Just listen," she ordered. "It started when Junior inherited all this land and decided to build condos—"

"Condos? Here?" Max exclaimed, shocked at the idea.

"Condos," she repeated. The battle had raged for weeks. She described it so well that he felt he was watching it all happen. He laughed so hard at some of the antics that tears rolled down his cheeks. As she spoke, he realized with growing sadness and dismay how much she loved these people.

From the time Jan had first called him, and over the past weeks, when he'd heard and seen for himself the intensity of the villagers' bitterness, he had assumed that the enmity was mutual. At the parties he'd attended, Farrell and Meg never failed to be mentioned and slandered in the cruelest possible manner.

For the first time, he realized how really devastated they must be. To care so deeply about the very people who were doing their utmost to destroy you seemed an ordeal almost too horrible to contemplate.

The more he thought about it, the angrier he became. How dare they do this to her, he raged. How dare they! She is so beautiful, so lovely. He'd watched her closely over the past weeks, sometimes with her knowledge, sometimes without. He'd seen how gentle she was with her animals, how much care she gave them. He'd persuaded Meg to show him around the studio and had been utterly floored by the beauty of Farrell's work. He'd stared at the statue of the woman escaping from her lover's desperate grasp. Turning to Meg, he'd asked her point-blank, "Is this a warning?"

She had looked at him appraisingly. "She's had her reasons for staying uninvolved." She had continued to stare at him until he'd answered her unspoken question.

"I won't give her any more," he'd promised. She had nodded, satisfied with his answer, and turned away.

He'd watched Farrell late one night when he'd woken from a sound sleep and walked out onto his balcony. She'd appeared suddenly out of nowhere, running down the dune. He had watched as she dove into the silver lake and disappeared beneath the surface. He had felt no fear as she swam for the horizon; once again he'd sensed that she was in her element, utterly secure.

"So," she said, finishing her story, "now do you feel like one of us?"

"Oh, exactly," he told her. "In fact, from now on, I want to be called Max O'Rosen."

"Cute, Max," she said sarcastically.

"Come on, Farrell," he challenged. "I'll race you to the lake."

"Sure!" she cried and took off, leaving him to eat her dust.

"Hey!" he shouted. "I never said go!"

From off in the distance, her voice choking with laughter, she called out, "Okay, Max! You can go now!"

He sprinted after her, wearing the hopeless, utterly befuddled expression of a man head over heels in love.

An hour later, Max sauntered out to the screened porch, interrupting Meg and Jan's conversation. "Hello, ladies!" he greeted them gaily. He was in an extraordinarily good mood.

Meg and Jan exchanged a conspiratorial glance. It was evident to both of them that something was happening between him and Farrell.

"What's up?" he asked, looking from one to the other. "Am I interrupting something?"

"Not really," Jan said. "I was just telling Meg how brilliant I think those tinted glasses are that Darla Laudin wears."

"Brilliant?" asked Max skeptically. "What's brilliant about them?"

"Well, it's not something a man would notice," Jan said, "but those glasses hide all the tiny lines around her eyes. Why, I bet they take years off. You know, at first I was surprised that a woman as well groomed as she wouldn't wear contacts, but then I realized how smart she was."

Max stared at her. "You know, you're right," he said softly. "Those glasses would hide a lot."

"Where's Farrell?" Meg asked, breaking his concentration.

"She's still swimming." Max grinned. "I swear that woman's part fish."

Meg laughed. "Part fish, part bird, part forest creature . . . it's humans she's had difficulty with."

Max nodded his agreement. "There is something wild about her . . . like a deer that ventures to the very edge of the forest and stares at you with those huge, compelling eyes. There's a timidness about her, too. Sometimes I almost have the feeling that she's afraid of me."

Meg and Jan exchanged a look, both of them aware that Max had completely forgotten their presence. He thought back to when he'd first met Farrell. He hadn't realized at the time how appropriate that meeting was . . . prophetic, really. And now here he was, afraid to make a move. As much as he longed to hold her, he sensed that if he moved too quickly, he would lose her irrevocably. He shuddered at the thought, then came back suddenly to the present. He looked down, almost in surprise, at Meg and Jan, who were staring up at him with amusement on their faces.

"Uh, well, ladies . . . if you'll excuse me, I'll go jump in a shower." He backed awkwardly out of the room.

"Max, wait," Jan called. "Before you go, I wanted to ask you to leave tomorrow night open. A friend of Farrell's is coming to visit, and I've invited him and Meg and Farrell to dinner."

Max stopped in mid-stride. His heart plummeted downward and landed with a resounding thud somewhere below his gut.

"A friend of Farrell's?" he asked weakly. "Funny, she didn't mention anything."

"Oh, she doesn't know yet," Meg piped in. "He just called today, and we decided to surprise her."

Max turned and left without a word.

"Max!" Jan called, then shrugged and looked at Meg. "Now what do you suppose could have gotten into him?"

"I can't imagine," Meg said, shaking her head. "You know, Jan, I really have to hand it to you. It's just amazing to watch the way you and Max relate to each other."

"I don't know what you mean," Jan said evasively, looking down at the floor.

"Well," Meg persisted, "it's like, oh, I don't know. You're just so easy together. It's like you've known each other forever."

Jan covered her face with her hands and sighed heavily. She looked over at Meg, considered a half-dozen reasonable explanations, discarded them all, threw her hands up over her head in total surrender, and cried, "I can't stand it! I can't stand it for one more minute!"

Meg stared at her. "What did I say?" she asked nervously.

"You just hit the nail on the head, that's all," Jan informed her. "Meg, the fact is, I have known Max forever—or for thirty-seven years, to be exact. Since the moment he was born."

"Jan, what are you talking about?" Meg asked.

"Meg . . . Max is my son."

Meg didn't even flinch. Her expression didn't change one iota. "Of course," she said calmly. "Your son Max, the writer, is Max Rosen, the famous novelist. How stupid of me not to have guessed!" she exploded. "But Jan, why in the world didn't you tell me? How could you keep something like this a secret? Why is it a secret, anyway? You must be so proud!"

Jan explained at great length.

"But Jan, I understood all about your arrangement with Norman before . . . why the secrecy now?"

"It was Max's idea," Jan confessed. "You see, he's not really here to visit me. He's here to find out who's behind all the talk about you and Farrell. He felt that he would do

better with no attachments . . . that people would open up
to him more easily."

"What makes you think he can help?" Meg asked.

"Because Max is part bloodhound, that's why! He's
really a frustrated detective. That's why his books are so
amazing. He can dig out secrets like no one else. Meg, I
don't blame you for being angry."

"Angry? I'm flattered!" Meg insisted. "I can't believe
that you and your son have gone to all this trouble for us."

"My God, this is a relief!" Jan cried. "It's been sheer
hell keeping this from you."

"Jan," Meg said, suddenly worried, "what about Farrell? How is she going to feel when she finds out that we
deceived her . . . that Max deceived her?"

"I think we'll have to let Max deal with that when the
time comes. In a way, it's been better this way. At least her
feelings for him won't be confused with her friendship with
me."

"Jan," Meg exclaimed, "just think! Wouldn't it be
wonderful if Farrell and your son—"

"Meg, I swear," Jan cried, her blue eyes sparkling, "I
could die happy just thinking about it!"

Max stepped out of the shower and padded naked to
the refrigerator. He swung open the door, grabbed a beer,
chugged it, and grabbed another. He couldn't remember
feeling so wounded, so angry, or so completely foolish.
Why, in God's name, had it never once occurred to him
that Farrell might be involved with someone else? He
squirmed in embarrassment when he thought of how ridiculous he must have seemed to her, like a callow adolescent.
He cringed at the thought of himself babbling like a sim-
pleton. Oh, God! he thought, reaching for another beer.

He walked to the bedroom and began dressing for
dinner. Another evening of dodging passes and soothing
egos seemed beyond him. He briefly considered leaving,
but immediately dismissed the idea. He'd come here to
help his mother's friends, and he'd stay until he'd finished.

"Damn!" he shouted, and took a swing at the closet
door, connecting soundly. The pain stunned him for a

moment. He checked to make sure that nothing was broken, shocked by the stupidity and violence of his action. He tried to shake off the desolation that gripped him, but found he couldn't. He flopped down on the bed and admitted to himself that for the first time in his life, he was in love, deeply in love . . . and her name was Farrell McBride.

At the coach-house door, Jan knocked again, wondering what could have happened. It had been hours since Max had left her porch. She wondered if he could have forgotten that they were expected at a party.

Suddenly the door swung open. "Mother!" he cried, "I salute you!" He raised his bottle, bowed slightly, and took a belt of his beer.

"Max, you're drinking!" Jan said in amazement. It was so unlike him to drink alone.

"You betcha, babe!" he told her, grabbing her arm and pulling her into the coach house.

"Max, you're drunk!" Jan cried.

"Perhaps," he said pompously, "but in the morning, I shall be ugly!"

"Oh, Max!" Jan laughed in spite of herself. "Come on, we're going to be late." She took his beer and poured it down the sink.

"You women are all alike," he groaned. "Take, take, take!"

"Oh, Lord," she muttered under her breath as she helped him into the car. She wondered how he would make it through the evening.

As it turned out, Max was the life of the party. He flirted outrageously with the women and regaled the men with shamefully embellished stories of his travels. He danced obscenely with Junior's daughter Kimmy, though Jan had to admit that it was Kimmy who was out of line. He continued drinking steadily throughout the evening, and when they finally left, he hung his head out the car window and sang "I dream of Kimmy with the bleached-blond hair" all the way home.

The Laudins, who had an engagement in Chicago,

had been noticeably absent. Without Darla, Jan thought, the women had seemed unusually subdued.

She pulled up in front of the coach house, fully expecting to have to help Max inside. Instead, he amazed her by climbing easily out of the car and then asking, "Did you happen to notice that Farrell and Meg weren't mentioned once all evening?" He turned and walked with exquisite care into the house.

"As a matter of fact, I did," she answered, but he had already closed the door.

Thirty-four

Max lay perfectly still, hardly daring to breathe. He understood perfectly that to move . . . was to die. Pain, blinding, searing pain, was his only reality . . . and darkness his only release. He lay immobilized for what seemed like an eternity, wondering what had happened.

Slowly, snatches of conversation came to him; then images flashed through his mind. His head began to clear, but the pain persisted. He realized that he had to do something; he couldn't lie there suffering any longer.

A picture began forming before his eyes. It was an Alka Seltzer! For a while, he was content to just think about it, to imagine the cold water, the round tablet, the gentle fizzing, the dancing effervescence, the profound relief!

Finally he could stand it no longer. He opened his eyes. Agony! The sun was high in the sky and blazing through the windows. He forced himself to sit up, and was vaguely interested to find that he was completely dressed, shoes and all. He groped his way into the bathroom, prepared and chugged his Alka Seltzer, and for the first time that morning, considered the possibility that he might live after all.

He undressed and climbed into the oversized shower. As the needles of water pummeled him from all sides, he decided that what he really needed was a bracing dip in the lake. He stepped out of the shower, pulled on his trunks, threw a towel around his neck, and tiptoed down the path to the lake.

The blazing sun was like an assault. He stopped at the top of the dune to rest, and squinted toward the beach. There was a young man in front of him, running down the slope. It sickened him to watch the runner showing such little regard for the effect his jarring steps would have on the contents of his stomach. He was yelling something; Max couldn't make it out. Then all at once he realized. The man was yelling "Farrell!"

Max scanned the beach, looking for her. It was so crowded that at first he didn't spot her . . . and then suddenly she was there, impossible to miss. She stood in knee-deep water, facing the horizon. She heard her name called and turned, her hair flying back behind her as her eyes focused on the dark young man running toward her. She yelled something and began to run, splashing through the water like a young gazelle, her arms extended, her face alive with joy.

"Jeff!" Max heard her cry. "Jeff, you're here!" She flew into his open arms, and he spun her around and around until they both fell to the ground, convulsed with laughter.

Max turned and walked away.

"Seconds, anybody?" Jan asked, holding up another blender of frozen margaritas.

"Well, as long as you're twisting my arm," Jeff said, offering his empty glass. "Just a smidge. These are delicious. Like slushes."

"Slushes with a kick," Meg teased. "Careful, she's a menace with that tequila!"

"Nonsense," Jan insisted. "I have a very light touch with alcohol. By the way . . . has anyone seen Max? He should have been here a half-hour ago." The mention of alcohol had brought him instantly to mind. She imagined that he was nursing quite a hangover after last night.

Jeff looked up innocently. "Seen him?" he asked. "Nooo, I haven't seen him, but ask me if I've heard about him." He glanced mischievously at Farrell. "Ask me anything. Religious beliefs, eye color, height, opinions on nuclear disarmament, world hunger . . . you name it!"

Farrell blushed furiously. "You are so obnoxious!" she cried, struggling to keep a straight face. Looking back, she realized that perhaps she had gone a little overboard in describing Max.

She had also taken much greater care than usual in dressing this evening. She'd swept the front strands of her hair back and braided them with a pale pink ribbon. Tendrils of gold escaped and fell in soft waves that framed her face. Her featherweight dress was of the palest pink silk. It fell from her shoulders in a romantic "Guinevere" style that complemented her slender figure and contrasted strikingly with her sun-burnished complexion. The effect was mesmerizing, her beauty so astonishing that even Meg and Jan, who were accustomed to it, had difficulty in keeping their eyes off her.

They were both mildly annoyed at Jeff for teasing her. It had been so long since Farrell had dared to care about a man that they were terrified lest she pull back or shy away before the feeling had a chance to grow.

They were seated in Jan's living room. She had given up on the idea of serving cocktails on the screened porch because the evening was simply too humid and uncomfortable.

"Did I hear my name mentioned?" Everyone turned as Max entered, looking like a refugee from skid row. His eyes were bloodshot and puffy; he was rumpled and badly in need of a shave.

"Sorry I'm late," he said as if this were the last place in the universe he wanted to be. At Jan's offer of a margarita, he shook his head and turned slightly green. He crossed the living room and slumped down next to Meg, smiling distractedly at her when she caught his eye. He looked down at the floor, up at the ceiling, out the window . . . everywhere and anywhere to avoid looking at Farrell.

His discomfort was contagious; soon all were shifting uncomfortably in their seats.

What's with this guy? Jeff wondered. This is the incredible Max I've been hearing about all day?

Jan disappeared into the kitchen and returned with a tall glass of V-8 juice, liberally spiced with Tabasco, and handed it to Max without a word.

"So," he said, taking the glass from her, "what's new?"

"Max?" Farrell spoke tentatively, confused by his appearance and behavior.

He ignored her and took a long swallow of his drink.

"Max, I'd like you to meet a friend of mine. This is Jeff Gibson. Jeff, this is Max Rosen."

Jeff half rose and extended his hand, but Max continued to study the bottom of his glass. After a long and extremely awkward moment, Jeff shrugged and withdrew his hand.

"Nice to meet you," Jeff said sarcastically, beyond caring about keeping up pretenses.

"Max!" Farrell cried. "What's wrong with you?"

Max knew that his behavior was unforgivable, but somehow he couldn't stop himself. What the hell did she expect, he rationalized; should I be delighted to meet her boyfriend?

He looked over at her for the first time all evening. Her beauty stunned him. The knife in his gut twisted and plunged even deeper, and he lashed out.

"Wrong with me!" he scoffed. "What the hell is wrong with you?" He spat out the words, his voice shaking with rage and frustration. He saw the tears spring to her eyes and instantly regretted his cruelty. Silently he cursed himself. He opened his mouth to apologize, but his pride kept him silent as Farrell sprang to her feet and ran out of the house.

He rose and stormed out to the screened porch, Jeff following at his heels. Meg and Jan sat staring at each other, shocked speechless.

Out on the porch, Max whirled and faced Jeff. "Aren't you a bit confused?" he asked bitterly. "Shouldn't you be running after Farrell?"

"I think you're the one that's confused, buddy. You know, Farrell's picked some real winners in the past for boyfriends, but I think you might just take the cake."

"Oh, really?" Max shouted, and then looked puzzled

as the words began to sink in. "What are you talking about?" he asked. "You're her boyfriend!"

"What?" Jeff asked, bewildered.

"Don't give me that," Max yelled. "I saw you on the beach."

All at once, it fell into place.

"You poor son of a bitch!" Jeff cried, shaking his head. "You are gonna be sooooo sorry for what you just did."

"What the hell are you talking about?" Max demanded furiously. "What the hell is so goddamned funny?"

Jeff pulled himself together. "Well, not that it's any of your business, but for Farrell's sake, I'll tell you. The only boyfriend I'm interested in is my own. Get it?" he asked. "My own."

Max's mouth fell open. "You mean . . . you mean you're . . ."

"Gay!" Jeff announced, grinning broadly. "Yep, now you got it."

"You're gay!" Max shouted. "Jesus, Jeff, that's great!" He grabbed Jeff's hand and began shaking it exuberantly. "I mean it, that's just great!"

Jeff was laughing openly now. "Well, I must admit that this isn't the usual reaction I get from straight men . . . but I do see your point."

"Oh, my God!" Max cried suddenly. "Oh, Christ! What have I done?" He flopped down on a chair. "Jeff," he said miserably, "she'll never speak to me again."

Jeff sat down next to him. "Well, it's hard to say. She did seem pretty taken with you this afternoon, but . . . well, that was before you made such an ass of yourself. Tell me, do you really care about her?"

"Care about her!" Max looked shocked. "I'm in love with the woman!"

Jeff nodded and then shrugged. "I don't know," he said honestly. "Farrell was burned pretty bad once before. It's hard to say."

"Jeff, tell me what happened to Farrell," Max pleaded.

Jeff looked at him, considering. Then he made his

decision. "Actually, I think you should know. It might help you to understand her better."

"Holy Christ!" Max breathed when Jeff had finished. "I'd like to kill the son of a bitch!"

"You'll have to take a number," Jeff told him. "He's made a lot of enemies along the way . . . but he's gained a lot of power, too."

"So he's the Illinois state's attorney," Max said.

"For the time being. Though between you and me, he's got a serious problem." Jeff proceeded to tell Max about Goldie.

"And the guy didn't press charges?" Max asked, incredulous.

Jeff shook his head. "He wanted to protect his aunt . . . except that now, as of two months ago, his aunt is dead. Of course the statute of limitations on the assault ran out a few years ago, so there's no question of pressing charges. But the story alone could destroy his career. And Goldie just might decide to talk."

"You know, Max said, thinking out loud, "we might be able to do some real good with a little leverage over the state's attorney."

"Like what?" Jeff asked, puzzled by the suggestion.

Max decided to confide in Jeff. "What the hell, you've known them a lot longer than I have. Jeff, doesn't the fact that Junior robbed them bother you?"

"Bother me!" Jeff cried. "It drove me crazy for a while. I can't tell you how many hours I spent going over those contracts. I even tried to get a look at the originals, but no way. Junior's lawyers advised against it, and Junior wouldn't budge. The fact is, Max, that Patrick Sweeney signed on the dotted line."

"I know, I know," Max interrupted. "My mother, I mean Jan— Oh, Christ." He realized he'd just let the cat out of the bag.

"Don't sweat it," Jeff told him. "Jan told me all about you this afternoon. She also explained why you're here. Go on," he prompted. "You were saying?"

"I just have a hunch that there's more to it than anyone thinks. Actually, my mother's had suspicions all along.

She mentioned that Junior had stopped you from seeing the original documents. Why would he do that? I mean, if everything was on the up-and-up, why would he care?"

Jeff shrugged. "Frankly," he said, "if I were his attorney, I'd have made the same call. As long as there were any questions on the floor, the estate had to remain open. Junior just wanted his money."

Max shook his head. "Lawyers," he muttered under his breath. "Still," he continued, "I have a hunch that those originals might tell us something. My mother insists that Junior isn't all that bright, and from what I've seen of him, I'm inclined to agree. I just can't believe he committed the perfect crime."

Jeff looked at him suspiciously. "Just what do you have in mind?"

"Well, if we could use some pull from the state's attorney's office, we could gain access to records . . . namely, Junior Sweeney's file cabinets. There's just no telling what we might find. I could also use Mr. Payne's help in another matter."

"Are you saying you want to put the squeeze on the Illinois state's attorney?" Jeff asked.

Max nodded. "Yeah, that's about it."

Jeff smiled. "Why don't I give Joe a call?" he suggested. "We'll see what Goldie has to say about helping us."

"This is great!" said Max, rising. "I'm going to go find Farrell and beg her to forgive me. Wish me luck!"

Jeff shook his head doubtfully. "It's gonna take a whole lot more than luck."

"Thanks for the vote of confidence," Max said as he headed out the door.

He had just started down the path when short, shrill screams of mounting horror pierced the night ahead. It was Farrell's voice, hysteria growing as sanity gave way to some unspeakable terror.

He started running. His eyes were useless as the thick foliage prevented the pale moonlight from penetrating. He held his arms out in front of him, feeling his way as he plunged on.

The screaming accelerated in short, staccato bursts, like machine-gun fire. "Farrell!" he yelled. "Farrell!" He raced headlong into a tree, slamming against the rough bark. He saw a flash of glaring white behind his eyes. Painfully, he pulled himself up and continued running.

"I'm coming!" he shouted, but his voice was swallowed by her screams. Her cries were the most terrifying sounds he could imagine. And then they stopped. The ensuing silence unleashed a fear in him so paralyzing that he had to will himself to breathe.

At last he broke free of the forest; he was running toward the house when a movement in the shadows caught his eye. It was the fine silk of Farrell's dress, rippling softly in the hot breeze. He could barely make her out, a black silhouette against the silver backdrop of the moonlit lake.

She was on her knees in the dirt, rocking stiffly.

He moved toward her slowly. "Farrell?" he called. She didn't look up. She was staring at a dark shape on the ground; he couldn't make it out. He went forward cautiously, fearful of startling her.

And then he saw.

"Oh, dear God!" he cried, tasting bile at the back of his throat as the sweet smell of freshly spilled blood assailed his nostrils. He pulled her to her feet and lifted her in his arms, desperate to shield her from the unspeakable scene.

The animal had been staked out and tied to chicken wire; its skin had been peeled back to reveal its entrails, which were now floating in a pool of blood. It was a rabbit, he realized.

Leading Farrell, he headed across the lawn to the house as Jeff came crashing out of the woods, followed by Meg and Jan.

"What happened?" Jeff yelled across the yard, gasping for breath as he approached.

"It's Farrell's rabbit," Max whispered. "Meg," he called, "I need blankets. Hurry!"

By the time he got her into the house, she was shivering uncontrollably. He looked down and realized that she was staring up at him, tears running silently down her

cheeks. He felt a wave of relief wash over him at the sight—
she was going to be all right!

Long after they had piled her high with blankets and
insisted that she drink a cup of hot chocolate, he sat watching her sleep. He had refused to leave; he would stay by her
side that night.

Before she had dropped off, she had told him that all
of the animals were missing from their cages.

"Do you think they let the rest of them go?" she'd
asked, her eyes wide with fear.

"Oh, sure," he'd said, careful to guard his expression
and his tone, not wanting her to guess at the horror he
imagined.

Tonight the final piece of the puzzle had slid into
place. As he watched his sleeping beauty, he contemplated,
with regret, the splintered psyche of a psychopath.

Thirty-five

Sunday dawned clear and hot. The cloudless sky was a pale,
washed-out blue, as though bleached by the rays of the
burning sun. The Village families rose and dressed for
eight o'clock mass. That would leave the rest of the day free
for golf.

Some walked to the services in the Village Hall, and
some drove cars, but most of them arrived in golf carts,
ready to hit the course at eight-thirty sharp!

This Sunday, however, at five minutes after eight, the
congregation was standing huddled on one side of the hall,
staring in shocked disbelief at the desecration. They were
unable to absorb what they were seeing. Finally, almost in
slow motion, they began to stir. A few women managed to
rouse themselves and began pulling children from the
room.

"This is blasphemy!" someone whispered.

"It's an outrage!" someone cried.

Father Dreason pulled a cloth from a table and covered the altar on which the slaughtered beasts had been

carefully arranged. The white cat lay on its back, the black
cat sprawled on top of it. The intended obscenity was
graphically clear. Both animals had been slashed open
from their necks down to their tails, and they, as well as the
altar and the floor beneath it, were drenched with coagu-
lating blood.

Father Dreason turned to the congregation and raised
his hands high over his bald head.

"There is evil among us!" he cried.

As usual, his words were well chosen, but his voice was
a curse. While he longed for a thundering baritone that
would command respect, the Lord had seen fit to saddle
him with an irritating nasal whine.

The villagers, however, were so distraught at the moment that they were willing—longing, in fact—to be led by
anyone who might feel up to it. They turned as one to the
diminutive priest and waited for some words of wisdom,
some guidance, some direction . . .

It was Father Dreason's shining moment. Finally, he
had them in the palm of his hand. This difficult flock of his,
so misguided, so willful—so insistent upon atoning for
their sins by paying for them with cold, hard cash—had
long confounded him. Now, at last, they were turning to
him. The spirit filled him, the power was intoxicating! He
opened his mouth to speak and realized in that horrible,
sobering split second . . . that he had nothing, absolutely
nothing of consequence, to impart. The silence was deafening.

It was broken by a child's anguished whisper: "What
happened, Mom? What happened to them? That's Dark
Star and Snowflake. Are they dead?"

Mary Dooley let out an outraged cry, lifted her son in
her arms, and ran from the hall. At the door, she turned
back to the villagers and called out, "The animals belong
to Farrell McBride! If none of the rest of you have the guts
to do something about this, well then, I guess it's time I did
something about it myself!"

The crowd erupted. The desecration of an altar was
beyond anything they had ever imagined. The fun and
games were over. What had seemed a faintly thrilling possi-

bility was now a horrifying reality. Those two women were not only mad, they were dangerous! It was time for action!

Max came awake suddenly in the chair beside Farrell's bed. He rose slowly, taking care not to wake her, and crept silently from her room. In the hallway, the distant thudding that had wakened him in the first place was louder. He walked on through the house, and realized that someone was pounding on the front door.

He pulled the heavy wooden door open and was confronted with a wild-looking woman who had been flinging herself bodily against the door. She cried out in surprise at the sight of a man and demanded that he bring Farrell to her immediately. "You tell her she can't hide from me, not after what she's done to my son!"

Max stepped out and closed the door behind him. He took the woman by the arm and led her away, talking softly to her as they went. Eventually he got the story from her. He shuddered at her description of the desecration of the altar and the mutilated animals. And he sympathized with her outrage over having her son, Timmy, exposed to such demented horror. He finally calmed her down to the extent that she agreed to go home, but not before she told him to warn both Meg and Farrell that they would find no peace in this community ever again, no peace and no goodwill.

When he turned back to the house, Meg was standing on the front steps. She looked tiny and pale, and frightened. Her eyes seemed as big as the beach stones that lay glittering and black on the water's edge. She had heard everything.

Their eyes met, and he knew that she understood.

"I'm going to Chicago, Meg," he told her.

She nodded. "Max, do you know what's happening?" she asked.

"I think so, almost everything . . . but I have to make sure."

"Then who—" she began.

"Meg," he said softly, "let me make sure first."

She turned away from him.

"Meg, I need something from you. Is there anyone you

can think of who'd remember the fire . . . the McBrides'
fire? Anyone at all?"

She nodded slowly. "The Captain would, my Dad's
best friend. He was there that night. He saw it burn."

"How can I find him?" Max asked. "Can I meet him?"

"I doubt that," Meg said. "He went back to Ireland
after Dad died. He said he was going home to die . . . but
he's still living. I have a number for him; it's the number
of a pub, actually. He doesn't have his own phone. You
have to call and leave a message."

"Will you give me the number?"

"Come on in," she said, and turned again toward the
house.

Max stuffed his belongings into a duffle bag and sat
down on the bed to place the call. He was lucky on the first
try; the Captain was in.

"Who is it, then?" the Captain demanded, his heavy
brogue crackling across the wires.

Max introduced himself as a friend of Farrell's and
explained a little of what was happening. He then asked
about the fire.

"I know it was a long time ago, sir, but I was hoping
you might remember—"

"Long ago, hell!" shouted the Captain. "I'm not
senile yet, my lad! You're talking to the right man all right.
Sure, I remember it like yesterday. If you're thinkin' there
was something funny about it, then you're a damned sight
smarter than a lot of people. Jim McBride's cigar never
started that fire. The house went up like a bloody torch!"

Max's pulse quickened at the Captain's words. I knew
it, he thought. "Why wasn't it investigated as arson at the
time?"

"Aahhh!" the Captain shouted. "They were Protes-
tants! All of them! Those inspectors wouldn't have known
a peat fire from a Molotov cocktail. And if you're wonderin'
why I kept me mouth shut, it was because Patrick asked me
to, that's why. It was bad enough as it was for little Eileen
and her young man, Luke."

Max thought it all over. It made sense, he decided.

"Thank you for the information," he said, ready to hang up.

"Don't be so quick!" the Captain bellowed. "I have a few questions of me own. Now, is it Farrell you're sweet on?" he asked.

Max smiled to himself. "Yes, sir," he answered, "it is."

"And are your intentions honorable, young man?" the Captain persisted.

Max bit back a laugh. "Oh, yes sir, they are," he assured him.

"Well then, that's lovely! Will you do me a favor then, lad?"

"Of course," Max agreed.

"Will ya let me know if there's to be a celebration of some sort?"

"Yes, sir, I will," Max promised.

"Because if there is, you can tell my girls that I'll be there with bells on!"

She broke free of the trees just as he was pulling out. "Max," she cried, sprinting after the car. "Max, wait!"

The distance between them widened as he began to accelerate out of the driveway. He adjusted the volume of the stereo, fiddled with the air conditioner, glanced in the rearview mirror, and slammed on the brakes.

He jumped out of the car. "Farrell, what's wrong?" he asked.

She stopped dead in her tracks. She had been so desperate to catch him, and it had seemed so hopeless, that now that she had his attention, she had no idea of what to say.

"Max," she pleaded, "don't go."

His heart melted. She had just jumped out of the shower, and her damp hair fell in glossy copper waves. Her face, innocent of makeup, looked younger than ever, and her eyes looked up at him beseechingly.

"I have to go," he told her reasonably. "It's the only way I can find out what's going on here and put an end to it."

"You can't find out if you leave," she insisted.

"Farrell, it's the only way, I swear it. I won't be long," he assured her.

"When?" she demanded. "When will you be back?"

"In time for your show," he promised. "I'll be back for that."

"That's not for eight more days!" she cried.

"I'll be back by then."

She exhaled deeply, as though the wind had gone out of her sails. She kicked at the gravel and buried her hands deep inside her pockets. She knew she'd lost.

"Farrell . . ." he said softly. She looked up, a study in dejection.

"I love you," he told her.

She stared at him incredulously, wondering if she'd heard correctly.

He turned and walked to his car.

"I love you, too, Max," she whispered, too softly for him to hear.

He opened the door and slid in.

"Max!" she yelled. "I love you, too!"

A huge smile lit up his face. "She loves me!" he cried.

She stood watching, and laughed out loud at his expression of joy when he turned and flashed her a thumbs-up.

"She loves me!" he sang as he cranked the stereo and roared out of the drive.

Thirty-six

At 9:01 A.M., Illinois State's Attorney Michael Payne sat waiting as his driver, Sammy, walked around the limousine and opened the door. Sammy had been working for the state for almost twenty-five years, and Payne was the only guy he'd ever worked for, including the governor, who wouldn't open his own goddamned door!

But then, thought Sammy, Payne was a real asshole right from the word go. He was the cheapest son of a bitch he'd ever met, even for a politician. He wouldn't spring for a McDonald's hamburger even if he kept you working right through dinner. He talked to his lovely wife like she was some kind of gutter-slut; no wonder she drank. And Sammy would be willing to swear under oath that the man didn't know the name of either one of his own little girls.

Sammy held the door open and stood at attention as Payne slid out and walked past him without a word. At the bottom of the first tier of stairs, Payne paused, turned back, and said, "Wait."

"Yes sir, Mr. Payne," Sammy called back cheerfully. "You asshole," he muttered under his breath.

Payne let himself into his office, making a mental note to dock his secretary for being late. It took a split second for his brain to register the fact that there was someone in his office; three men, in fact, and one of them had his feet on his desk!

"What the hell!" yelled Payne, instantly furious. "What's going on here?" he demanded.

"Don't you remember me, Michael?" one of the men asked. "I'm crushed."

Payne studied him more closely. "Joe Brown!" he exclaimed, his face registering his surprise. "Okay, Joe," he said, "I remember you. Happy now? Now take your friends and get the hell out of my office!"

"Sorry, Michael, we can't do that." The man behind the desk spoke softly. "Not yet, anyway. First we're going to need a favor . . . well, two favors, actually."

Payne's eyes narrowed into dark slits. He walked to the edge of his desk and leaned over so that he was inches from the intruder's face.

"You're not getting a fucking thing except arrested!" he screamed. "Do you know who you're fucking with?" He was beside himself with fury and disbelief. How dare they? How *dare* they?

"Michael, Michael . . ." The man behind the desk shook his head and spoke consolingly. "Don't get so excited." He lounged ostentatiously in Payne's swivel chair.

Payne looked ready to explode.

"Does the name 'Goldie' ring a bell?" the third man asked.

Payne spun around and glared at him. "What is this shit?" he spat. "You guys are about six years late on this. Get the hell out of here."

The man behind the desk let out an exaggerated sigh, cocked his head slightly, and gave Payne a disappointed look. Then he reached forward and pressed a button marked "Speaker." "Goldie," he said, "say hi to Michael."

For the first time, Payne was shaken. He paled slightly and bit his lower lip, but he recovered well. "Fuck you!" he said menacingly.

Goldie's voice came over the speaker. "Oh, don't be so hostile, Michael. After all, I'm in mourning . . . or didn't they tell you? My aunt died, Michael, over two months ago, in fact. I've been meaning to get in touch ever since."

Max, sitting behind the desk, noted with relief that Payne was beginning to look nervous. A muscle just below his left eye was starting to twitch, and tiny beads of perspiration were forming on his upper lip and forehead.

"Listen! All of you!" Payne said, his voice beginning to sound more desperate than angry. "I don't know what you're trying to pull here, but if you think you can prove anything after all these years, you're crazy."

"Oh, well, that's not exactly true," Goldie chirped. "My videos would be more than enough to ruin you, Michael."

"There are no videos!" Payne shouted. "We always erased everything we made."

"Well, not actually." Goldie giggled. "You know how sentimental I am. What we erased were blank tapes. I just never could stand to throw anything away."

Payne felt himself go numb. He was certain his heart was going to burst, it was beating so loudly. He stumbled across the room and sank down onto his leather couch. He leaned over, buried his face in his hands and tried to pull himself together. Slowly, he forced himself to assess the situation sanely. What was the worst they could do to him if indeed Goldie had the tapes? The answer was obvious. Exposure. Well, he tried to rationalize, so what? It's not the Dark Ages anymore. After all, we're entering the nineties, and other politicians have come out of the closet and survived.

But even as he formulated the thought, he knew he was kidding himself. Maybe a politician running on a gay platform, with a gay constituency, could survive in certain areas of the country. But the State of Illinois was nowhere near ready to embrace a gay state's attorney, and certainly not one who'd been exposed by his flamboyant ex-lover. Christ! The farmers downstate would murder him! He shuddered to think of what his backers would do. He'd be better off dead.

On the other hand, he reasoned, what if Goldie was lying? After all, it had been years. What if there were no tapes? He'd be giving something away for nothing (God knew what they wanted) and making himself vulnerable in the process. There was only one thing to do. He glared at the man who was lounging in his leather swivel chair.

"Fuck you."

Max just managed not to flinch. Damn, he thought, we almost had him! "You're sure you want to play it this way, Payne?" he asked. "It's a long fall."

"You're the one who's gonna take a fall, asshole," Payne began, with some of his usual arrogance.

What happened next was so unexpected that later no one could agree on the details. It must have been the word "fall."

"Shall I send the tapes, Max?" Goldie's voice inquired over the intercom.

Max looked at Payne's sneering face and wished by all that was holy that such tapes really existed. He sighed theatrically. "I guess so."

That's when Joe suddenly sprang to life. "Yeah, send the tapes!" he ordered as he bounded across the room and grabbed the neck of Payne's shirt. His astonishing strength was made evident by the ease with which he yanked Payne up from the couch.

Max's jaw dropped. What in the world? he wondered. He shot Jeff a look, but the shocked expression on Jeff's face showed that he was equally in the dark.

Max turned back and was horrified to see that Joe was dragging Payne toward the window.

"Send the tapes!" Joe yelled. "We'll use them for his epitaph! Then everyone will understand why such a prominent fellow as he jumped from his sixteenth-floor office!"

"Joe," Jeff cried, taking a step toward him, "this is crazy! Stop it!"

"What's happening?" Goldie's voice demanded. "Joe, Jeff, Max, is anybody there?"

"Joe, stop it!" Jeff pleaded. "Stop it right now!"

"Help me!" Payne screamed. "He's crazy, he's crazy!" His eyes were wild and bulging horribly from their sockets. They rested on Max's face. "Stop him!" he begged.

Max returned his stare and allowed the corner of his mouth to creep up, ever so slightly.

Payne, reading his expression as a positive sign, relaxed somewhat. The terror in his eyes gave way to the faintest hint of insolence.

Joe paused and turned to Max. "Well?" he asked.

Without taking his eyes off Payne, Max spoke. "Kill him," he said, almost casually.

Jeff stopped dead, frozen in place.

The expressions that played across Payne's face were like nothing any of them had ever imagined. Then Joe reached the window. Just when Max expected Payne to explode, he did just the opposite. He completely broke down and sobbed like a baby. A sudden stench alerted Max to the fact that the Illinois state's attorney had lost control of his bowels.

A half-hour later, the threesome was riding the elevator down to the main floor.

Jeff, white and shaken, turned to Joe. "What the hell got into you?"

"I don't know," Joe answered, still shaken himself. "I guess I held a bigger grudge than I realized. I just saw red at the thought of him coming out ahead again."

"A grudge?" Max asked.

Joe shrugged. "I used to work for Payne, and we were friends . . ." He paused. "Forget it."

"Friends!" Max said. "Remind me not to get on your bad side."

"You should talk!" Jeff cried. " 'Kill him,' " he said, mimicking Max's casual tone. "I almost died! I thought you'd both flipped!"

"Well, I knew the windows wouldn't open, and they're shatterproof, too," Max explained.

"How the hell did you know that?" Jeff demanded.

"I don't know; it's code for high-rises, isn't it? Anyway, it worked. We got what we needed."

"Right." Jeff held the door as they stepped into the lobby. "I still can't believe what just happened."

"Once we get the I.D.'s, we can dive right into Junior's files."

Jeff stared at him, thinking, the man's relentless. "Well, I've got to get to my office."

"Drop me off, will you?" Joe asked.

"Sure." Jeff turned to Max. "Need a lift?"

"No. I'll be in touch. Great job, guys," he said, then strode off.

"By the way," Jeff called, "who's the woman you're having them track?"

"Oh." Max turned and shrugged. "Just an old friend of Farrell's father's. I'll tell you about it later." He started off again.

"Oh, and Max," Joe called.

Max stopped, sighed, and turned again. "Yes?" he asked politely.

"The windows do open." Joe smiled. "But great job anyway, 'guy'." He wagged his fingers in a distinctly unmasculine manner, and strode away.

"*What!*" Jeff cried, jogging after him. "What did you just say?"

Max stood with a thunderstruck expression on his face, watching as the receding figures entered a revolving door and disappeared from view.

"I'll be damned!" He whistled softly.

There were only five days left until the show. Max had been gone for three whole days, and still she hadn't heard from him. She was beginning to think he'd just skipped out on her. And why not, she asked herself; he probably thinks we're all crazy!

Of course, the fact that they were keeping the phones off the hook didn't occur to her. They had been so inundated with threatening calls that they'd finally gotten fed up with answering the phone. Then the callers had simply transferred their hostilities to Jan, until she, too, had had enough.

Farrell stood back to look at the piece she was working on. "Oh, shit!" she cried just as Meg entered the studio.

"What's wrong?" Meg asked.

"Nothing. I just can't work, that's all. I can't keep my mind on what I'm doing. How's your chin?"

Someone had thrown a rock through the kitchen window the night before, sending glass flying in all directions. One of the slivers had embedded itself in Meg's chin.

A mindless rage had gripped Farrell at the sight. She had run out after the culprits, but they had had the advantage of darkness and a reasonable head start. She'd heard them, though, off in the distance, and knew they were Village teenagers, just following their parents' lead.

She and Meg had sat up half the night discussing their options. They had finally decided to leave the Village. Clearly, they couldn't stay with things as they were, and they'd both grown tired of being treated so abominably. The horror of what had happened at the altar was exceeded only by the horror of the fact that people whom they had known as friends for years actually believed them responsible!

"I'm fine," Meg assured her. "It's really just a scratch." She turned toward the door, listening. "There's Jan," she said, as Jan's familiar "yoo-hoo" floated in through the front door. They walked down the hall to greet her.

Jan was smiling, wearing her beach gear and carrying a picnic basket. "I decided we needed some cheering up," she told them hopefully, lifting the basket. "Come on, let's escape to the beach for a while."

"I'm game," Meg announced, surprising Farrell. As a rule, Meg wasn't a beach person.

So once Farrell had jumped into her suit and they had located Meg's beach umbrella, sunscreen, bathing suit, sun hat, sunglasses and cover-up, they were on their way.

"Finally!" she whispered to herself. She had been watching the house for days now, waiting for the right moment. Farrell ran every morning, but she was beginning to think that Meg would never leave the house.

She pulled brazenly into the driveway, no longer terribly concerned about discovery. Success, she'd come to realize, was her destiny. Life had taught her that. But then, what could one expect? The world was filled with such tiny, common minds. Her secret power was growing . . . and growing . . .

After tonight . . . She paused, unsure of how to complete that thought. She really hadn't planned beyond this evening. She now realized that everything she had done up to now had been merely a dress rehearsal. Faces, frightened and surprised, flashed before her eyes . . . each face had been only a step, a necessary step, drawing her ever closer to this one, unalterable conclusion.

She climbed out of her car and smoothed her tailored white trousers. A navy blazer with an anchor insignia and a navy-and-white-striped silk blouse completed her nautical ensemble. Her blond hair was caught up in a wide navy bow. She could have posed for the cover of *Palm Beach Life.*

She walked around to the west wing and chose her point of entry. Though most of the windows were open to admit the cool lake breeze, this one was especially appealing. Partially concealed by heavy, overhanging branches, it was shaded now, and later it would be immersed in darkness. Carefully, she slit the screen along the edge, and entered. It would be a simple matter to tape the slit corner before she left. She patted her trouser pocket and was instantly reassured. The spool of electrical tape was safely nestled there.

She sauntered through the house, taking her time and looking in every room. She stopped in Farrell's room—it

was a simple matter to guess which was hers—and lay down
on Farrell's bed, imagining how it would be. Then she rose
and walked into the living room. A noise startled her, but
she realized that it was just the disgusting goat, curled up
in a box. Should she kill it now? She liked the idea of their
coming home and finding bloody bits of it strewn here and
there. But then they might be too upset to eat her brownies. My God, but she was clever to think of these eventuali-
ties!

She left the brownies on the table, and with them a
note that read, "Love, Jan."

Thirty-seven

Max was waist-deep in file folders and beginning to get
discouraged. He'd been digging through Junior's records
for almost three days, and still . . . nothing.

Gaining access to the records had been a piece of cake.
He'd simply walked in, flashed the I.D. that Payne had
provided, and demanded to see the files. Of course the fact
that Junior was out of town for the week had helped matters enormously.

He was reaching in to scoop out another armload of
files when a red-tagged folder caught his eye. It read "Con-
fidential."

He reached for it, his hand shaking slightly. Something told him that this was it. Slowly, he opened the file
and began leafing through the papers. Soon he was scanning each page. Finally he slammed the file shut.

"Damn!" he cried, utterly discouraged. It was the correct file all right, and all of the documents were there. But
they were copies, albeit clearer copies than those that Jeff
had shown him; probably they had been the second sheet
behind the carbon . . . Something occurred to him.

Reopening the file, he checked the bottom of each
page. There, they were barely discernable, but there nonetheless. Faint blue initials identifying the typist: "p.t." Max
was certain that there were no such initials on the papers

that Jeff had shown him. They probably hadn't penetrated the carbon to the third copy.

He turned to Sally, the secretary who was assisting him. "Who's P.T.?" he asked.

She looked at him blankly and gave her gum a particularly definitive crack. "Who's what?" she asked, placing her small hands on her tightly skirted hips.

"Whose initials are P.T.?" He held up the file. "The secretary who typed these."

"Oh, that's probably Patsy Thompkins. She's Junior's, um, Mr. Sweeney's private secretary."

Max looked at her in astonishment. "I thought you said you were Mr. Sweeney's secretary."

"His secretary," she snapped, "not his private secretary." Her hard black eyes glinted in accompaniment to her innuendo.

"And where do I find his private secretary?" he asked.

"She's home packing this week," Sally said. "Some people can afford a new condo every two years, even if they don't lift a finger!"

"Do you know how long she's worked for Mr. Sweeney?" Max asked.

"Did I say she worked?" Sally shot back. "But she's been here for at least eleven years, 'cause that's when I came."

"Sally," Max asked, "can you think of any reason that Patsy would use carbon paper to copy these contracts, rather than the copy machine?"

"That's a good one," she laughed. "Sure, I can think of a reason. 'Cause the old man didn't like copy machines, that's why. He didn't trust them. Before he died, we all had to use carbon paper to make copies . . . Hey!" she called as he brushed past her and ran out. "Who's gonna clean up all this mess?"

Twenty minutes later, Max picked up Jeff in front of his office. "Any word from Payne's office?" he asked as Jeff hopped in the car.

"You mean since you called twenty minutes ago?" Jeff said. "No, no word."

"Did you try—" Max began.

"Still busy," Jeff interrupted. They'd both been trying to get through to Meg, Farrell, and Jan for three days.

"I just don't understand why they'd be keeping the phones off the hook."

Jeff shook his head. It didn't make any sense to him, either. "So what's up?" he asked. "What's so important that you had to drag me out of my office in the middle of the afternoon?"

Max smiled slyly and glanced sideways at Jeff. "Well, I'm not positive about this . . . but I think we're about to meet Junior Sweeney's mistress."

"No way!" Jeff cried. "Please, spare me. Junior Sweeney? That's disgusting!"

Max laughed. "Don't get your hopes up," he teased. "My source is totally unreliable."

When Max announced their arrival through the intercom, Patsy Thompkins immediately buzzed them in. While they rode up in the elevator, she flew into her bedroom, pulled on her tightest sweater and quickly ran a brush through her hair. Take every advantage, she reminded herself.

They breezed into her apartment and introduced themselves as though they owned the place. Max glared suspiciously at the numerous packing boxes that littered the front hall and asked, doing a pretty fair imitation of *Dragnet's* Sergeant Friday, "Moving far, ma'am?"

"Oh, no," Patsy answered, startled by his implication. She bit her plump lower lip and fiddled nervously with the enormous sapphire on her right pinkie. "I'm just moving to a more spacious apartment in this building."

More spacious apartment, thought Jeff; nobody talks like that.

"Been looking for these, ma'm?" Max dangled a huge ring of keys between his fingers.

"Oh! I didn't even know I'd lost them." She took the keys from Max and tossed them on a packing box.

"Not a very safe practice," Max warned, ". . . leaving them in the door like that. Let's sit down, shall we?" He walked past her into the living room and gestured for her to sit down.

Jeff noticed the Sergeant Friday imitation, rolled his eyes heavenward, and concentrated on not laughing.

Max sat across from Patsy, only inches away. Jeff sat on the radiator cover that doubled as a window seat and stared out at the lake.

"Let's get down to business, shall we, Miss Thompkins?" Max suggested. He took a note pad and a pen from his inside pocket.

She pouted energetically and once again began twisting her pinkie ring. She's holding up pretty well, Max thought. She reminded him a little of Bridget, but a younger, softer, more alluring version.

"Is Junior, I mean, is Mr. Sweeney in trouble?" she blurted, unable to restrain herself.

Max glanced suspiciously around the room, presumably searching for hidden agents. He leaned in closer to Patsy and said in a conspiratorial whisper, "Quite possibly, Miss Thompkins. Quite possibly."

Patsy gazed at him earnestly, leaning in a little to give him a better shot at her cleavage. "Can I ask you something?" she whispered breathlessly.

"Certainly, Patsy."

Her eyes flickered momentarily, registering his use of her first name. "Well," she began, pausing briefly to smooth her stockings, "if someone worked for someone else who did something wrong . . . could the someone who only worked for them get in trouble?" She looked up at him innocently.

Max ventured a quick look at Jeff, whose mouth was gaping. "Well," he began, stifling his own surprise, "I suppose that would depend entirely upon how cooperative the, uhm, the someone who worked for the person was."

"Oh!" Her eyes slid from Max's to a large trunk that sat among the packing boxes in the foyer.

"With that in mind, Miss Thompkins, is there anything you'd like to tell us about certain records dealing with company assets during a period of time approximately six years ago?"

Patsy twisted her ring frantically. She looked desperately from Max to Jeff, and then back to the trunk again.

Finally, agonizingly, she made up her mind. "Ummm, wellll, nooooo, nothing comes to mind right exactly at this moment."

"Oh, Miss Thompkins," Max sighed, sounding like a disappointed father, "are you absolutely sure?"

Looking about as unsure as a person could, she hedged. "Well, not right precisely at this moment . . ."

Max saw the light. She was going to squeeze Junior! He closed his note pad, rose, and stood menacingly over her. "Very well, Miss Thompkins, if that's the way you want it."

He started for the door, and then turned back. "Oh, by the way, you're not planning on leaving town for any reason, are you?"

Her eyes widened with alarm, her plump lips pouted defiantly. "I'm being picked up in half an hour!" she cried. "I'm going to Lake Geneva for the weekend."

"Really?" Max frowned, reopened his note pad and clicked his pen. "You'll be staying where?"

"I feel unclean," Jeff said, climbing into Max's car.

"Man!" Max agreed. "Ten to one she's planning to put the screws to Junior. I swear, I could hear the wheels turning."

"That's because her brain's rusty from lack of use," Jeff said. "Now, let's go!"

"Go?" Max looked shocked. "Go where?"

"Well," Jeff said ironically, "it did occur to me that I might stop back by my office . . . you know, just for a lark."

"We can't go," Max insisted. "Didn't you see the way she kept looking at that trunk?"

"Sure, but—"

"But nothing. We have to get into that trunk!"

"Max," Jeff said, "how the hell do you suggest . . . ." His eyes widened in horror. "Oh, no!" he cried.

"Well," Max said defensively, waving the key he was holding, "there were several like it on the ring. I don't think she's the type to miss it. *And* she is leaving in half an hour . . ."

Forty-five minutes later, after watching Patsy pull away

in a silver stretch-limousine, Max was inserting the key in the lock of Patsy's front door.

"Eureka!" he cried as the bolt turned.

"I don't believe I'm doing this," Jeff whispered, glancing nervously over his shoulder. "Do you realize that I could be disbarred?"

Max looked at him incredulously. "Do you realize," he demanded, entering the silent apartment, "that you lawyers are all nuts? Jeff, get a grip! We're committing burglary here. Two days ago, we broke into the state's attorney's office and threatened to kill him. Arguably, we are accessories to attempted murder. Disbarred, hell! You could go to jail!"

Jeff shook his head. "Oh, thank you, Max. I feel so much better now." He crossed the foyer and knelt to help Max peel off the masking tape that sealed the trunk. "I don't know what's gotten into everyone lately," he grumbled as he worked. "You, Joe, the world's gone mad. Especially Joe . . ."

"Well," Max pointed out, "he's your life partner, or whatever you call each other. What the hell did Payne do to him, anyway?"

"He won't talk about it," Jeff admitted. "I really don't know what happened."

"Well, it must have been bad," Max said, pulling away a final strip of tape. "There, that's it." He lifted the lid and revealed an assortment of linens.

Together they began lifting out hand-embroidered tablecloths, quilts, fine India-cotton sheets, and finally, a manila file folder.

Max opened the folder.

The original contracts were there, in perfect order, all of them signed by Patrick Sweeney. Nothing in them appeared to be incriminating, or even the slightest bit irregular.

What were incriminating were the attached notes directing Patsy to insert whole paragraphs into signed contracts.

In each case, the additional paragraphs transformed routine inventory transfers between affiliated companies into total inventory takeovers. The end result, of course, was that the transferring companies (those later inherited by Farrell and Meg) were rendered valueless, while the receiving companies (now Junior's) doubled, sometimes even tripled, in value.

All of the notes bore Junior's signature.

"Bingo!" Max whispered.

"And she kept them in her hope chest," Jeff said. "Think of it!"

They rode the elevator down in silence, each of them lost in his own thoughts.

Once in the car, Max spoke. "You know, I almost feel sorry for Junior. That is one scary woman."

"Don't waste your pity," Jeff said with contempt. He turned to face Max. "Do you realize what you've done?" he asked.

Max smiled contentedly. "Yup."

"How do you want to handle this?" Jeff asked.

"I don't know, Counselor," Max answered. "What are our options?"

"That's a loaded question. It really depends on what you want to accomplish. If you're talking about pursuing legal channels, certainly it can be shown that Junior is guilty of fraud. Assuming due diligence on Meg and Farrell's part at the outset of the contract—in this case, the will—the statute of limitations is generally one year from the date the fraud is discovered. That's today. I think we can pretty much bank on favorable treatment from the State's Attorney's Office." They exchanged knowing looks.

"We might, however," Jeff continued, "have some difficulty in explaining how we came into possession of these files. I must tell you, Max, that this could get pretty messy. After all, we are talking about a closed estate. On matters of probate, the statute of limitations can be a myriad of things. As a general rule of thumb, which I hesitate to resort to, but as a conversational tool—"

"Yes?" Max glared.

"Seven years. Maybe."

"So you're saying the estate could be reopened?"

"Possibly," Jeff hedged. "It would depend—"

"Jesus Christ!" Max exploded. "Do you guys ever give a simple, straight answer?"

"Maybe."

They laughed, easing the momentary tension.

"Jeff," Max said seriously, "skip the legal mumbo jumbo for a minute. Whatever we do, I mean, if we come out with this, Junior's going to jail, right?"

"Almost certainly." Jeff nodded. "Wait a minute. What do you mean, 'if' we come out with this?"

"Well, think about it. How do you think Farrell and Meg will feel about sending Junior up the river?"

Jeff opened his mouth to argue, then sighed. "What do you suggest?"

"Well, we could go to him ourselves and see what he's willing to do on his own. It'd be a lot faster. I happen to think that Meg and Farrell have waited long enough. What do you think, Jeff?" Max turned and looked him in the eye. "Do we go through proper channels?"

After a moment, Jeff conceded, "Well, we've gone this far. We'll try it your way."

"Good. Now—" Max handed him the car phone "—do me a favor. Call your office."

Jeff dialed the number. "Hi, Sara. It's Jeff. Any messages? He did? Hold on a second." He covered the mouthpiece. "Payne called."

Max came to attention. "And?"

Jeff removed his hand. "Okay, Sara, shoot. Uh-huh, really? He did? Oh, no, she did? When? Mmm-hmmm, I see. Where?"

"What?" Max yelled.

"Hold on, Sara." Jeff set down the receiver and turned back to Max. "Payne sent over a file on your mystery woman."

"Where is she?" Max demanded. His voice was strained, every muscle in his body tense.

"That's the problem—"

"Damn!" Max pounded his fist on the dashboard.

Jeff gave him a searching look, then continued. "It seems she dropped out of sight six years ago—"

"Shit!"

"Will you let me finish?" Jeff shouted. "She has a mother."

Max paused. "A mother? Alive? Here?"

"Alive, but not here." Jeff said. "She lives in a nursing home in Littletown, Vermont."

"Littletown, damn! I'd have to fly to Boston and rent a car. That would keep me away for another two or three days."

"Why don't you just call the woman?" Jeff suggested.

Max shook his head. "No way. I can't do this over the phone." He jammed his hand through his hair and frowned. "I guess I don't have much choice. Jeff, can you have Sara book me a flight to Boston?"

"Sara?" Jeff picked up the receiver. "Sara, are you there? Oh, good. Sorry. Listen, will you book a flight to Boston for a Mr. Max Rosen? Yeah, round trip. Oh." He turned to Max. "When do you want to leave?"

"The first available flight."

"But—" Jeff started to object, before he was silenced by the look in Max's eyes. "Sara, he can make O'Hare in about thirty minutes. See how close you can come to that. Yeah, I'll hold."

Thirty-eight

They spent the entire afternoon on the beach. It was the most fun any of them could remember having had for quite a while. Not wanting to encounter any villagers, they hiked along the shore past the Village boundaries and made a silent pact to put their worries on hold, to enjoy the day one minute at a time.

They read, they talked, they ate, they even managed to salvage a little of their former enthusiasm for the impending show. At one point, before Farrell went for a long run along the shore, she and Jan persuaded Meg to join them in the water. The sight of her, daintily tiptoeing into the lake, had them laughing so hard they almost drowned!

It was early evening when they finally trudged back to

the Village and up the dune to Jan's house. Jan fixed a tray of sandwiches, and they sat in comfortable silence, watching the sun set.

At ten-thirty, Meg declared that she was completely done in. Farrell agreed, and they thanked Jan for her inspiration and headed home.

When they entered, Meg was the first to notice the brownies.

"Oh, how decadent! Farrell, did you know that Jan had left these?"

Farrell shook her head. "She must have set them down when we were searching for the umbrella. I wonder why she didn't just bring them along."

"I don't know." Meg smiled sheepishly. "But as long as they're here . . ."

"Oh, go ahead," Farrell urged. "You can certainly afford the calories."

"You've convinced me." Meg smiled, biting into a dark fudge brownie. "Oh, they're fudge," she exclaimed. "They have chocolate chips in them." She polished off the brownie in four bites.

"That's it. That really did me in," she said, heading off to her room. "Good night, Farrell. Sweet dreams."

"Sweet dreams, Meg," Farrell answered softly. She then went down to the living room to check on Chevo. He was sound asleep in his box. She stroked his tiny head for several minutes, then rose, switched out the lights, and went to bed.

The moment Farrell lay her head on the pillow, she knew she wasn't going to be able to sleep. Horrible images of the splayed rabbit and the cats on the Village Hall altar assailed her each time she closed her eyes. Finally she sat up and stared out at the lake; the silver surface was smooth and glassy. A late-night swim ought to help me sleep, she decided. On her way out, she grabbed half a brownie. What the hell, she told herself, a little bit won't hurt.

It was time. At last the moment was upon her. The wait had been almost unbearable. Minutes had crept by so slowly that they had seemed like hours . . . like years.

The house was dark, as dark as a tomb. She smiled at the thought, slipped out of her car and reached in back for her supplies. As she walked between the stone walls and up the driveway, her heart was beating furiously, not with fear, but with excitement.

At the window, she removed the tape.

Farrell plunged into the lake, her sleek body causing hardly a ripple as she cut knifelike through the surface. Soon she was immersed in the rhythm of her swim; the cool, black depths, the velvet sky, and the silver splash of her steady strokes became her only reality.

She went to the living room. She could scarcely believe it was happening. Nothing could stop her now. Her mission had been decided years ago, she was bound to act. Her only regret was that she wouldn't see their faces . . . wouldn't watch as their surprise registered, and then their fear . . .

Meg fought her way to consciousness. The room seemed to be shrouded in a dense fog, and her entire body ached with fatigue. The urge to sleep was almost irresistible, but as she struggled to the surface, she felt the stark awareness of the evil that had awakened her.

Light footsteps in the living room, the hollow slam of the screen door, and then a low-pitched moan.

Danger! she thought. Farrell's in danger! She tried to lift her head, to call out a warning, but was capable of only an inaudible whisper.

The fog was closing in, her eyelids were growing heavy. I'll rest for just a moment, she promised herself, just for a minute or two . . .

Reluctant to allow the moment to pass too quickly, she set down her supplies and stepped out onto the balcony to breathe the soft night air. But as she slipped out, the screen door escaped her grasp and closed with a bang. She waited, hardly daring to breathe. No one came.

She turned and faced the water. Her heart was racing.

As much as she'd looked forward to tonight, nothing had prepared her for the sensations she was now experiencing: heightened awareness, sharper vision, keener touch and hearing—and the power! A massive strength was coursing through her.

A sudden movement out on the water caught her eyes. A silver flash. She leaned over the balcony, squinting. Just a bird, she decided finally, probably a seagull.

She was enchanted by her heightened abilities. She imagined that she could see not only the surface of the lake, but right through its depths to the wavy ridges of sand that lay beneath.

Her hands gripped the thick wooden railing. If I squeeze, she thought, I'll snap it.

She felt herself growing warm again. The soft wind, the intoxicating strength, and the awareness that, once again, she held the power of life and death . . .

She closed her eyes. The knuckles of the hand still clutching the railing protruded and turned white; her body, strung as tight as a bow, arched, and then shuddered. The orgasm that shook her was so profound that a moan of ecstasy escaped her wide, sensuous mouth.

When her trembling ceased, she turned and reentered the house.

She lifted the can she had brought and unscrewed the top. Then, patting her pocket for her book of matches, she heard a faint rustling sound from the wooden crate that sat in the far corner.

She smiled and crossed the room, unaware that she was humming a strange, discordant tune.

Still surging with excitement, her entire body pulsing with the power, she raised the can of gasoline and began to pour . . .

Farrell had swum only a short distance when her arms grew tired. She accelerated her pace, deciding she would swim out the lethargy, but after a short while, she sensed that the fatigue was getting worse. Her arms were heavy and leaden, and her legs didn't want to kick. Her whole body was sluggish. She realized that she was suddenly and overwhelmingly on the verge of exhaustion.

She felt a sharp pang of fear, but quickly calmed herself. After all, she reasoned, she was more comfortable in water than out, and she could always float on her back if she had to. As if to prove it to herself, she rolled over and found, to her growing horror, that she had to struggle to stay afloat. Her body felt as buoyant as a stone, and for the first time in her life, the black water began to seem menacing.

She searched for the shoreline. What's wrong with me, she wondered as she fought to stay afloat. The shore . . . there it was. It took every ounce of her will to keep herself from panicking as slowly, painfully, she began to swim toward land.

Every stroke was an enormous feat; her arms felt as though hundred-pound weights had been attached to them, weights that had to be lifted and lowered, lifted and lowered, over and over again. Her breaths came ragged and irregular, and soon she longed to close her eyes and let the darkness enfold her.

She stopped swimming for a moment to check her progress, and saw to her dismay that she'd barely made any headway. It almost looked as though she had drifted farther away from shore!

Is the current against me? She began to panic at the thought. If it was against her, she knew she would never make it to land.

She set out once again, struggling against the deadly lethargy, unaware that the harder she worked, the more quickly the drug was pumped into her system.

Suddenly she saw a bright light up ahead, and the water all around her seemed to glow. She decided with relief that she must be getting close; the light from the house was already reaching her.

But no, she realized! There were no lights on in the house. She looked again. At first she was confused by what she saw. There were lights on in the house! Every window was lit up. The house looked as it did when the sun was setting and the golden colors were reflected in the windows. Then she knew what she was seeing.

"Meg!" she screamed, and immediately choked on a mouthful of water. She began to swim again, fighting the exhaustion and the black depths. Her tears flowed into the lake as she swam . . . and prayed.

When she looked again, she saw that flames were shooting through the roof. The house seemed to be collapsing inward as she watched, and there were explosions going off inside, like bombs.

"Meg!" she screamed. "Meg!" She started swimming again, but this time her arms refused to move and she felt herself slipping slowly beneath the surface. The water closed in around her, covering her mouth . . . and then her feet touched bottom.

She struggled to the shore, screaming for Meg, dragged herself across the beach and started up the dune. Scrambling on all fours, she fell frequently; sand clung to her shivering body and her wet hair.

She made it to the top of the dune and stumbled down the path toward the house—toward what used to be the house. Now there was nothing there but a raging fire and an immense cloud of smoke that was blacker than the night sky.

Someone was screaming, and suddenly she realized that it was herself. She felt herself drifting away from the scene; she was watching herself watch the fire, hearing herself scream, and she knew with certainty that if she ever stopped screaming, it would all be real.

Someone grabbed her from behind. Then they were shaking her, and calling her name. She tried to pull away, but they wouldn't let her go. It was making her angry! She spun around to face them, but couldn't make out who they were. She would never have believed it possible to be blinded by her own tears. She wiped her eyes with the backs of her hands, forgetting about the sand, and now she was really blind! Someone handed her a cloth. It took a long time for her vision to clear. When it did, she saw that it was Jan who had been shaking her, and beside her . . . beside her stood Meg. Unharmed. Farrell fainted.

Minutes passed before she opened her eyes. Meg—
Meg!—was bending over her.

"I thought you were dead," Farrell managed to whisper.

"I know," Meg said. "You were screaming my name
the entire time."

"What happened?" Farrell asked, staring at the house.

"I don't know," Meg told her. "I thought I heard you
in the living room. Then I realized it was the sound of
flames crackling. I ran to your room, but of course you
weren't there. By then it was so bad that I had to climb out
your window." Meg shuddered at the memory. "It was as
though the whole house just exploded."

For the first time, Farrell noticed that the fire department had arrived and that most of the Village was gathered
outside the walls . . . watching the action. Some of the
onlookers stood apart, staring mutely at the flames. Others
were gathered in little clusters, pointing here and there at
the wreckage. They seemed quite animated and excited.
She turned away from them; they didn't matter anymore.

"Oh, my God!" Farrell cried suddenly. "Chevo!"

Meg turned and walked unsteadily to the woods.
There she put her hand on a tree and retched. Finally she
turned, leaned against the trunk, and watched their home
burn to the ground. She wondered if Farrell had realized
yet that their entire year's work had burned as well.

Thirty-nine

The woman straightened her back indignantly, clearly of-
fended at Max's choice of words.

"I beg your pardon!" she told him, slamming her
paperback down on the front desk. "This is most certainly
not an 'old people's home.' This happens to be the Robert
Frost Retirement Residence for the Elderly!"

She was so pleased with her proclamation that Max
had little doubt that she had invented the name herself.

She began rummaging in a drawer, taking time out

every few minutes to glare at him suspiciously. She was a
tall, dried-up stick of a woman, all sharp edges and elbows,
somewhere in her mid- to late sixties. Her hair was dyed an
improbable shade of red and piled, twisted, glued, and
looped in a style that he realized, to his amusement, was
identical to that of the curvaceous redheaded heroine de-
picted on the cover of her book. Her skin was sallow, her
cheeks gaunt, but her eyes, which were now down-turned as
she continued her search through the drawer, were shaped
like almonds and were the same reddish color as acorns, if
you polished them on your sleeve. They were large and
deep-set and quite lovely.

At last she looked up triumphantly and thrust an ancient business card under Max's nose.

It read, THE ROBERT FROST RETIREMENT RESIDENCE FOR
THE ELDERLY—Proprietor, Miss Emily Shacklebun.

She looked as though she'd just scored match point.

Max reached in his pocket and pulled out the state's
attorney I.D. He made a great show of glancing suspiciously around the empty parlor before sliding the I.D.
across the counter.

She glanced at it, then picked it up and studied it
intently, a confused look on her face.

He leaned in and whispered, "Emily, we need your
help."

"We?" she repeated.

"Government business, Emily. We're looking for
someone." He whispered a name.

"Oh, well! I see!" She leaned in even closer, her acorn
eyes glittering hopefully. "Is she in some kind of trouble?"

Max pantomimed locking his mouth and throwing
away the key. His expression remained deadly serious.

"Do you know her, Emily?" he persisted.

"Know her?" she cried. "Know her? I like that! Let me
tell you something, young man; she deserves whatever's
coming to her! That hussy wheedled her way in here, took
advantage of my trusting nature, ate at my table, slept
under my roof for over a year, and look what happened!"

Hussy? Could she possibly be talking about the same
woman he was looking for?

"Emily," he interrupted her, "how old is she?"

"Eighty if she's a day," Emily said, "and doesn't she just think she's the whip in the cream!"

Max nodded sympathetically. "So she's not here anymore?" he asked.

"Not her! And good riddance to both of them, I say!"

"Both of them?" Max asked, lost.

"Why her and that Clarence Simmons, of course. Both of them living in sin on Sugar Hill! I'll say this for them," she added, "they chose the right neighborhood, anyway."

"Do you have that address, Emily?" he asked.

She looked at him as if he'd sprouted an extra head. "Well, I have to send their mail, don't I?" she asked. "But you won't find them there now."

"I won't?"

"No, dear. They're off to visit his daughter for a couple of days. They're always running here and there and every which way." She sighed. "And he was such a nice man before she came," she said wistfully.

"Two days!" Max exclaimed.

"That's right, dear," she answered. "You're not in a hurry are you?"

In the midday sun, the enormous magenta and tangerine daisies on her crisp cotton housedress were so bright that he found it painful to look directly at her.

She had busied herself almost desperately, preparing coffee, setting out a plate of cookies, pouring fresh cream, topping the brimming sugar bowl. Now she stood by the sink, staring into the sunlight that poured through the curtainless window.

She sighed, and he saw her sag inward almost imperceptibly with the sad resignation of one who has learned long ago to endure the unendurable.

She turned to him, and in her eyes he read her suffering and her strength. Life had taken its best shots at her, but she had survived, and she was sane.

"What has she done?" she asked simply.

"Mrs. Madigan, I'm so sorry—"

"Jean," she corrected him. "Just call me Jean, and

don't be sorry. It doesn't help me, and it won't change anything. Just tell me what she's done and what you need, and I'll help you all I can."

He nodded. "Has she been institutionalized?" he asked.

"Institutionalized, her? Never! She found one doomed fool after another to marry her. This one's got more money than God—they all did. She never came home much, just every few years or so. She told her father and me never to visit her . . .

"Course I didn't mind, I saw what she was. But it . ." Her eyes filled, and her voice got husky. "It killed her father. Just plain broke his heart. He never could see her the way she is. Never could accept it. He just kept right on seeing his baby girl and the illusion."

"The illusion?" Max asked.

She looked him in the eye, assessing him. Apparently she found him acceptable, for she continued. "I've heard stories, seen a movie on television not too long ago about that Bundy boy, so I know there are others like her. Not just bad, wholly and completely bad, though Lord knows, that would be enough . . . but smart. Oh, she's real smart! Always made straight A's in school. And always knew just how to get around people, especially men, but everyone, really. Why, she could charm the stars down from the sky! Even when she was a child, she always got just what she wanted."

"Mrs. Madigan. Jean." Max paused, hesitant to ask the next question. "Did she set the fire? Did she burn down Jim and Moira McBride's home?"

She closed her eyes. "Of course it never occurred to us at the time. But then, after Duke and the baby . . ." Soundless tears slid down her cheeks. She looked hopelessly at Max. "My grandchild."

They were silent for several minutes.

"Jean?"

She looked up and met his gaze. She had read his tone. She looked away.

"I don't know," she whispered. The naked fear in her voice belied her words. "I don't know," she repeated insistently. "I never once thought it. All these years, the idea just never occurred to me. Why would it?" she asked defensively, and then added sadly, "No one ever suggested anything of the kind.

"But then," she continued in a low monotone, "then I heard about the senator . . ." She took a long, deep breath. "He drowned in his own bathtub." She whispered finally, so faintly that her words sounded like a sigh, "I believe she killed my son. My only daughter murdered my only son."

The horror of those words took his breath away.

She stared past him, seeing nothing. "You know, I felt it in her the day she was born. Call me unnatural. Lord knows, I've said it myself, but I swear to you that from the moment I first held her in my arms, I knew. Course I told myself I was crazy . . . that my hormones were actin' up, but they weren't. I just knew.

"It wasn't until my son was born that I was absolutely certain. Oh, you should have seen the hate in that child's eyes! We caught her with the animals then. Just seven years old and killing things! But she lied her way out of it, and we let her. Her father loved her so, and I just let him go on believing and convinced myself I was wrong. You know," she said, "there was another one, too."

Max looked up sharply. "Another one?"

"Besides Duke and the senator."

Max waited for her to continue. He knew that she would. A twisted sense of loyalty, or maybe just plain fear, had kept her silent for nearly fifty years. Now that she'd started talking, she wouldn't stop until she'd told him everything.

"She was married to the senator at the time. Charles." She smiled bitterly. "She didn't want us showing up and embarrassing her in front of all her fancy friends, but she didn't mind showing up at our home with her young lover. I think she actually enjoyed shocking us. Course she said she was going to leave the senator and marry him, and Shane, silly name, he was fool enough to believe her."

"But she was lying?" Max prompted.

Jean looked at him. "Mr. Rosen, he was one of those

body-builder types, her personal trainer she called him."
She shook her head. "She'd have never left a senator for a
penniless pretty boy." She looked up. "But he had other
qualifications."

"Other qualifications?" Max repeated.

"Wait, I'll show you." She rose and left the room,
returning in a moment with a stack of photographs.

She put one down in front of him. "There, that's
young Luke McBride."

Max stared at the picture. Farrell's father. The image
smiled up at him: clean-cut, rugged good looks; dark, wavy
hair; white teeth. Movie-star material, he decided.

"But she didn't kill Luke," he objected.

"Oh yes she did," Jean insisted. She put another photograph down. "She killed him over"—she put a third one
before him—"and over"—she put the final picture on the
table—"and over again."

Max stared at the four smiling faces. They differed
slightly. Duke was a bigger, brawnier version. Charles was
finer-boned, and more aristocratic looking. Shane tended
toward pretty, where Luke had been handsome. But the
differences were negligible; the four men were cut of the
same stone. He'd seen adult twins with less striking resem-
blance.

Max was speechless. He whistled softly.

"The strange thing is," Jean continued, "the one she's
married to now doesn't look like him at all."

"What happened to Shane?" Max choked out the
question.

She left the room and returned again, this time with
an old newspaper clipping. The headline read, "Apartment Fire Kills Two." Along with a seventy-four-year-old
woman, a twenty-six-year-old man by the name of Shane
Forester had died.

Max handed the clipping back to her. "You mentioned that she'd married again," he said, "but there's no
record of it."

Jean shrugged. "She's married all right. Sent me a
picture from Mexico. They got married on a boat down

there. Maybe Mexicans don't keep those kinds of records,"
she suggested.

"Or maybe they lose them," he muttered.

"It's strange, though, her marrying him. He's rich
enough, but he doesn't look like Luke at all. He must have
something else she needs. Lord knows, it can't be money.
I guess she just wanted to be back home again. She was just
desperate to be back home . . ."

Forty

The day seemed to sparkle. The vivid blue sky was stuffed
with billowing fat clouds, white and black and every shade
of gray in between. The wind had kicked up overnight, and
the air was so clear you could pick out the sharp outlines
of skyscrapers across the lake.

A small-craft warning had been issued, and the waves
were bigger than anyone in the Village could remember.
They slammed furiously against the shore and sucked back
everything within reach, sand and rocks, washed-up trees,
beached sailboats. They sucked them back and pulled
them down to where the undertow was waiting.

It had been four days since the fire. On the second day,
the shock of the loss was still reverberating through Meg
and Farrell, but they had begun to formulate a plan: to
head back East with Jan once their insurance was settled.
Then the next blow came.

The insurance inspector and his crew had been on the
job for less than a day when they made the discovery that
the fire had not been electrical in nature as previously
assumed. No, indeed. Inspector Sloats wasted no time in
informing them that the incineration of their home had,
without a doubt, been the result of arson.

Sloats was a tough, wiry little man, slightly built and
solid, like a jockey. His face was permanently tanned, and
as shriveled and ridged as a brown walnut. He looked out
at the world through hard little black eyes with all of the
cheery optimism of a fifty-year-old hooker. Sloat's job had

taken its toll. He had long since boiled all of humanity
down to its lowest common denominator, which, from his
point of view, was pretty damned low. He'd seen it all, and
one thing he'd seen time and time again was that in a pretty
fair percentage of arson cases, the victim was also the per-
petrator.

Meg and Farrell not only might be deprived of any
insurance benefits, but they were in danger of being prose-
cuted for insurance fraud.

It was a living nightmare. For the past two days they'd
had to endure humiliating interviews with Mr. Sloats, who
completely disregarded the fact that they'd lost everything
they owned in the world.

"So, ladies," he sneered, "a couple hundred thou
wouldn't be a bad take for two ladies on their own, now
would it?"

"That's ridiculous!" Meg argued. "Why, it would cost
more than twice that for us to rebuild."

"Ya' think so?" He wrinkled his nose doubtfully.
"Lucky break, wasn't it? I mean, ya both bein' up and about
at midnight."

Sloats had also begun interviewing the villagers. After
speaking to a few of them, he got what he called his
"hinky" feeling. A guy didn't work for twenty years in the
business without developing an instinct. All the pros had it.
Some guys' arm hairs stood on end, some got tingly feelings up and down their spines. For Gil Sloats, it was in his
gut. And this one had his gut tied up in knots.

There was something funny about this case that Sloats
hadn't figured out yet. Everyone wanted to knock these
broads, like there was some kind of vendetta going on or
something . . . especially that one blond babe he'd talked
to. But it made for an interesting case, and the only thing
Sloats liked better than making a bust was solving a puzzle.
And this one was a doozy! Oh, it was arson all right, he'd
stake his reputation on it. But there was something else
going on besides—something shadowy. He knew it. But
more important, his gut knew it.

Meg and Jan were on the screen porch, listening to the

waves crash against the shore, when Farrell appeared wearing a new swimsuit, a towel fastened around her hips.

"You're not going swimming!" Meg cried in alarm.

Farrell shook her head. "No, it's too rough even for me," she said. "I'm just going for a walk. Anyone interested?"

She'd asked for politeness' sake, and was relieved when they both declined. For the past few days they'd all been clinging to one another as though they were afraid to be alone, which, in a way, they were. There was no escaping the fact that someone had deliberately burned their house down. It was only reasonable to surmise that whoever it was had intended for them to burn with it.

As Farrell walked down the path to the beach, she could hear the insurance team calling to one another as they sifted through the rubble. One of them yelled, "Hey, Gil! Get a load of this!" She tried unsuccessfully to block out the horror of strangers pawing through the remnants of her life.

She headed up the beach. From the porch, they watched her, a solitary figure against the raging lake. Her hair, whipped and tossed by the wind, trailed behind her like gold and copper streamers. Her towel snapped around her thighs until she yanked it off and slung it across her shoulders.

The day had a magnificence about it. Everything seemed somehow more than itself; colors were more vivid, shadows darker, edges sharper, cleaner, deeper. It was the kind of day you'd like to take a bite out of—a great, hunking bite—and let the juices spurt and run right down your face. The kind of day that brings the savage out in all of us . . .

She could feel the storm brewing, though it would still be hours before it showed its hand, tingeing the air with that eerie shade of yellow that blows in right before the silence. She always felt it early. Sometimes she thought that the gathering electricity sought her out and used her. By the time it broke, she would be so pumped up that the hair on her arms would be standing on end. On days like this—

there weren't many—she could run for miles on the excess energy without the slightest effort.

Today she walked. Enough, she decided, enough pretending not to care, enough trying not to think of him. Her world was falling down around her, had fallen down around her, and still she found herself wondering. Where is he? Is he coming back?

She was almost upon them when awareness set in. She'd been so preoccupied that she hadn't even noticed the crowd. Horrified, she realized that she had blundered right into the midst of the annual lobster party. She'd forgotten completely about it!

Thankfully, no one seemed to notice her. They were all staring out toward the horizon. As she turned to make her escape, she realized that something was terribly wrong. Their faces were masks of fear. Several of them were shouting something; she could see their mouths working, but the wind snatched the sound from their throats and flung it out across the water. A woman was jumping up and down frantically at the water's edge, her arms bent in supplication, her face contorted, and her mouth was gaping open to allow the escape of her soundless screams. It was Mary Dooley.

Farrell followed her gaze out past the surf and found the focus of her agony. *"Timmy!"* Farrell shouted as she watched a monstrous wave reach in and flush the child out of his little boat and fling him fifteen feet farther away from shore.

She had time to locate him as she ran. He was just a tiny speck, bobbing on the surface . . . and then he disappeared from view. She never hesitated, never really even made the decision; she just acted.

No one had known she was there until she flew past them in a blur, plunging headlong into the roiling water. She propelled herself downward, timing her dive to cut below the six-foot wave. If it had caught her head-on, it would have slammed her back to shore and crushed her before it sucked her down.

She broke the surface and was swallowed up whole.

* * *

Gil Sloats hunkered down to inspect Stan's find. After eighteen years, it still amazed him to see the things that would survive a fire, even one of this magnitude. He'd once found a porcelain vase perfectly intact in a pile of smoking ashes. He'd seen a child's paper notebook survive a three-alarm fire, and once he'd even found a woman's pocketbook with a fresh book of matches inside. There was simply no telling when it came to a fire. But this was something else again . . .

He examined the still-smoking carcass of a small animal. Nearby they'd found the charred remains of a ten-gallon can of gasoline.

He wasn't yet sure what it all meant, but it looked like some kind of demented ceremony. Had they burned the place on purpose, or had the fire somehow gotten out of control? He did know one thing—his employers wouldn't have to lay out a dime for those screwy broads.

With a triumphant gleam in his eye, he marched down the path to Jan's house, wondering as he approached who the speeding maniac in the red Mercedes was.

Max roared up Jan's driveway. Jeff had met him at the airport, and they'd managed to make the drive in less than an hour.

As Max screeched to a halt, Jeff unpeeled his fingers from the door handle and tried to shake some blood back into them. His knuckles were completely white and stiff.

On the way, Jeff had filled Max in on what had happened. He and Joe had paid Junior a visit, armed with Patsy's records. At first Junior had blustered and threatened to have them thrown out of his office. But the minute they'd mentioned Patsy and produced the evidence, he'd seemed to wither right before their eyes. As they stood and watched, all the fight had just fizzled out of him.

"I think the realization that Patsy had betrayed him upset him even more than getting caught," Jeff told Max. "The real knockout punch came when we informed him that in all likelihood, charges would not be pressed."

"In all likelihood?" Max asked. "I thought we decided—"

"Max," Jeff reminded him, "this entire arrangement is subject to Meg and Farrell's approval."

"You haven't told them yet?"

Jeff shook his head. "We both know Junior is a liar. It seemed prudent to wait and see if he comes through as promised before getting their hopes up. He has until the end of the month to come up with the money."

"Cash?" Max asked.

Jeff sighed. "Max, we're talking about six million dollars."

"Ho-ly mackerel!" Max whistled.

Jeff shrugged. "It's what the son of a bitch stole." He went on to describe the details.

Jeff wisely waited until they were free of the city-bound traffic and on the open freeway before mentioning the fire. Even so, Max turned so pale at the news that Jeff ordered him to pull over.

"Thank God Farrell was out of the house!" he said.

"Which brings me to another matter," Jeff began. "Farrell almost drowned that night, and it's a miracle Meg ever got out alive. They were drugged, Max."

"Drugged!"

"Whoever set that fire wasn't taking any chances. Someone left a plate of brownies in the house, drugged brownies. They left a note saying the brownies were from Jan, but Jan knew nothing about them. It wasn't until the next day that Meg and Farrell put it all together. There isn't any question about it."

"What did the police have to say about all this? I assume they were notified."

"Of course," Jeff continued, his frustration plainly evident. "There's surprisingly little they can do. After all, we can't prove they were drugged, and until the arson inspector files his report, Meg and Farrell are considered suspects."

Max floored it all the way to Jan's house. They leaped from the car and hurried into the house. Meg and Jan were out on the porch.

"Where's Farrell?" Max asked abruptly.

"She went for a walk on the beach," Jan told him.

"You let her go *alone?*" he cried. "Which way did she go?" He ran out the door, collided with Gil Sloats, glanced at him vaguely, literally lifted him by the shoulders and set him out of the way.

"Toward the lake!" Meg called after him. He ran on.

Sloats was trembling with rage. He resented men who were taller than himself, and that son of a bitch had just picked him up like he was some kind of rag doll! He spun on Meg, eager to take his anger out on her.

"Does this look familiar?" he snarled, holding up the charred can of gasoline. He watched her eyes, waiting for her to register fear or anger. Instead, she looked only mildly irritated.

"It's obviously a gasoline can, Mr. Sloats," Meg snapped. "A rather badly burned—oh, dear God! Is that—was that in our house?"

Sloats was thrown by her reaction. He prided himself on his ability to read people, and either this broad was ready for an Oscar or she was truly in the dark. A new thought occurred to him; could the young one have set this whole thing up by herself? After all, she had been safely in the lake on the night of the fire. Attempted murder, as well as arson? That would certainly explain his "hinky" feeling. "Where can I find Miss McBride?" he demanded.

"Farrell!" Meg cried. "I'm going with Max!"

Jeff and Jan followed her out the door, leaving Gil Sloats alone.

"The hell with this," he snorted, and took off after them.

Farrell came up for air beyond the reach of the crashing surf. It took everything she had to stay afloat and draw a solid breath of air. The enormous waves rose and fell with such seemingly random violence that it was impossible to calculate where the next assault would originate.

While struggling for breath, she focused on where she had last seen Timmy. Aiming for that spot, she dove again, heading straight down to the bottom. It was easier to make some headway down there, just inches above the sand. Though the water still bucked and rocked, pummeling her

from side to side, and the undertow was a constant threat—
if it caught her in its deadly grip, she'd never fight her way
out alive—at last she reached the point that she'd been
aiming for . . . she thought; it was impossible to know for
sure. She surfaced again to take a breath, and saw nothing
but the waves. Her determination hardened. She swore to
herself that she would not give up until she found him.

From the beach, the crowd watched in silence. When
her head poked above the surface, they breathed a collective sigh of relief. When she dove again, they held their
breath along with her, and prayed.

Mary Dooley and her husband stood together, staring
at the spot where their son had disappeared, waiting to find
out for sure if their lives were over.

Junior stood rigid between Bridget and Kimmy, his
eyes scanning the lake's surface.

"What does she think she's doing?" Bridget scoffed.

Junior didn't bother to look at her. He'd done a lot of
soul-searching in the past few days, and had come to the
conclusion that his greatest crime had been in listening to
his wife. "Something, Bridget," he responded coldly.
"She's doing something."

"Something stupid, if you ask me," Bridget snapped.

"Really," Kimmy agreed.

Max arrived on the beach, saw the crowd staring out
at the horizon, and wondered what was happening. He ran
up to a stranger and asked him.

"The Dooley boy is out there," the man told him
grimly.

Max scanned the surface of the lake.

"The McBride girl went in after him," the man added.

The words sank in like daggers. "How long?" Max
grabbed the startled man by the shoulders. "How long has
she been under?"

Before the man had a chance to answer, Max let go of
him and started running to the water, stripping as he ran.
He pulled off his sport coat and shirt and flung them to the
wind, then stood on the shore hopping on one foot as he
pulled off his shoes and pants.

He dove into a wave just as Farrell's head appeared

above the surface. He didn't hear them call out "There she is!" The wave slammed him back onto the shore so hard that it knocked the wind from his lungs.

She reappeared, and this time she stayed on top, on her back, kicking toward the shore.

"She's got him!" someone yelled. "She's got him!"

Jan ran to her son, shaking with fright. Kneeling, she held him briefly and then stood to stare at him in disbelief. "You damned fool!" she cried. She'd arrived just in time to see him lifted as though he were weightless and thrown through the air.

His wind was coming back. "Farrell!" he gasped.

"She's all right, Max. Look!" Jan pointed to where Farrell was crawling out onto the sand and handing Timmy's limp body over to Dr. Small. Meg stood a few feet away, weeping openly in reaction to her fright.

"Farrell!" Max staggered to his feet and ran to her.

"Max," she whispered, still fighting for breath. "Max, you're here."

He pulled her up, wrapped his arms around her trembling body and buried his face in her wet hair. "Thank God. Thank God you're all right!" he whispered.

Farrell disengaged herself and took his hand. On shaking legs she led him to the group that crowded around Dr. Small and Timmy. As they watched, Timmy suddenly began choking and regurgitating enormous amounts of water. A few minutes later, he started to cry.

Dr. Small looked up at Mary Dooley. "He's going to be just fine, Mary," he assured her.

Mary Dooley turned to Farrell and barely managed to whisper, "Thank you, oh, thank you for saving Timmy," before she broke down completely.

Farrell dropped to her knees and wept tears of relief. Max, deciding that her warmth was his first priority, ran to retrieve his jacket.

Gil Sloats, who had arrived in time to see Farrell pull Timmy to safety, had been waiting for this moment. He sidled up next to her. "Nice hero routine," he said softly. "My, but you're a strong swimmer! Just think, two near-drownings in such a short period of time. Amazing!" He leaned down, looked her in the eye, and whispered, "I'm on to you, Farrell McBride."

Farrell rose. Physically and emotionally spent, she tried to make sense of his words. "I'm sorry, what are you—"

"What the hell are you talking about?" Max roared. He brushed by Sloats, gently wrapped his jacket around Farrell's shoulders, then turned and towered over the man. "Who are you?" Max demanded. "Mother," he addressed Jan as she approached with Meg and Jeff, "who is this guy?"

"Mother?" Farrell whispered.

"Max." Meg spoke up. "Mr. Sloats is an insurance inspector. He suspects Farrell and me of burning down our own house."

"I never said that!" Sloats insisted. "I never said anything like that. You're not getting me for libel!"

"Well, that's just plain stupid," Max said. "What possible reason—"

"Two hundred thousand reasons, friend," Sloats snapped, forgetting himself. He didn't like being called stupid. "That's how much she hoped to make on the fire."

"Excuse me." All of them turned as Junior stepped forward.

Meg sighed. "Junior, I don't think—"

"Wait, Meg," Junior pleaded. "Give me a chance. Another one," he mumbled. "I, uh, I couldn't help overhearing. Mr. Sloats, listen. My sister and niece have no reason to perpetrate such a fraud." He glanced at Jeff. "They are each wealthy women in their own right."

"Oh, really, Mr.—uh, I didn't catch your name." Sloats had the appearance of a cobra who'd just spotted a plump white egg.

"Sweeney, Junior Sweeney."

"Right," Sloats nodded. "I thought so. That your wife over there?" He pointed to Bridget, who stood several feet away in a cluster of women. She looked up at the mention of her name.

Junior frowned. "Yes."

"Well then, may I ask why your wife told me, and I

quote, 'Those two are as poor as church mice. They'd do anything to get their hands on two-hundred thou.' " He stared at Junior.

By this time, the villagers had tuned in to the increasingly loud drama. All eyes turned to Bridget.

"Well, I might have said something like that." She shifted uncomfortably. "But it's true, isn't it? I don't know what you're prattling on about, Junior."

"What my wife is unaware of, Mr. Sloats," Junior explained, "is that on the morning of the fire, I met with Meg and Farrell's attorney, Mr. Gibson, and signed documents whereby I agreed to make them each a gift of three million dollars."

At that announcement, the villagers turned first to Meg, and then to Farrell, to check their reactions. They both looked stunned. No one thought to look at Bridget, who had half-collapsed into Kimmy's arms.

Sloats blanched. His mouth went completely dry. "They were aware of this gift?" he asked.

"They were," Junior lied. Beads of perspiration formed on his brow.

Jeff and Max exchanged shocked looks. Both Meg and Farrell gaped at Junior.

Bridget found her voice. *"What?"* she screamed. "Junior, how dare—"

But instead of cowering as he usually did, Junior turned on her and roared, "Oh, shut *up*, Bridget! Just shut your big mouth!"

Then Kimmy threw her arms around her mother's neck and cried, "Daddy! How dare you speak to Mother that way?"

To which Junior responded, "Oh, you shut up, too."

Max had had enough. He put his arm around Farrell's shoulders. "My God, you're still shivering." He turned to Jan and said impatiently, "Let's go." Then he called, "Oh, Mr. Sloats."

Sloats turned. "Yeah?"

"I think you'll want to join us. I have a lot to explain."

* * *

Max stood in the upstairs hallway at eight o'clock that evening and tapped on the door. "Farrell, are you about ready? The sheriff is downstairs."

"Come in, Max. I'm decent."

He pushed the door open and stood in the threshold, watching her. She sat on the edge of an oversized four-poster bed tugging on a pair of argyle socks. She wore stone-washed jeans and one of Jan's bulky fisherman sweaters. Her damp, copper hair curled around her face. Her cheeks were still rosy from the heat of the shower. She glanced up and met his gaze. Her eyes were the color of . . . "Leaves," he muttered.

"What?" she asked.

"Leaves," he repeated. "Your eyes are as green as leaves."

She smiled. "My grandfather said that once." Then her smile disappeared. "Max, what's going on?"

"Jeeze, Farrell, there's so much I have to tell you—"

"Well, how about starting with Jan?"

He cringed. So she had caught his slip on the beach. "I really wanted to tell you sooner. It started so innocently. We didn't want to alarm you and Meg. It just didn't seem like a big deal at first. But then, I didn't know I was going to fall in love with you . . ." Farrell glanced up again, but Max rushed on. "Somehow it got to be this huge thing. Farrell, can you understand? I couldn't just blurt it out. And there was so much else happening. Can you forgive me?"

She ignored his question. "And Junior's gift?" she pressed. "Three million dollars! Was that a secret, too?"

"We were going to explain all that, but we didn't want to get your hopes up until . . ." He sighed, and turned to go. "I don't blame you for being angry. Look, I'll just wait downstairs . . ."

"Max."

He stopped in his tracks.

"You're going to have to quit protecting me—"

"Farrell," he objected.

"Listen to me," she insisted. "You're going to have to stop protecting me from the truth. I can't spend the rest of my life with someone who doesn't even trust me to—"

"What did you just say?" he asked.

"I said you're going to have to trust me."

"Not that. The part about spending the rest of your life with someone."

Her cheeks flushed. "I never said that!"

"You certainly did!" He strode across the room and took her hands in his. "Marry me, Farrell McBride. I swear, I'll protect you only from harm."

The look in her eyes was all the answer he needed.

Sheriff Tucker McClean leaned against the wall, his muscular arms folded casually across his massive chest. The expression on his craggy, chiseled face was that of a man who didn't have a care in the world. Patience was just one of his virtues.

Fifty-three years had affected neither his height nor his excellent posture. Erect, he stood just over six-feet-six. His mop of graying, sandy hair contrasted sharply with his ruddy, tanned complexion. His thick dark brows seemed equally incongruous juxtaposed to those well-trimmed but undisciplined locks. His deep-set eyes were such a pale shade of blue that they were impossible to read, and in certain kinds of light, he looked stone-blind.

He smiled when the couple entered the living room. It was nice to see young people in love. While the young lady joined the others on the couch, the young man approached him.

"Sheriff McClean." Max extended his hand. "I spoke to you on the phone."

"Mr. Rosen? It's a pleasure." The sheriff smiled pleasantly and extended an enormous hand. There was the memory of a bayou in his softly drawling baritone. "I'm a big fan of your books."

As Max shook the sheriff's callused hand, he read the intelligence behind the pale blue stare and breathed a sigh of relief. His impression on the phone had been correct. The man was nobody's fool. Max was well aware of the fact that all of his information, as damning as it was, was purely circumstantial. "I'm flattered, Sheriff. You pros are my toughest audience."

Sheriff McClean nodded. "Why don't we get started?"

Fifteen minutes later, when Gil Sloats started to interrupt for the fourth time, Sheriff McClean overtalked him. "Mr. Sloats, from what Mr. Rosen here has managed to tell us so far, I'm inclined to think that we just might have a dangerous character on the loose. Now, why don't we all just keep quiet, and if there are any questions to ask, I'll ask 'em." He nodded for Max to continue.

At eight-thirty, Max was relating his conversation with Jean Madigan. He handed the sheriff the photographs Jean had given him.

Sheriff McClean glanced at them, then stood and walked to the phone. "Ma'am," he said to Jan, "would you happen to know the Laudins' number?"

Jan rose and found the number in the directory.

He glanced at the page and dialed. There was no answer. "Do you know anyone who might know their whereabouts?"

"Bridget," Jan said, and immediately found her number. "Bridget Sweeney."

He dialed the number, and after several minutes of low conversation, hung up and turned to the group. "It seems that the Laudins have gone off to Lake Geneva for the weekend; Mr. Laudin's family reunion. They left first thing this morning. Mrs. Sweeney seems to think that Mrs. Laudin has been depressed about something for the past few days." He frowned. "Mr. Rosen, I'm sure you're aware of the fact that all of your information is of a circumstantial nature. However, your lawyer friend here will tell you that cases can be tried on circumstantial evidence, and I'm inclined to agree with your conclusions. On the face of it, I'd say that Mr. Sloats here has his arsonist, and that Miss McBride and Miss Sweeney are in serious danger. If Darla Laudin was in town, I'd pick her up for questioning. But she isn't, and that frustrates me. Now, if y'all don't mind, I'd like to use that phone again and call an ol' buddy of mine who happens to be on the force up there in Lake

Geneva. Just to make sure that Mrs. Laudin is where she's supposed to be. That way, we'll all sleep better tonight."

He placed the call.

While they waited for the sheriff's colleague to confirm Darla's whereabouts, Jan prepared a plate of sandwiches.

At nine-thirty the call came.

The sheriff spoke for several minutes. "Well," he said as he hung up, "ol' Billy swung by and spoke to the housekeeper. Looks like the Laudins are out for the evening. They're not expected home until late. Mr. Rosen, I'd like to borrow your file, if you don't mind. I'll make a few copies, fax one up to Billy . . . Think I'll send one over to the federal boys, too." He took the file from Max and walked to the door. "I'll be seein' y'all tomorrow, bright and early. In the meantime, I'd suggest you get some sleep. Try, anyway. Darla Laudin's three hundred miles away, and the minute she crosses my state line, I'll get her. Ol' Billy might even decide he wants to talk to her, once he sees all this." He tapped Max's file. "Well, good night now."

He walked out the door, then stuck his head back in. "You comin', Mr. Sloats?"

Forty-one

Sheriff McClean switched off the burner, lifted the squealing teapot, and poured the steaming water into his mug. Stirring the black decaffinated coffee, he walked through his unlit house to the back room, where he'd set up a makeshift office.

The little two-bedroom cottage had been as cute as a dollhouse before his Grace had passed away. But now, after fourteen months of Tucker McClean all alone, the rooms were beginning to look more like the Sheriff's Department than a home.

He sat down at his desk—comprised of a plywood board and two end tables—and stared out the picture window. He sat there for a long time, listening to the thunder crash and watching as the lightning illuminated the five acres of blue spruce trees that had been his and Grace's pride and joy.

When the phone rang, it was as though he'd been expecting it. He knew who was calling before ol' Billy ever said a word.

"Tuck?"

"What's up, Billy?"

"I think we got ourselves a little problem."

"She's not there," Tucker said. It wasn't a question.

"That's right. That report you sent up made me uneasy, so I went back just to have a look-see. Mr. Laudin got in 'bout a half-hour ago."

"When did she leave?" Tucker asked.

"That's just it, Tuck. She never came here in the first place. Mr. Laudin says she was feeling poorly this morning and refused to come with him. Said he didn't like leaving her, but she insisted he not miss his family reunion. He hasn't been able to reach her all day."

"I got to go, Billy."

"Right. Oh, Tuck, in case you're wonderin' . . . I asked that housekeeper why she didn't mention that the Mrs. didn't show. Guess what she said."

"What's that?" Tucker asked.

"Said it wasn't her place."

Tucker depressed the button, then dialed the operator. He didn't have time to search for numbers. He identified himself and instructed her to put him through to the Tenholm residence in the Village.

A minute later, she was back on the line. "I'm sorry, Sheriff, I can't seem to get through. It must be the storm. It's funny, though. No one's reported any lines being down . . ."

He hung up and dialed his office. "Betty, get on the wire and round up the boys. We've got ourselves an emergency."

It was well after midnight, and Farrell was wide awake. The wild events of the day, and the disturbing knowledge that Darleen was still out there somewhere, were enough to keep her tense and restless.

Finally giving up on sleep, she rose, pulled on the terry-cloth robe Jan had loaned her, and tiptoed down the hallway. She assumed that Jan and Meg were sleeping, for there was no light showing beneath their closed doors. Max and Jeff had finally retired to the coach house, bleary-eyed and exhausted.

She crept down the darkened stairway and stood at the westward window, watching as lightning slashed the sky, fitfully illuminating the inky blackness like some massive strobe.

Far below, the lake roared and thrashed, a maddened beast newly wakened after months of sleep, and starving. She felt the house shudder with each assault upon the shore.

And then it happened! A huge wooden-framed screen panel ripped free from the porch and came, thrust by a violent blast of wind, hurtling toward the window where she stood. It came so fast that her mind barely had time to register terror before it catapulted forward, and then, at the last possible second, was lifted by an updraft, crashed harmlessly above the window, and ricocheted back to lean precariously near the gap it had torn in the planking.

She took a moment to collect herself, leaning heavily against the back of a chair, then peered out the window. She realized she would have to retrieve the panel before the wind took hold again and sent it crashing through the glass.

"Betty? Tuck. You get the boys?" Sheriff McClean flipped his windshield wipers to high and cracked his window to relieve the humidity. The goddamned defroster wasn't working again. "Good. I'm on my way, too. Get Robbie on the radio. I want him to make a call for me. Well, go get him out of there, Betty. Now!"

The instant that Farrell stepped out on the porch, she was completely soaked. She shuffled across the rain-slick planks, her progress hampered by the sodden terry-cloth

robe that now seemed to weigh a ton. She reached the
opening in the screen and, bending down to retrieve the
panel, felt a wave of vertigo as the lightning flashed and
illuminated the sickening drop to the rocks below.

With the back of her arm, she tried to wipe her dripping hair from her eyes, but succeeded only in wringing the
terry-cloth sleeve onto her face. The howling wind was so
loud and fierce that she was afraid of being blown over the
side. She gripped the wooden edge of the screen and began
to inch backward, dragging it toward the house.

And then she froze.

She heard the screen door slam in the side entrance of
the porch, and turned awkwardly in her heavy garment.

It was too dark for her to see until a jagged bolt of
lightning tore the sky apart, and revealed Darleen.

Her glasses were gone; her chic, blond hair was plas-
tered to her head in tangled strings; she was bleeding from
a deep scratch in her forehead. Her designer clothes were
torn, and wet and filthy; her eyes were lit with a mad intensity, and she was smiling.

Then, as quickly as she had appeared, she was gone.
Swallowed up in darkness.

When the lightning flashed again, she had moved
closer. And this time, Farrell saw the long steel blade glint-
ing in the terrible light.

The ringing phone fit perfectly into Max's dream. He
was back in high school, and the bell was ringing. He ran
down an endless corridor. "I'm coming!" he shouted out
loud.

He awoke and glanced around the room. He couldn't
believe he'd slept! He'd been so sure that he would toss and
turn all night. The ringing phone beside his bed startled
him. He picked it up. "Yeah?"

"Mr. Max Rosen, please. Sheriff's Department calling."

Max's adrenaline surged. "Rosen speaking."

"Mr. Rosen, Deputy Robert Drew here. Sheriff
McClean asked me to contact you. He's on his way to the
Tenholm residence—"

"What happened?" Max demanded. He grabbed the jeans he'd left on the foot of his bed and yanked them on.

"Sheriff McClean instructed me to inform you that Mrs. Laudin never left town. He was unable to get through to the Tenholm residence. Apparently the phone lines are down."

"But I'm in the coach house," Max argued. "It doesn't make sense . . . *She cut the lines!*" He dropped the receiver and ran, barefoot and shirtless, out the door and into the violent storm, completely forgetting Jeff, who remained sound asleep in the next room.

With the crash of thunder, Meg came instantly awake. Outside, lightning streaked across the sky, throwing her room into sudden sharp relief. Then utter darkness.

She gasped aloud. It was back, the feeling, so strong that the ground seemed, for a moment, to have dropped beneath her bed. It was the old sensation, the rushing wind like a falling dream . . . the awareness of something about to happen, like a thought not yet formed. It was stronger than ever before.

"Farrell!" she shrieked. She realized that her face was damp with tears.

It was dark again. With panic welling up inside her, Farrell crept backward, then stopped and almost cried aloud with fright as she remembered the opening. She groped behind herself and realized with sickening clarity that another step would have sent her over the edge and onto the jagged boulders that rose up so ominously from the beach below Jan's deck.

Lightning flashed again, and Darleen was inches from her. The horrible smile was fixed, her expression so insane and her eyes burning with such consuming rage that Farrell was struck dumb with sheer heart-stopping terror. Darleen took one step closer and raised the blade.

"*You!*" she whispered savagely, her voice a hoarse, rasping scrape. She stood for a moment, poised to strike . . .

"*No!*" Meg screamed from the open doorway. "*No!*"

The sound of Meg's voice freed Farrell from the paralysis that had gripped her. She ran, in the sudden welcome darkness, toward the doorway.

Furious, Darleen spun toward the voice and slipped backward, regaining her balance only to look up as lightning flashed again.

Meg faced her defiantly. Though terror gripped her, she knew she would face this challenge. This was her gift—at last it made some kind of sense. She could alter this one horror. She met Darleen's insane gaze. Trembling uncontrollably, her knees weak and rubbery, she took a step forward, and then another . . .

Then, slowly, her fear was replaced by confusion as she watched the inexplicable play of emotions on Darleen's face.

Meg would never know that some trick of light in the momentary flash of lightning had turned her wide black eyes as red as burning coals, her dark hair blacker than the night, and given her pale skin an eerie, bluish tinge. She would never know that in that instant, she looked as mad as Darlene, and more, possessed by the evil Darleen had courted.

In that fleeting instant, all of Darleen's malignancy and hatred turned to wrenching fear. She jumped back to escape from the nightmare that suddenly confronted her, and fell screaming, grasping at the air, into the terrifying void.

In the distance, sirens wailed, barely audible over the shrieking wind.

Max found Meg and Farrell clinging to each other, as stiff as petrified wood. Blue strobes and sirens competed with the thunder and lightning. He crossed the porch and encircled both of them in his embrace. Together, they inched to the edge and waited in the darkness. Finally, a roar of thunder and a blinding flash of light revealed the broken body on a boulder far below.

Farrell cried out, and Max led her away, but Meg, held by some deeper instinct, waited for another flash. In a moment it came, following a deafening crash, and illuminated the rocky beach . . .

"The empty beach," Meg whispered.

Great waves crashed against the rocks and washed them clean; they sucked back everything in reach . . .

They'll find her body, Meg reassured herself, ignoring the flicker of fear. Surely it will wash up with the tide.

Epilogue
(The Following
Spring)

The early mist has lifted from the springtime world outside my window. The sun, having finally risen higher than the trees, illuminates my tiny room and the transparent curtains that float on either side, as chaste as a bride's white underthings.

I hear the telltale bang and sputter of the mailman's Jeep, and I wait, counting . . . giving it not more than ten. One, two, three and *slam!* There she goes! I hear the slap of her bare feet across the wooden porch and I close my eyes, imagining . . .

In my mind's eye, I see her running, graceful still, across the soft green lawn. Her red-gold locks fly out behind her and catch the morning sunlight. Her laughing eyes, alight with anticipation, will first scan, then read, every single letter before she returns to the house.

The time has passed so quickly, but then it does when life is sweet. We were married very grandly. As Meg had hoped, it was an outdoor wedding.

Everyone came: Junior and Patrick III, even Sheriff Tucker McClean. I saw the sheriff and Meg dancing together several times—not that I'm suggesting anything.

The only ones who didn't show up were Bridget and Kimmy, who were said to have splitting headaches.

Jeff was my best man; Meg was Farrell's maid of honor. And between Meg and Mom and Jeff, and Joe and the Captain (who arrived with a string of bells around his neck), there were enough tears shed that the runoff posed a definite threat to Lake Michigan's status as a body of fresh water. (To be honest, I shed a few tears myself, especially when I heard her say "I do.")

She was so beautiful on that day that as she walked toward me on the Captain's arm, I could hear them gasping in the aisles.

We're renting now; we look out over the golf course. Our house won't be finished until August, and neither will Meg's. She's building on the same spot as the old house, and we're right next door, on a five-acre lot that was part, a small part, of my mother's wedding gift.

Oh, did I mention that my own sweet mother turned out to be the mysterious investor behind the infamous blind land trust? She set up the trust in my name and held it through all these years for the day I married, or for the day she died. Needless to say, we were all delighted that it turned out to be the former.

Between the two houses there will be a cottage for the Captain. He was so quick to leave Ireland and so reluctant to return that we knew he was longing to stay—but his pride wouldn't let him admit it.

We actually almost lost him. He was booked on a flight and packing to leave when Farrell saved the day. She floored me by announcing to him that if he left, she would have no one to act as godfather to our child!

So it should be quite a summer. Not only will we be meeting our firstborn, but Jeff and Joe are renting the Marlin estate for July and August—which we fully expect will raise a few eyebrows.

Furthermore, Goldie is planning to visit, which should raise a few roofs! He'll be passing through the Midwest on his cross-country tour to publicize his memoirs. As you can well imagine, the publication of his book directly coincided with Michael Payne's unprecedented resignation as state's attorney.

I hear the screen door slam and Farrell's feet flying up the steps.

"Max!" she calls. "Max!" She appears breathless in the doorway. "Wait 'till you see!" She hands me a letter and a photograph from Meg and Jan, who are off traveling. "Look," she laughs, "they're riding camels. God, I bet they're having fun!"

Suddenly her expression changes. "Oh, Max," she says, dismayed. "You're writing!" She turns away, then back again. "Are you almost finished with it?" she asks.

"Just about."

"Well then, tell me just one thing. Does this book have a happy ending?"

I look at her, and my heart swells with love. I wonder how many men in all the world are so moved at the sight of their own wife.

She studies my expression; I cock my head and smile. I open my arms, she comes to me, and with my cheek against her swollen belly, I answer her . . .

"The happiest."